"Jeff Kass's *Center-Mid* paints an intimate picture of the complexities of modern adolescence while highlighting how sport can ground individuals and provide a platform to address difficult topics. Kass's female characters battle their inner and outer demons, yet at the end of the day these same characters find that those who may be different from them really aren't. *Center-Mid* is an absolute page turner where the reader roots for the success of females both on and off the field."

- MAREN LANGFORD, FORMER USA NATIONAL TEAM FIELD HOCKEY PLAYER

"Champions make winning look easy. But behind every perfect team is a group of imperfect individuals battling to make sense of their messy, complicated lives. Jeff Kass captures the journey with humor, heartbreak and electrifying field hockey action. *Center-Mid* is everything I love about Y.A."

- PATRICK FLORES-SCOTT, YA AUTHOR OF *AMERICAN ROAD TRIP* AND *JUMPED IN*

"Jeff Kass deftly captures the complicated, raw, beautiful, and profoundly impactful time of young adulthood, through the refreshing perspective of Allison, a dedicated, determined female athlete discovering what wins and losses look like both on and off the field. With a powerful examination of what defines right from wrong, how mistakes shape and guide us, and the confidence that arises from standing together as a team, *Center-Mid* scores."

- SARAH GRACE MCCANDLESS, YA AUTHOR OF *GROSSE POINTE GIRL*

CENTER-MID

JEFF KASS

FIFTH AVENUE PRESS

Center-Mid

Copyright © 2021 by Jeff Kass

This is a work of fiction. Names, characters, business, events and incidents are the products of the author's imagination. Any resemblance to actual persons, living or dead, or actual events is purely coincidental.

All rights reserved. This book or any portion thereof may not be reproduced or used in any manner whatsoever without the express written permission of the author, except for the use of brief quotations embodied in critical reviews and certain other noncommercial uses permitted by copyright law.

Fifth Avenue Press is a locally focused and publicly owned publishing imprint of the Ann Arbor District Library. It is dedicated to supporting the local writing community by promoting the production of original fiction, non-fiction and poetry written for children, teens and adults.

Printed in the United States of America

First Printing, 2021

Layout and Illustration: Ann Arbor District Library

Editor: Nichole Christian

ISBN: 978-1-947989-91-7 (Paperback); 978-1-947989-92-4 (Ebook)

Fifth Avenue Press

343 S Fifth Ave

Ann Arbor, MI 48104

fifthavenue.press

For Sam and all the teammates and coaches who help her grow.

[1]

Mallory's laughing, which is my second favorite sound in the world.

"Stop staring," I say. "He'll see us."

The "he" is a hairy man in a minivan next to us at the stoplight. He looks old, at least fifty. His beard's gray and sloppy and his van's the burgundy color of the wine my mom drinks. He's got flabby, fat arms that look like ugly pigs attached to his shoulders and he's wearing a tank top. You can see his pale, hairy chest and, spanning across his clavicle, part of a tattoo that looks like the bright-orange bill of a duck —which is why Mallory's laughing.

"Who cares if he sees us?" she says. "He's your boyfriend."

Game on.

"That's not my boyfriend," I say. "My boyfriend weighs eight hundred pounds *more* than that guy and *his* drunk Donald Duck tattoo goes straight across his face and wraps around his neck. And it's greasy. And three-dimensional. It has chunky bumps in it, like pyramids of really bad acne."

"Yeah, well, my boyfriend, just last week, had *two* greasy, bumpy duck tattoos across his face that even crawled into his nostrils and his ears, or tried to, but they couldn't make it because both are already so clogged with, like, forty pounds of earwax. Plus, he couldn't keep the tattoos anyway because he chewed them off when he was hungry and his refrigerator was empty because he actually doesn't have a refrigerator because he has no patience, like zero, and he eats all the food he buys—which is a lot, like seven bags of Hot Cheetos every three minutes—inside his creepy stalker-van before he even gets home."

"Gross." I laugh. "But my boyfriend can't even chew because he only has one single tooth and it's so big it looks like a snow shovel and it takes up his whole mouth. Even his mother calls him Shovel Face."

"OK, but my boyfriend doesn't even have a mother. He just emerged from a swamp with mud and slime and dead frogs and mucousy snot-snails dripping from his skin."

"That's kind of sexy though."

Mallory laughs again, that beautiful music, like an orchestra of flutes, and the light changes and I floor the gas and we're dust, leaving the man in the minivan behind so he can finish texting or taking a selfie of his disgusting beard or whatever else he was doing with his phone.

We get quiet because the truth is our game is actually sad, and we both know it. We've known each other since preschool and neither of us has ever had a decent boyfriend. Of course, neither of us has had many boyfriends, and we didn't start having them until the middle of junior year—we got started pretty late due to no free time ever—but the situation still seems bleak enough that we play the game in order to make ourselves feel better.

We should have more boyfriends, and better ones, or at

least ones who aren't totally offensive. Mallory is gorgeous. Tall and graceful with thick, blond hair and a face with curves and angles in all the right places. A lot of people think I could be her sister, though I'm a bit shorter and hippier, and I know I'm not bad—my *mom* always tells me I'm beautiful—but I don't think I'm anywhere near as pretty as Mal. My mom also says boys are intimidated by us, especially the nice ones, and I think she might be right because every boyfriend we've ever had has been emotionally deficient.

Mallory's last boyfriend, Jake, is the kind of d-bag who inhabits the extreme and—unfortunately—not-lonely-enough end of the d-bag spectrum. Two weeks ago, he blew her off *on her birthday* in order to smoke weed with his friends. Promised he'd meet up with her but never texted, left her looking at her phone every twelve seconds while he was sucking on a bong at the same playground where we used to play groundies in elementary school. They broke up a week after that, but I can tell she's still thinking about him because she's curling and uncurling her fingers, making a fist and then unmaking it, which is what she does when she's mad but doesn't want to say exactly what she's mad about.

"Jake's an asshole," I say.

"I know."

I don't think she really does.

I want to say it and I don't want to say it.

I don't like it when she's hurt.

But I've also seen her running into the smallest space on the strong side of the field and taking my pass and swinging hard, making solid contact on the dead run and sending the ball smacking into the board like somebody hit it with a sledgehammer. I need to see that again, hear that again, and in order for that to happen, we need to trust each other in every possible way. So she needs to know the truth.

All of it.

We pull into the parking lot we've pulled into a million times, not just every school day at 7:15 a.m. when we promised each other as soon as I got my license we'd never head inside the building without turning around and watching the sun rise over the trees on the cemetery opposite the school, but early September Sunday afternoons like this one too, when the lot's empty and everyone else is at home watching football, eating potato chips or pizza. We're tired too, want to be in our houses relaxing, but we are also the one and only Womack Warriors and we want to win states again so we're not in our family rooms wrapped in blankets, zoning out with the TV on. We're about to be sweating like fiends, burning our knees on the turf when we dive for balls most people think are out of reach, churning our thighs through a two-hour practice, working our corners and inserts.

"It's not like he didn't text anybody that night," I say.

"What? Who'd he text? How do you know?"

I still don't want to tell her.

The thing is—Jake's cute.

Really cute.

Sharp cheekbones.

Deep, brown eyes.

Rock-hard six-pack.

Round, squishy lips.

Ringlets of dark, floppy hair like one of the hobbits in *Lord of the Rings*.

He's also the best ice hockey player in our school, with a wrist shot that slams off the edge of his stick like a bullet, and the person he was texting to see if she wanted to, you know, hang out later, was definitely tempted, or more flattered actually, that such a cute boy would be willing to devote even a sliver of attention to her instead of her best friend, who was taller and less hippy, and she wasn't totally sure if he was kidding or what, if he was only making fun of her to try to get a laugh out of his friends, who were probably all stoned and clustered around peering at his screen, so she just texted back, *Don't be an ass. It's your girlfriend's birthday, remember? She's waiting for you to text her.*

He never did.

"I'm just saying," I say. "I know for a fact Jake texted someone that night and tried to hook up with her."

Mallory curls her hand into a fist again, then uncurls it. Tilts her head toward the window. Won't look at me. I turn off the car but don't get out. It's quiet without the radio.

"How do you know?" Mallory says, the words squeezing out slow, like a tire losing air.

I stay quiet.

"Who told you?" Mallory says, and turns away from the window to peer at me, her eyes watery. Her eyes asking the question her mouth is afraid to give birth to, to make present and alive and hovering between us in the front seat's stale air.

Neither of us moves to leave the car even though practice is about to start and it's our job to lead warm-ups.

"Nobody told me," I say. "Nobody had to tell me."

I put my hand around her fist. Her skin feels hot and angry. She knows what I mean and also knows two other things—I won't lie to her, and she's more important to me than any boy. We sit in silence a few more seconds.

"He's an *asshole*," I say, harder than before. "That's all that matters."

She nods.

"You're the best person ever," I say, squeezing her hand again. It's a ball of heat inside my fingers, itching, like a grenade, to explode. "Listen to me, Mallory. He's not worth one minute of your time."

"We're going to be late," she says, and I can see her shoulders regaining their strength, the fifty push-ups she does each morning working their way into her voice. "Let's go."

[2]

IN WARM-UPS, Mallory runs away from me.

Like always.

She's not trying to beat me. She's trying to beat herself. Has always tried to do that, ever since fifth grade when we got serious about this game and she decided when the coach said we had to run a lap around the field, she'd run every inch of the field.

No shortcuts.

Around the entire rectangle of turf, she stays on the outside of the sideline and I battle to keep up. We try to set the tone so no one on our team will cut corners, but inevitably someone does, and that someone will briefly pull closer to Mallory and me, but then Mal will find another gear and speed up and make that girl small in the rearview and I will speed up and try to catch Mallory and usually I won't be able to, but my best friend can't cheat even if she wanted to, and she makes me believe that about myself too.

After stretching, we drill two-on-ones. Mal and I against one defender. That's not a fair fight. In my dreams, almost every night, I see Mallory run, cutting toward the middle on a sharp line that looks like a sleek sailing boat homing in on the regatta's finish. I move my wrists when I'm sleeping, flick a pass and, without slowing down, she swings and then it happens—my first favorite sound in the world—the ball resounding off the wooden board at the back of the goal like a great gong, a song that says we did it, we conquered, game over, we won. I'm not lying when I say I move my wrists when I'm asleep. I dream the dream of passing to Mallory as many nights as I can. It's the dream that keeps me from dreaming about being the sad girl with no college scholarship, the lonely, loser-all-the-time girl, the tough girl nobody likes, or worse, the dream of my mother passed out in a ditch.

In real, wide-awake life, we kill it.

The defender rushes toward me and when her hips move past the point where she can't go back, that's the instant I flick the pass. Mal's open and her booming shot never misses. If the defender chooses instead to block the passing lane, I fake and then I'm gone. My own booming shot smacks the wood. Nobody stops us. Even Julie B.—super wealthy and super hard-core gender warrior who was all-state last year and is going to Princeton—can't stop us. We score every time.

After practice, we go with Julie B. to Subliminal Burrito. It's a basically lame burrito haven because this is the Midwest and not many people know how to make burritos the way they do, for instance, in California. Still, we are hungry and we smash. I cover my burrito with so much guacamole it looks like a mountain of green mud avalanched all over it. Julie B., with great pride, tells us how Tamara broke up with Edwin. We all agree this is progress. Edwin's a graduate of the same school of how-to-be-a-horrible-boyfriend as Jake, so score one for humanity. Julie B., with less pride, tells us how her whole AP stats class cheats on every test, even the kid who has the golf scholarship to Notre Dame.

"Isn't golf the sport where you're supposed to be honorable?" Mallory asks.

"No one's honorable," Julie B. says. "No one anywhere."

[3]

AT HOME, my mother's drunk. Why not? It's Sunday evening. She's outside, in the backyard, sitting on a metal chair with chipped white paint, her wine glass and ashtray on the table next to her, also metal with chipped paint. Her hair is pulled back into a ponytail and her face features so much sunscreen, it looks like somebody slathered her with the kind of paste we used in elementary school to glue felt squares to construction paper. Even though she smokes way more than necessary, she's always lecturing me about how I'll get skin cancer if I don't lather up as much as she does. I kind of believe her, but I still don't do it.

"Did you eat anything?" I say when she hears me open the sliding door on the porch and turns her head so I can see her ghostly face, her pupils dilated from sun and alcohol.

She ignores my question and smiles like she's the light of the world. Which she is. Still beautiful, even with the pasty layer of sunscreen, my mother is disappearing. She's probably lost fifteen pounds in the past year. And she wasn't overweight before that. She doesn't, as far as I know, throw up her food. At least not when she's sober. She just doesn't eat.

She cooks for me, won't let me consume anything labeled "microwaveable," then goes outside and has a cigarette and when she comes back in, doesn't do anything more than nibble a few bites of whatever she prepared.

"How was practice?" she says.

I sit down next to her and watch the birds in the trees, which is what she was doing before I got home. She feeds them too, with a half-dozen feeders she built herself and spread around the yard. There's a cardinal pecking at the one in the pine tree and we watch it for several minutes without speaking. If it were 1992 and our story were a two-hour movie on cable, this would probably be the time where she tells me my father, or that moody boy I like, called while I was gone, but that was a different world and now anyone who wants to reach me calls or snaps or, most often, texts directly. My mother is not in the middle. She never has to relay me messages, never has to know who I'm talking to, or not talking to.

Not that it matters. My father never calls anyway. It's too late for him to care and, honestly, I no longer want him to.

"Are you hungry?" she says.

I shake my head. "We stopped for burritos. Practice was great. Mallory killed it. She hit all my passes. Total Mal and Al show."

"That's good. I would've cooked."

"I know."

For a while we don't talk again. A blue jay cuts across the yard and chases the cardinal from the pine tree. Then the cardinal doubles back and bullies the blue jay. It's like the country's national mood—the red party, then the blue one, then the red again. I make a joke about it to my mother. She acts like she doesn't hear me, so I have to snicker at my own cleverness, which feels terrible.

Part of me wants to take my phone and throw it at the

birds. I'd miss them, of course—no harm, no fowl, ha ha—but then my phone would shatter against a tree or somebody's rooftop and then my mother would have to take my messages from the ancient house phone and she'd know who I was talking to, and maybe she'd be worried about me more, or at least ask me something beyond whether I need food.

"I'm going out later," she says.

"Where?"

"I'm not sure. That guy I went out with last week? Harvard? He's picking me up."

Harvard isn't the man's name, just where he went to school. He works in the same law firm my mother does, and he recently got divorced. My mother's not a lawyer, but a legal secretary who takes dictation. That means she types a lot while the lawyers talk. Like our house phone, which I don't understand why we still have, it's an ancient, obsolete custom. Why don't lawyers type on computers like everyone else? Maybe in some firms they do. But most of the lawyers my mom works for are old and bald and wear bow ties and drink brandy after work from glasses the size of salad bowls. They can do that in our kind of medium-sized city-town and still be respected and go to theater productions and street festivals and smile at the hordes they pretend to recognize because their families have lived here for four hundred years and they have cul-de-sacs named after them.

When my mother's dating someone she feels like there might be a future with, she practices her own kind of naming ritual, coming up with a nickname for the guy, like Harvard or Cleveland or Buffalo or School Psychologist. He lasted the longest. Almost a year. I didn't like School Psychologist. It felt like he constantly wanted to analyze me, even though I don't go to the school where he works. That's not appropriate. Harvard is one of the younger, non-family-street-name attorneys at the firm and probably does his own typing, but I still don't like him because he shaves his face every day and always looks like he just got out of the shower. I can't trust anybody that well-groomed.

"I have a lot of homework," I say, "so I'll probably be up when you get home."

"Don't worry about it," my mother says.

We're quiet again and watch the birds.

We're quiet for a while.

"I don't like the cardinal," I say. "He's a bully."

"I hate him," my mother says. "I always have."

[4]

I WASN'T LYING to my mother.

I do have a lot of homework.

We've only been back in school for, what, a week and a half? But the teachers, who, like usual, don't understand people have lives outside their classrooms, are already piling it on.

I check my planner and what I have already failed to complete could masquerade as a mound of oozing, half-chewed food stuffed into a restaurant's dumpster. Forty differentiated equations in analysis, twenty pages in a novel called *In the Time of the Butterflies*, a worksheet for Spanish, a rewrite of a physics lab report, and—the worst—a dozen pages to read in my online econ textbook. It's not that I don't like economics. I'm kind of neutral, to be honest. It's interesting sometimes—if I'm in the mood, for one specific example, to explore why most of my T-shirts cost ten dollars and some of Julie B.'s seventy-five—to learn about supply and demand and elasticity, and micro and macro and bubbles and slumps, but I hate online textbooks. I get that it saves trees not to have to print seven hundred pages multiple times, and that it saves money for the school, and, no doubt, I like not having to carry around a fifty-pound, hardcover monster, but I also get the feeling some of the people in charge of my life think kids just like to do stuff more if it's on computers.

The truth is we like to do on computers what we *like to do on computers*. The device doesn't make anything more—or less—fun. I like to play field hockey, but it's not like I'll dreamily adore any other activity that happens in the same place where I play my sport. It wouldn't be any more fun, for another specific example, to get a flu shot on the field hockey field just because it's the field hockey field.

In fact, when I'm on the computer doing something I don't want to be doing, I'm more likely to want to do something *else* on the computer that I'd rather be doing because I'm already on the device that lets me do that. In other words, if I'm reading an econ textbook online, it's too tempting to think about what else I could be doing online. Like, instead of reading the econ textbook, I could, with a swipe of my finger, be watching Beyoncé wear a yellow dress and swing a baseball bat at automobile windshields, which is very satisfying. I could also be tempted to do that if I were reading out of a real textbook, but it would take more than a swipe of a finger. I think there's actually an economic theory for that—the convenience of doing something more fun instead of the required and righteous task you're supposed to be doing—but, since I don't have a real authentic (and righteous) textbook to investigate, I forget what it's called.

After I finish my math and science—STEM subjects first, gotta take 'em seriously, according to our governor and other important people on television—I text Mallory and we mess around with our Spanish vocab, telling each other how our boyfriends have heads as big as gabinetes de archivos and ears that stick out like grapadoras because, for some reason, in our first unit of the semester, we're learning the language of either the workplace or office-supply stores, it's unclear which.

Mallory takes too long to respond to one text, which means she's busy texting someone else.

Jake says he wants to hang out, she finally says. *What should I do?*

Tonight? I ask her.

Affirmative, Captain Allison. I know it's just a booty call, but I kinda feel like it, you know?

I do know. But it's Jake. Why is she even texting with him? Did his having an interest in me make Mallory *more* interested in him? Mallory doesn't back down from any competition, and I don't either. Is that what's happening here? If it is, I bet Jake sensed it and that's why he went after me in the first place. Just to piss Mallory off and make her want him more.

Maybe let him do more.

I don't respond right away.

I think about Jake's big shoulders and his eyes that know how to laugh in a way that makes everyone getting stoned around a bonfire pay attention, that way that eyes have of being noisy, which is something my mom's eyes have too, even when they peer out of her ghost-pale face.

I don't have that.

Which is probably why Mallory's not listening to me about Jake.

Outside, a woman who got divorced two months ago walks her well-groomed Lassie-dog down the block. It's something she does five or six times a day, the dog's coat so shiny it looks like a brand-new Mercedes.

His heart is a paplera de reciclaje, I type into my phone. *When he's done using you, he'll take you back to the grocery store and cash you in for cinco centavos.*

But I don't send the text.

And I don't hear anything else from Mallory either.

[5]

I FINISH ALL MY HOMEWORK, even the econ, just before midnight and my mother's still not home.

The house feels as empty as my stomach.

I remember the burrito from so long ago, it seems like a prehistoric era. I think about getting a snack from the kitchen. Probably some cereal. With chocolate milk. Low-fat. A boy whose nickname is Rugger sends me a text that says, *Hey*.

Rugger didn't get the nickname from playing rugby. He got it from drinking too much tequila the first time he tried it and puking on the thick living-room carpet at Jake's house. It happened in ninth grade and Rugger's actually a nice kid. Even though he smokes weed every day, I've never heard of him being an asshole to anyone. He says he wants to be a ranger in a national park after college. Wants to party a lot when he's a student and then get serious post-graduation and be a good shepherd for trees and rivers. Possibly verdant savannahs. I kind of understand that idea, but I doubt I'll be partying a lot in college, not if I want to keep playing hockey and also enlighten myself on the academic side.

There's an economic concept for that too. It's called too-much-partying-equals-a-waste-of-tuition, which is something my mom can't afford to pay anyway. It's a field hockey scholarship or nothing for this girl. I don't want loans. I can't owe anybody anything. I just can't.

Rugger's not dumb, even though he parties. He's in my analysis class and we've worked on homework together—sometimes he even understands concepts I don't—but he's never texted me this late at night.

Hey at midnight can be a deep thing.

Especially on a Sunday when there's a whole new week of school looming with its ugly, mean-looking eyebrows.

It doesn't necessarily mean *I'm lonely*, but it might mean that.

It might also mean *I'm bored and the prospect of another boring week is intimidating, are you the person who can make life interesting?*

It could mean *I miss you* or *Let's hook up again*, but neither of those make sense because Rugger and I are not a couple or even close friends, and we've never hooked up.

So maybe it means *Do you think there's any potential we might hang out at some point?*

Which is an interesting question.

I've never really thought about Rugger like that because, even though he's nice, he smokes too much, and, well, the puke thing, and also he always seems to have a lot of ninth- and tenth-grade girls around him. He's not as cute as Jake—his shoulders are about half the size—but he's not *not* cute and he's definitely smarter and nicer.

Because I can't actually answer the potential-hang-out question, I choose to believe *Hey* means *It's late on a Sunday night and I'm still up and I'm wondering if you're still up because being human is a strange existence and maybe it's a little less strange if someone else is out there who maybe wonders about certain random elements of the universe in a similar way and I believe you might be just such a person so I'm reaching out to you. I'm taking a chance that, while we spin through these vast, swirling cosmos, maybe you and I can connect in a way that's interesting to both of us.*

I decide to text back.

Hey, yourself.

[6]

THE NEXT DAY in school my own head feels like a gabinete de archivos, an overstuffed and rusted domicile for files no one's looked at in twenty years. I can barely keep my eyes open. I ended up texting with Rugger until two a.m., and my mother still hadn't come home. She got in sometime before three. I only know because it was three when I heard her retching in the bathroom, then the sound of something glass, probably her expensive eye cream (which is her asleep-during-the-night version of sunscreen), falling to the floor and shattering.

Here's something Rugger texted me that's kind of thrilling. We were talking about whether it's worthwhile to believe in God and he said, *I don't know if it's worthwhile not to believe. I'm not sure I do believe, but what's going to happen if I'm on an airplane and it's about to crash and there are only two minutes before we hit the ocean, and I want to believe then? I don't want to think about whether it's my fault the plane is going down or if it's too late to redeem myself. I don't want to have my last two minutes being full of feeling stupid just because I didn't believe in something.*

I'm not sure I feel the same way about religion, or a

higher power or whatever else might be out there, but let's be honest, Jake has never said anything that thoughtful in his entire, beautiful, I-presume-to-be-sex-soaked existence and, also, I know what Rugger means about feeling stupid about not believing in something.

It's like with Mallory.

I need to believe if I pass the ball into a certain area, she'll be there to receive it. If I don't believe she'll be there, I'll never make the pass, and then what happens when she *is*? Then I'll feel the kind of stupid Rugger's talking about. I'll fail my team because I failed to believe. I can't handle that. It's like the Great One, the immortal Wayne Gretzky, said, you miss one hundred percent of the shots you never take.

Which makes me think of Jake, who has such a bullet shot.

It's sublime to watch, in fact. It ripples the back of the net from no matter where he shoots it, and it makes me think how, when he aims to do something, he nails it.

Which means he believes in something too, even if it's only himself.

And let's be honest, even if he's an asshole, there's something about his gigantic self-confidence that makes me understand why Mallory can go back to him.

When I hit the practice field, I'm so tired I'm awful.

The Mal and Al show sputters, then ceases to function altogether, a circus caravan stuck in a rut in the road. I didn't sleep much after listening to my mother throw up and break things, so my stomach's wobbly and unfocused and my legs are two heavy logs. I'm slow and my passes are off, and Mallory keeps looking at me like, *Why do you suck*, and I never ask her if she snuck out to hook up with Jake because she's running like her feet are made from a Katy Perry song and that means she probably did.

After yet another horrendous pass where I turn the ball

over directly to Julie B. and she dribbles back the other way and scores, Coach tells me to take a break. I wander over to the sideline as if I'd like to erect a lakefront cabin there and stretch out on a hammock made of nothing but air, as if my legs could float off the ground, weightless. I take a drink from my water bottle and Aaliyah, who has an ankle with a nasty high sprain, hobbles over on her crutches and asks me if I'm all right.

"Fine," I say, because I don't want to talk about how terrible I'm playing or why I'm playing so terribly and I also don't like to be around people who are injured. It's silly, I know, but I always feel like the injury, the bad luck of it, can rub off on me.

Without me on the field, Mallory takes a couple perfect passes from Sydney and beats Julie B. twice in a row and scores goals. "You didn't look like yourself out there," Aaliyah says, as if she's some kind of coach.

"Who did I look like, Miley Cyrus?"

I say it to be mean, and also because I remain pissed off at Miley Cyrus for dumping her Hannah Montana persona. Nobody likes to watch people on television grow older. They turn into demons who strut around with stainless-steel coffee containers and talk about STEM subjects.

The alarm I wake up to is still the opening chords from "Party in the U.S.A." Only Mallory knows that.

Also, to be honest, the main reason I like that song at all is that people *have* told me I look like Miley Cyrus. Personally, I don't see it. I mean, I kind of have big eyes like she does, and I sort of have a semblance of cheekbones, but my lips are totally average, if not slightly below that, and, let's be real, she's beautiful and I'm past the point of exhausted and my passes sucked.

Aaliyah's hurt by my snippy tone and hobbles away without saying anything else and I feel worse for being a jerk.

I follow and tell her I'm sorry and that I'm overtired and have been having a terrible day.

"I know how that feels," she says, peering down at her ankle, which is still swollen, and I feel like even more of a jerk.

I gaze at her hair, which is beautiful, with these springy, spiraled curls that look like the kind of curlicue pasta you can buy in fancy packages at Whole Foods. I wonder what it would feel like to touch it.

"You know what I really don't like?" Aaliyah says. "When white people stare at my hair."

She's kind of smiling but her eyes look harsh, so I can't tell how serious she is. My stomach, which already bites, hardens like I ate a bowl of clay. And I hate clay. I'm a mess around clay. I'm the worst artist in my ceramics class and I also feel like the worst captain in the history of all sports teams everywhere.

"I'm sorry," I stammer, "it's just, it's really pretty."

"Pretty or exotic?"

"Pretty." I feel myself getting angry, like I want to stand up for myself and try to win an argument I didn't even know I was involved in. "I think Mallory's hair is beautiful too, and Sydney's, and Coach's—even though it's short. Pretty much anything's better than this boring clump." I run my fingers through my own itchy, sweaty mane and pull at a few split ends. Aaliyah can choose to believe me or not. I'm having a shitty day and if she wants to hate me, if she wants to think I'm racist, she can go ahead.

Her eyes soften.

Sort of.

"It's just usually when white people look at my hair, the next thing they want is to reach out and touch it."

I feel ashamed of my fingers.

"Really?" I ask, as if I'm shocked, offended.

"Yeah, even teachers sometimes." She shakes her head. "Actually, a lot of times. You'd be surprised. It's like they think I'm a dog."

Coach's voice chimes from the middle of the field. She's upset with Sydney about something and gestures toward the scoring circle with her left hand as if she wants her to understand something she isn't quite getting. I don't know if I should be happy about that, but I'll be honest, it makes my stomach feel a bit better.

"Look," I say to Aaliyah, "I'm sorry. I'm being a huge jerk today. We'll probably go for burritos after practice. You want to come with me and Mal?" I'm trusting Mallory will still want to go with me after my horrid passing.

Aaliyah examines her ankle some more and I can tell she's thinking about whether she should forgive me or not, whether it's worth it to alienate one of the senior captains. "To tell the truth," she says, "you *do* kind of look like Miley Cyrus. Except you don't have those toothpick thighs. More muscle in your hips too."

I laugh and we spend time talking about how it sucks to have bad days and Coach high fives Sydney after she figures out what she wants and after practice Aaliyah comes with us to get food.

[7]

THE ONLY PROBLEM is Julie B. and Sydney come with us too. I wish Sydney hadn't, because I'm still upset about my disgusting passes and her good ones, but she just moved here from a nearby town where they still have beauty pageants and a foofy homecoming court so I'm willing to swallow my insecurities and cut her some slack. There's not a whole bunch of room in the car though, and Julie B. and Aaliyah are the two biggest girls so they battle it out for shotgun.

Then Julie B. says, "Girl, I'm a senior. You get the back of the bus."

Nobody says anything for a few seconds. Aaliyah is the only African American player on our team. The only African American player, actually, we've had on the team in like five years. And she's on crutches. I feel the clay in my stomach harden and Sydney looks like she wants to scurry back to her town with beauty pageants.

I think about how I almost reached out to touch Aaliyah's hair and the overflowing-garbage nature of my overall day and I hear myself say to Julie B., "You can't say that."

Everybody stares.

I feel a chill coming from Mallory, as if she turned into an icicle. The sharp, pointed kind.

My voice quivers and it sounds like somebody else's, but I keep talking. "That's not acceptable, Julie B. You can't say something like that to her."

The parking lot, the seagulls circling around it, everything grows blurry.

Nobody talks.

"It's OK," Aaliyah says to break the silence, but I know it isn't.

"Oh, Christ, lighten up," Julie B. says, climbing into the back seat. "First off, you know I was joking. And second, you know I didn't mean it *that* way."

Mallory looks like she wants to punch me in the face.

[8]

AT SUBLIMINAL BURRITO, we eat burritos and quesadillas, no chips. No sour cream either. Mallory and Julie B. are loud and laugh a lot and go to the machine and refill their small soft drinks numerous times without paying. Sydney laughs a lot too, but doesn't really say much. Aaliyah and I are quiet and I can't tell if it would be better to say something else to Julie B. and put the whole conversation on the table—like how can she be so pro-woman and so Princeton and so rich and such an overall feminist badass and still make such an insensitive comment—or if I should just try to move on and be happy and friendly and make Aaliyah laugh so she feels more like part of the team. Since I can't figure out what to do and Mal's ignoring me, I tune out and think about better times, like when her father built a special field hockey room for her, or maybe for both of us, in her basement.

I say maybe for both of us instead of just her, because after my father left and my mom started to drink and be out more, it sometimes seemed like Mallory's dad wanted to be a dad for me too. He's the tallest adult I've ever encountered, probably around six-eight, and he used to be a minor league baseball player but busted one of his knee joints and had to stop. He's the only injured person who doesn't make me uncomfortable. He has Mallory's enormous brown eyes and the male edition of her face and when we were younger and still played softball, he'd take Mallory and me to the park every weekend and pitch us batting practice from a gigantic and dusty bucket of balls. Then, even though he was limping around like an old man, he'd hit us grounders and flies. Afterward, he'd take us to Dairy Queen, and while I don't like that kind of artificial, soft ice cream now, back then it was the best of all possibilities, and Mallory and I would always get chocolate cones dipped in additional chocolate with chocolate sprinkles on top and we'd eat them like we believed nobody in the world was more important than we were.

He built the field hockey room after we tried out for our first club team in sixth grade and even though we made it, it was obvious we didn't have the same stick skills as the eighth graders. When I say built, what I mean is he cleaned out a storage room so it was totally empty and put artificial turf on the floor. Then he knocked down one of the walls, stripped it to the wooden jousts, and put up netting instead of sheetrock so we could blast away and not dent anything solid.

"When it's cold or raining outside, you can come in here and work on your shots," he said. "You can shoot as much as you want."

That's not what we did.

We worked in there every day, cold or not, rain or not, and even though the room was too small for us to do long passes, we worked on quick give-and-go plays and played defense against each other as if we wanted to tear each other's throats into pieces. We worked on our flicks, pushes, pulls, reverse chips, and aerials and made up some other moves there aren't names for. Then her dad made small targets out of orange duct tape in the upper and lower corners of the net and we practiced aiming our shots at them. In a few weeks, we could do what the best eighth graders could do, and a few weeks after that, we were better than they were. They pretended they still liked us, but they didn't, never hung out with us in the hotels at tournaments—would like, leave the swimming pool as soon as we got into it and go sit in the hot tub—and never put us in the text group chat, either, or invited us to gatherings at the bubble-tea place on Orange Street. We hated how they snubbed us, and that's another thing Mallory and I promised each other, that no matter how good any younger girls were, we'd always reach out to them and try to make them feel wanted.

Which means I'm shirking my promise if I don't somehow reach out to Aaliyah.

Like, in the next thirty seconds.

Mal's dad comes to every game now, home or away, and he never cheers or yells from the stands, never publicly puts pressure on her, and that's great, but I also think it's part of why Mallory's so intense. She told me once she sometimes hates the field hockey room. "It's always there," she said. "After you go home, it's still there, I can still use it if I want and it makes me feel like if I'm not down there shooting at the corners when you're sleeping, I'm not working as hard as I could be."

"Do you mean not as hard as *your dad* thinks you should be?" I asked.

"That's not it," she said, but I didn't totally believe her because another time she told me she thought I was lucky my parents never came to games.

I also asked her why she cared if *I* were home sleeping when she was thinking about the room unused and dark, like if she were measuring herself against me.

"I always measure myself against you, Allison," she said, "but that's not a bad thing. It's a compliment. Because you're amazing."

Yeah, sure I am.

When Sydney goes to the bathroom and Mal and Julie B. head to the soda machine to steal more beverages and giggle, Aaliyah and I are the only two left at the table. Well, our silence is there too and it feels like a flipped-over train laying on top of us.

"Do you like the Divergent movies?" I blurt out of nowhere because I can't think of a single other thing to say.

At first, Aaliyah doesn't say anything, looks at me like I should stop pretending we're at day camp and I'm the counselor whose job it is to make everyone feel included. Then she smiles. Her teeth are a little crooked. One of the lower ones in the center of her mouth looks shorter than the rest, like it got chiseled down with a file. "Are you kidding?" she says, and her smile grows bigger. "I'd say they're the best, except they're not. The books are better."

I high five her like we just won states because I also love books more than movies—not absolutely always, but mostly—and we spend the next few minutes talking with our mouths full about Tris and Four and what it means to be Dauntless and everything feels warm and hearty until we are ready to leave, when Jake bounces into Subliminal with two friends from the ice hockey team. Mallory is not surprised so I know she texted him to tell him. The other two boys are Robbie and Connor, and they are so tall they are shy. Connor has acne that goes all around the bottom of his face like a chinstrap beard and teeth that are large and bright. I've heard he's nice, but I don't know him except to wave and say hi. He also has a reputation for being the toughest fighter who no one wants to mess with. Robbie is the tallest, and so skinny he looks like a delicate bird, maybe a flamingo. He almost never talks, but he's supposed to be a good fighter too.

I am not interested in talking to any of them because I hate Jake for texting me on Mallory's birthday and then for roping her back into his bullshit, but she is delighted he's there in his floppy shorts, which show off his tan calves, and his neon tank top, which illustrates the striations in his massive shoulders. He is a cheeseball, but he is also a very gorgeous and dazzling cheeseball. I am tired of Subliminal Burrito. It's too loud and I ate too much and there's nothing else to say about the Divergent series. Also, I have homework and my mother to deal with when I get home.

"You guys want to come to the Meadow?" Jake says, and Robbie giggles. It's kind of a titter and super awkward, and I kind of feel better and want to kiss his long, skinny face.

But there's no way in hell we're going to High Oak Meadow.

It's amazing there, with the river flowing by and all the trees that offer shade and the lush grass and the glacial boulders. It's also the place where a boy with floppy shorts and tan calves goes with his friends to smoke, and we are in-season so, no, we're not doing that. The boys already know we're not doing that, and it's actually an insult to ask.

Even Rugger, who smokes every day, wouldn't ask.

"Not today," I say, trying to make it sound light and whateverish, but I know it doesn't.

Mallory gives me another I-want-to-punch-you look because she doesn't like that I'm speaking for all of us, but that's too bad. I *am* speaking for all of us, showing my teammates that even the cutest boy with the prettiest shoulders can't tempt us to do something that could screw up our season. For a second, I think she might decide to go with them just to spite me, but she doesn't. She's worked harder than anyone and, tan calves or no tan calves, there's no breaking up the team.

"Jake, you'll have to excuse us," she says. "We've got a state championship to defend."

"At night?"

"It's called homework, which leads to good grades, which leads to staying eligible. Also, *as you should know*, we have a game tomorrow."

"Same homework as last night?" he says, and Robbie titters again but there's nothing cute about it because it means he already knows what happened between Jake and Mallory and that means Jake's an even bigger dumb-ass than I thought.

"How about a celebration blunt after the season's over?" Jake suggests.

It's celebratory, I think, *the adjective, you idiot*.

"How about you never talk to me again?" Mallory says and flips her hair like she's Regina George and starts to lead us out to the parking lot. Sydney and Julie B. follow as if boys our age will never have a chance with any of us—which they shouldn't, not really—but I hang back so I can open the door and hold it for Aaliyah and we're the only ones who can hear Jake say, "If I can't talk to you, I can still text, right?"

I turn to give him a dirty look, my dirtiest, in fact, the kind I normally reserve for my mother if she drinks too much at a restaurant and starts flirting with waiters and talking so loudly it's embarrassing. But then I am startled. Jake is fast, a quick, agile skater, and he's managed to slide right up to me while my back was turned. Before I can ratchet up the necessary acid in my eyes, he's got his hand on my face. Just the knuckles brushing against my cheek. They feel warm and strong and my skin tingles. I can't help it, I want to put his fingers in my mouth and lick them. "Last night was magic," he whispers, "and it could have been you. In my heart, I wanted it to be you."

"Don't be an asshole," I say, but my voice is small, the kind that fits inside someone's back pocket, and he knows it, and his smile is large and disgusting. I want to say more, to feel my fire and make every beverage machine at the burrito place vibrate with my anger, but I don't. I push through the door and feel the sun on my forehead like a needle jammed between my eyes, and I kick my foot—hard, one time—into the parking lot gravel, then hustle to catch up to my squad.

In the car, Julie B.'s already sitting in the back. With Mal and Syd. I lunge to hold the car door for Aaliyah—that's two doors in about forty seconds—and she struggles to fold her swollen ankle into the front seat.

Nobody says anything during the ride, as if we're teammates of nothing, not one single thing.

[9]

AFTER WE DROP the other girls off, Mallory climbs up front and can't wait to talk.

"You doubted me, didn't you?"

"No."

"You did. You thought I wanted to go to High Oak and smoke with Jake. I saw it on your face."

"Only for a second, I swear."

She laughs and it seems like everything's good again, like we could keep driving all the way across the Midwest, blasting pop songs out the window, singing along as if we're celebrities with ten million YouTube subscribers and jewel-studded sunglasses.

We can't though, because when I get close to her house she starts to unbuckle her seatbelt before we even reach the driveway, as if she's got somewhere much more essential she needs to be.

"Lot of homework?" I ask.

"Fair amount."

"English essay?"

"Just a lot of stuff to do."

She reaches for her backpack on the floor by her feet, grabs it by one of the straps, and ducks her head to swing out of the car.

"I'm sorry," I say, trying somehow to slow her from leaving so quickly. "I shouldn't have doubted you. I know how much you care about the team."

"No, you don't," she says, "not really."

I'm stunned and want to cry.

It sounds like the world is a giant vacuum cleaner and there's an ear-splitting whoosh and I'm being sucked away from everything I know. Is this my car I'm driving? Is this my best friend telling me I don't really know her? I don't know what to do, so I stare through the front windshield at an ugly plastic mailbox and a tree beyond it with a falling-apart treehouse. Mallory is out of the car, ready to jog up the stairs to her front door, but she turns back and ducks her face in.

"I love you, Allison," she says, "but you need to get your act together."

"I don't understand," I say, reaching to brush her hair from her face so I can see her eyes. For an unsettling moment, my knuckles trace across her cheek the way Jake's did mine. "I had a bad day, my passes were off, so what? You think I don't know how much you care? You think I don't care as much as you?"

"You basically accused Julie B. of being racist. That's the kind of thing that can destroy our team. You see how no one talked on the way home? Why do you think that was?"

I don't say anything about Jake touching my face or Robbie's creepy giggle. Or, for that matter, about Mallory sneaking out to hook up with Jake on a school night. "What is? *What* can destroy our team? The actual racism? Or speaking up against it?"

"You know what I mean."

"No, I don't. I actually really don't."

It's the kind of day where the afternoon heat sticks onto us long after it's gone. Even though we ate our burritos amidst well-functioning air-conditioning, we are both still wearing our sweat.

"Who's our best defender?" Mallory says.

"Julie B."

"You know why?"

"Because she's tough and can't stand letting anyone get past her."

"Yeah, because she's *defensive*. You ever won an argument against Julie B.?"

I'm not sure. It's probably true I never have. Once, I tried to explain to her that her older brother wasn't as big a loser as she thought he was just because he worked scooping cones at the ice cream parlor with the worst-tasting ice cream in the city. Even worse than the soft, fake stuff. It's weird when ice cream, soft or hard, tastes bitter or stale, like a nap that went on too long. Julie B. had acted like it was her brother's fault, like if he didn't have those stooped shoulders and the pimples on his forehead, he'd be working at the dairy where the ice cream was frothy and thick and made your lips swell like too much kissing.

She'd asked me if I'd be willing to date him and I said maybe, even though there wasn't a chance in hell, and she knew it. But that's partially because you don't date your teammate's brother, period. *That's* the kind of thing that can totally destroy a team. Any team.

"He's definitely a loser then," she told me. "See? You'd pretty much date anyone and you still wouldn't date my brother."

I knew she was kidding, sort of, about my being willing to date pretty much anyone, because I'm actually not, not at all. I don't like boys who talk too much about video games, for instance. I mean, please don't inform me about the survival statistics of your avatar or whatever—but I guess Mallory's right. There's no point arguing with Julie B.

Thinking about dating, and actually, how picky I am about it, makes me wonder whether Rugger's planning on texting with me again tonight—but hopefully earlier in the night and hopefully not for as long—and I lose my track of thought—or is it my train of thought or the track of my train of thought?

Mallory looks at me as if she's been waiting frantically for several minutes for me to vacate the lone stall in a public restroom—like, *Houston to Satellite Allison, get with the program*—and I know I shouldn't have been thinking about Rugger right now either, and I should probably tell her about Jake whispering to me too, but it doesn't seem like the right time. And now Mal's curling and uncurling her fist and I remember I'm supposed to be focusing only on Julie B. and whether I've ever won an argument against her. "No, I guess I haven't."

"And you won't either, because she won't let you. Do you really want to have a debate with her about whether she's racist? Because all you'll do is make her hate you and if she hates you, and you're a captain and she's our best defender, that means she starts to resent you more than she already does and then our team falls apart."

The anger in me surges from somewhere I didn't know about, as if I've got a secret basement where there's a rage that's been incubating since I was born, or at least since the first time a boy snuck up behind me in middle school and snapped my bra strap.

"Did you see Aaliyah's face when she said that?" My voice is rising, ringing like a tardy bell. The lawns in Mallory's neighborhood aren't that big, though they're perfectly gardened. Her neighbors can probably hear everything. "Did you see the way her shoulders slumped when she got into the car without saying a word? As if she knew there was nothing she could do, that there might not *ever* be something she can do. I don't care how good Julie B. is on defense. She can't make someone feel like that. Some things are bigger than a state championship."

"Really?"

"Yeah, really!" I say it like I'm in a courtroom on television, shouting my objection at the judge.

"How about you keep your voice down? You think the whole city wants to hear this?"

"Maybe it needs to. Maybe our pretty little community needs to have a conversation about race if a senior in our high school, who has a four-point and who everyone loves and who is going to the Ivy League, thinks it's OK to tell the only Black girl on the team she should sit in the back of the bus. I don't know about you, but I saw Sydney cringing too."

Mallory almost makes a laughing sound. Instead, she shakes her head.

"OK, say you're right. I'm not saying what Julie B. said was cool—"

"Cool? Come on, Mal. It wasn't even close to cool. You know what Aaliyah told me? Teachers at our school touch her hair because they're curious. They reach out and treat her like she's a goat at a petting zoo. We have no idea what it feels like to deal with something like that."

Mallory gazes at the ground.

I wait.

"OK," she says, looking up to meet my eyes, "it was shitty for Julie B. to say that. No question. But what do you want to do about it?"

"I don't know that I want to do anything. I did what I thought was right at the time. I called her out and let Aaliyah know she wasn't the only person upset."

"Yeah, but how did that make Aaliyah feel? Did she hug you? Give you a high five? If I remember correctly, she just felt more awkward and wanted to hide the whole time at Subliminal. So what did calling Julie B. out accomplish?"

"A. She didn't hide the whole time at Subliminal, just at first while you were laughing with Julie B. and stealing beverages, and B. it made Julie B. understand she can't talk like that. C. It made Aaliyah understand that at least someone on the team is willing to stick up for her."

Mallory shakes her head again. "Thanks for your little lesson about the alphabet, and for being a judgmental bitch. It's not like you haven't stolen drinks before. You're the one who taught me, remember?"

I do. It was before my mom got the job at the law firm and after when my dad disappeared and stopped paying child support for like, two years and we had no money. I'm not proud of those days.

"OK, forget about the drinks. I don't know why I said that. I just wanted to make Aaliyah feel like part of the team."

"Yeah, but maybe you just made Julie B. mad at you and made Aaliyah mad that you felt she couldn't handle it herself. Maybe you made her feel like a little sibling who needs the big, bad white girl's protection. Did you think about that? And maybe you reminded her she's the only girl on the team who doesn't look like everyone else."

"*I* made her do that? You don't think she thinks about that every second of every time she's with us?"

"It doesn't help for you to point it out in front of the group."

"Julie B. already pointed it out."

"Look, Allison, you can think that all you want, but even if it was wrong for her to say, I'm going to choose to believe she didn't mean it in a nasty way."

"Really? How did she mean it?"

"As a joke."

"Not a funny one."

"Allison, I'm with you that it was wrong. It was thoughtless, but I don't think you needed to make a big deal out of it in front of everyone. We could have talked to Julie B. on our own, told her she can't say stuff like that, maybe even asked her to apologize to Aaliyah one-on-one. Now, though, it's already in Julie B.'s head that you're uptight about it and she's going to be defensive if we bring it up again. You know she thinks she should have been named captain instead of one of us. Now she's going to think it even more."

It's true what Mallory's saying. I probably shouldn't have embarrassed Julie B. like that. Then again, she shouldn't have said something racist. Also, I wonder if Julie B. thinks it's me or Mallory who shouldn't be captain.

Probably me. *Nobody* thinks Mallory shouldn't be captain.

"Do you get what I'm saying, Allison? There's a way we could have handled it that would have been better for the team. You didn't think about that. That's what it means to be a leader, to think about how everything you do and say affects the team."

"Aaliyah's part of the team too," I say.

"I agree. And I want her to feel like she's an important part, a natural and organic part, not an *issue* everyone has to tiptoe around. There was a better way to handle this, Allison, that's all I'm saying."

"I get it, Mal."

"Do you?"

In my mind, I see a bus and Aaliyah and I sitting at the front of it, quiet and alone, with the rest of the team in back howling, Julie B. leading them in a rousing chorus of the Rolling Stones' "You Can't Always Get What You Want," a song, to be honest, Julie B.'s probably never heard of. I only know it because my mom plays it when she's tanked and thinking about my dad and about how her job isn't what she wants, and about the unfinished furniture she never touches in the garage. She used to build chairs, or rebuild chairs, I should say. Find them on the side of the road broken and splintered, and rehab them as if they were birds with broken wings, rebolt them and sand them and paint them in an array of bold colors and then sell them at art shows. Now the broken chairs just sit in a pile, a tangled, neglected mess.

I told Rugger about them in one of the texts last night, explained how much they bum me out, how they sit there like a plan to go somewhere cool that always got talked about in an exciting way, but never actually happened. It felt weird to talk about them with a boy I hardly know since I've never mentioned them to anyone else, but he said I should just forget about them. They're not a metaphor, just old chairs.

Since I haven't said anything, Mallory walks away from the car. Without looking back, she says loud enough for me to hear, "It's the Mal and Al show, remember? Don't make me have to take passes from Sydney at the game tomorrow. I hate that."

"I won't," I whisper, not loud enough for her to hear.

I hate that too.

[10]

Rugger wants to hang out.

He texts me early this time, shortly after I leave Mal's, but he wants to meet up late, after he finishes his homework. Not to smoke or anything, just to talk in person, face to face. I want to, just to see what it's like—what his face feels like for talking and other subversive activities—but I tell him no. Sneaking out wouldn't be a problem, my mother would probably let me go anyway or be too drunk to notice. And I'm tempted. But I don't want a repeat of today's horrid practice at the game tomorrow, so I'm going to bed at a reasonable hour. Before eleven.

I tear through my analysis homework and my terms for the online econ. I'm supposed to be working on an English essay, but it's not due until next Monday so I blow it off. I write up the summary I took notes for in physics lab this morning and it's only 10:30 so I brush my teeth, shower quickly, and am ready to say goodnight to Mom by 10:50.

That's the hard part.

I can hear the TV downstairs, but that doesn't mean she's awake. She could be passed out on the couch already, which happens about fifty percent of the time during the week. I don't know how she wakes up for work every morning, but she always manages to. Maybe she doesn't get as drunk as I think she does. Maybe she's just tired and doesn't like sleeping in her bedroom if she's the only one in it. I, personally, can't sleep in a big room like the living room with all that space around me and no door to close. I like my room, how it's small, secure. Posters of national team players that I clipped from USA Field Hockey's magazine, *FHLife*, hang on the wall. My favorite is of Rachel Dawson, midfielder for the Olympic team in 2008 and 2012. In the poster, she's playing in London and has her stick pulled back and ready for a backhand sweep. She's low to the ground, her face no more than two feet above the turf. Her back leg is fully extended behind her and her front leg is bent so she can get maximum leverage when she whacks the ball. When I focus on the muscles in her arms, I see hissing snakes. That's what I like to think about before I go to sleep in my tiny room with too many clothes on the floor and the door closed, how my own arms can be hissing snakes too. How I can be a different creature, not the girl who sits quietly in class, hesitant to raise her hand, but the girl who can crack her stick against the ball and send it all the way down the field.

When I get downstairs to the living room, I see my mother's not asleep yet. She's sitting bolt upright on the couch, but nothing about her is moving, so it's really scary. The television is playing a reality show, one about people earning the chance for free cosmetic surgery if they lose enough weight to show the surgeon they're serious about improving themselves. I can't stand shows like that and I have no idea why my mother would be watching one. She is already beautiful and the only improving she needs to do is the kind that includes eating actual food and putting down her drink and leaving it on the table.

I sit on the couch next to her and take one of her hands in mine. It feels cold and damp. She still isn't moving or saying anything. There are strands in her hair that are bone white. She has told me she doesn't want to dye them, but I'm betting, one day, she will. We are quiet and the sound on the television is low and we are bathed in its blue glow. My mother squeezes my hand, so I know she's alive. I wouldn't say she's crying, but her eyes are glassy. On the program, a woman steps on a scale and celebrates. She'll be able to have a new nose now, she tells her best friend, and fuller lips. I want to swing my field hockey stick into her forehead, make her really need the surgery she's so excited about getting.

Commercials for local cosmetic surgeons and expensive moisturizers assault us for several minutes and my mother does not turn to look at me or say anything. I am terrified and cold. A new show comes on about losing weight in order to get a new car. Thin people apparently deserve everything. My mother does not talk and her eyes don't dry up. I sit with her for a long time. The night gets too big for me, like it's only space, only drifting and no gravity. When I finally go upstairs, it is almost one a.m. and I don't have the energy to text Rugger or look at Rachel Dawson's coiled arms.

Tomorrow is the first game of the season and my legs feel like sinking boats that can no longer float.

[11]

AT SCHOOL, I see Rugger talking to a sophomore named Delaney.

She is cute with sandy-blond hair and a blue, sophisticated sweater that looks like a tight skin, like she's a blue-skinned creature from a science fiction movie. Additionally, her curves fill her leggings nicely. I'm a little pissed because it seems like Rugger must be all about immediate gratification if, just because I didn't hang out with him last night, he turns right away to a tenth grader. But that is fine. He can talk to anyone he wants.

I walk past them and do not say hello, even though Delaney is in my ceramics class and we often stand next to each other at one of the overlarge sinks at the end of the hour when we are scrubbing the clay from our fingers and forearms. I hate clay and am only taking ceramics to earn my mandatory art credit, so I tend to scrub it off with ferocity and Delany tends to laugh at me, but in a sweet, empathetic way. Rugger shows her something on his phone and she laughs about that too, but it is not her real laugh. I have heard her real laugh at the sink and, one time, when she was spinning a bowl on the wheel and she was distracted and her putty knife slipped and clay flew up and splashed her cheek. She is one of those beautiful girls who does not play sports and has muscles that are mostly soft. I'm not trying to hate because she's nice, but maybe Rugger prefers that look. If so, he would not prefer me.

And my snakes.

That's OK, he smokes too much anyway.

About ten seconds after I pass them, I get a text and it's him. That means he texted me while he was talking to her. I don't respect that kind of behavior. The text says he thinks I look shimmering today. What gives him the right to tell me how I look? And what does it mean to look shimmering? Am I a dying star fading out? My light too distant to mean anything? Maybe he meant to say sparkling or glimmering.

That boy better brush up on his vocabulary if he wants to make the leap from sophomore fake-laugher with soft muscles to senior defending state champ.

My phone buzzes again.

Jake.

Want to sneak off-campus for lunch and hang out?

[12]

TODAY'S GAME is our home opener, against Westgate. They are gritty and tough and made state semifinals last year, so no one can score in the first half. A girl named Lauren Metcalf who has a full scholarship to Northwestern is their center-mid and we battle for the ball like two runt puppies trying to nurse their mother's last available nipple. I can't believe I just compared myself to breastfeeding dogs. That's gross.

Also true.

I think of her more as an elbow, a giant elbow with feet, because that's what I feel when we're trying to nudge each other out of position—her elbow in my chest. All game long. It's sharp and hard, like the corner of a brick and I know I'll have a bruise when I get home, a purplish mark between my breasts. I briefly wonder what Rugger would think if he saw it. Then I wonder why I'm thinking about him during a tight game.

Of course, it's better than thinking about Jake.

I didn't sneak out with him for lunch. There's no way I would. But I thought about it a lot during ceramics, how his lips might taste and what his hands might feel like on my back, and the coffee cup I was allegedly working on turned into a pencil holder, then a bathtub for a doll house, then nothing.

We've had almost zero opportunities in the scoring circle. Mallory's been open a couple times, but I haven't been able to get the ball to her. If I lift it, they knock it out of the air with their sticks. If I push-pass, they are quick enough to get their sticks down on the ground and block it. I look for space, but it's scarce. I don't feel slow because I'm blocking everything they try to get into our end too, either that or cutting off angles so they have to pass into the Julie B. zone—which basically means we're getting the ball back because she is eating their passes the way she eats burritos—but the game is still frustrating.

At halftime, Coach advises us not to get frustrated.

At halftime, Coach tells us to believe in the hours we've put in, to trust our instincts, to play to win instead of playing not to lose.

At halftime, I grab my water bottle and drain it and look around to see if anyone has a bigger jug, one that might still have extra water in it I can use to refill my own. Aaliyah sees me searching and I notice she's got one that's at least a half-gallon, and she's not playing because of her ankle so it's probably still mostly full and I gesture with my empty bottle, mime pouring it out on the ground so she can see there's nothing in it, and she thinks for a few seconds and then gives me a slow nod. I bring my bottle over to her and she uncaps hers and starts to pour.

"Thanks," I say. "Hot out here."

"Be Dauntless," she says, instead of *you're welcome*. "Get a goal."

[13]

WITH JUST UNDER two minutes left and the game still scoreless, the giant elbow digs into my chest again, this time as hard as she can, and I've had enough. We are chasing a loose ball at midfield and I do the thing I have been waiting to do all game. Instead of lowering my center of gravity, pushing back into her and painting my own abstract art onto her ribs with my shoulder, I step back slightly and don't resist her momentum. In basketball, they call it "pulling the chair." Because she thinks I'll be pushing back and I'm not, her force has no way to be absorbed and she tumbles. I slip around her and she is quick to recover, but not quick enough. I have open space for half a second and that is all I need.

I reach the ball with the tip of my stick and lift a pass to Mal sprinting down the right side. She fields it clean and beats her defender and is in the clear. Their goalie is all-state and fearless, so instead of sitting back in the net and waiting for Mallory to home in on a corner, she rushes out like a huge roadblock and tries to cut the angle. But I haven't stopped running. When Mal sees the goalie's charge she raises her stick as if to drive the ball past her on the right side, then reverses her wrist and swats it back to me across the middle. The net is wide open and I don't even have to swing hard. I just flick it into the board and then Mal and I are hugging and everyone is running to join us, except for Aaliyah, who stays on the sideline because it will take her too long to hobble out and enter the scrum.

It is the worst thing that can happen for Westgate, a scoreless tie broken with less than two minutes left. The giant elbow is furious I tricked her, but she also gives me a chin nod to let me know she appreciates the move and that she will try even harder to beat me next time. For the rest of the game they come at us like ferocious lions or other kinds of large and untamed felines, but we take no chances because we have already scored and our defense is a fortress they can't penetrate. With twenty seconds left, I stop another charge and send a pass backward and across the field to Julie B. She runs around with the ball while their attackers swarm after her and the clock ticks down to the horn.

When we get back to the sideline, our coach congratulates us for our patience and tells us we did a good job not letting our frustration overwhelm us. "Great combo work," she says to Mallory and me.

Mal gives me a fist pound and I nod my head and finish drinking the water Aaliyah gave me.

She limps over and says, "You did it. I knew you would."

"Thanks," I say, and mean it.

"You're welcome," she says.

[14]

I heard about your goal, Rugger texts me at a reasonable hour. *Sorry I couldn't make it to the game.*

Why couldn't you? I text back, then erase what I wrote before I send it. I'm not his mother. I don't need to know why he can or can't do things. I eat a few slices of seaweed from a package, teriyaki flavored. People make fun of me for eating seaweed. These are the same people who can't fall asleep without first smoking a plant rolled up in a piece of paper and sealed with somebody's spit.

I had to watch my brother, Rugger writes, answering my question as if I'd sent it. *My mom had a job interview.*

He told me before how his mom lost her job because of the recession, which I can identify with, and how she's been freaking out, which I also can identify with, so I guess it's OK for him to miss the game because of his eleven-year-old brother, who is autistic. *Pretty mildly*, Rugger also told me, *but still someone has to be around to watch him all the time.*

I got beat up pretty bad, I write. *Have an ugly bruise on my chest.*

I don't know why I wrote that. Am I fishing for him to say something suggestive, that he'd like to see the bruise?

He doesn't say that though, just, *Ugh, sounds nasty.*

Now I wonder if I'm repulsive, if he's grossed out by the thought of my purple-bruised chest. *It's not that bad*, I write, then erase that too, because it sounds slutty, like I'm begging him to say, *Want me come check it out, rub it, kiss it, etc.?* Do I want that? I know I definitely don't want to sound like I do, so I change the subject. *Do you think a lot of people in our school are racist?* I write.

While I'm waiting for Rugger to text back, guess who I get a text from?

Jake.

Of course.

You might think Mallory's not hanging out with me at night, but you're wrong. You might think she's all dedicated to the team and at home eating milk and cookies and doing homework like you are, but she's not. You don't know what you're missing, Allison. You can still be the one if you want to.

Jerk, don't ever text me again, I text back, though I probably should've just ignored him, pretended I never got his text or that I'm too busy to answer or care.

My mother drops a glass downstairs and I hear it shatter against the kitchen floor. Soon we will have nothing breakable left in our house. Then I hear her cursing, then crying. By the time I get to the kitchen, she's running cold water over her hand, sopping up the remaining blood with a cloth napkin.

"Are you OK?" I say.

"Fine."

I feel like telling my mother she's not fine, that I'm not fine either. That a beautiful, nasty-minded boy just accused me of being a milk-drinking goody two-shoes and I feel like going to his house and running him over with a motorcycle, then kissing him. Also, that she needs to stop drinking or I'm going to start hating her soon.

Instead, I ask how everything's going with Harvard.

She makes a kind of *who knows* gesture with her hand wrapped in the bloody napkin and then I ask if she ever dated anyone she shouldn't have, someone she knew was a bad person, but she did it anyway.

"Besides your father, you mean?"

She seems to squeeze the bloody napkin tighter when she says it, so I don't want her to think about him anymore. I don't want to think about him either.

"Yeah," I say, "besides him. Like somebody in high school."

She turns toward the window above the sink as if she can see through it in the dark and watch the birds battle for prime position at the feeders. She can only see her own reflection though, which, lacking a frosted layer of sunscreen because it's nighttime and indoors and she hasn't lathered on her eye cream yet, her cheeks ruddy from her wine, looks almost joyful, even though her hand's still bleeding.

"I used to know a boy named Mortimer," she says, as if I'm supposed to believe something like that.

"Mom, stop making stuff up. I came down here because I heard you destroy another glass–of which, soon, by the way, we're not going to have any–but am I harping on that? No. I asked you a serious question because I need perspective from somebody older and wiser. That's you. Be honest, nobody names a child Mortimer. That's a cartoon name for a kid with a talking dog who gets beaten up by his younger sister."

My mom doesn't know what to say at first. Should she respond to what I said about the broken glass? Is she shocked I called her old? Or wise? Am I working myself up to a rant she doesn't want to hear right now?

"Actually," she says, after squeezing the bloody napkin for a few more seconds, "this Mortimer was a basketball player. Not very good, he rarely got into games, but they called him

Morty, or sometimes Mortician, and everyone on the team loved him because he sold the best marijuana."

My mom knew a weed dealer in high school?

"I know what you're thinking," she says. "No, I never smoked anything with him, but I did kiss him once, and he was mean. He was somebody cruel. A bunch of us were on a camping trip where everyone was drinking beer around a bonfire, and I was maybe fourteen, and I'd never really drank anything before so I got woozy pretty quickly and there he was, next to me. His skin smelled like the fire we were sitting in front of. He was playing guitar and singing Zeppelin songs, and it was all really terrible—screechy and off-key and horrendous—and everyone was laughing and he was laughing too, but I could tell he felt bad about it, so I told him he was pretty good, even though he wasn't."

I kind of feel like I know the rest of the story.

The boy was probably named Chuck or Benji and not Mortimer, and a year or two older than she's claiming, and not a basketball player or a drug dealer. My mother was probably fifteen, at least, and did a lot more than just kiss him. She probably hurt him badly, left him in ribbons for several months where he did nothing but mourn and explore the deserted island of his heart, but she won't tell it to me like that. She'll be the victim. There'll be some kind of lesson I'm supposed to learn, some warning about how boys can hurt you if you trust them when they don't deserve it. Since Dad left, that's the lesson she always teaches. Or tries to.

"He asked me to take a walk with him," my mother says, "and I went, even though it wasn't really clear what was happening. We probably only walked a couple hundred feet away from the fire, but it felt like a different world. The trees were dark and the ground felt squishy and he led me to a rock to sit on and I remember thinking, *How did he know this rock was here? Has he taken other girls here before?* And I thought he was going to roll a joint and ask me if I wanted any and I was thinking I was maybe willing to try it, but he didn't, we just sat down on the rock and he said, 'Tell the truth, my singing is awful, isn't it?' I nodded and then we were kissing. It was kind of nice but I'd heard he was a boy who lied to his girlfriends, so I didn't let him put his hand on my shirt and so after a few minutes he stopped and we went back to the fire. That was it and I was going to write it off as whatever, silly night in the woods, but then on Monday in school, there was a rumor we'd had sex."

"And you didn't have sex?"

"Not even close. I didn't like him that much, but the boy I did like, his name was Samuel and he was in my biology class. He had this lovely, sandy hair and soft eyes—just like your father, I guess, now that I think about it, weird—and he believed the rumor so he acted like I'd betrayed him, and he wouldn't talk to me anymore. It's not like we'd been in a relationship either. Christ, we weren't even lab partners. I told him nothing serious happened on the camping trip, but it didn't matter how much I insisted. In his eyes, I was a fallen woman."

"Forever?"

"Yes, I was a fallen woman forever."

It's too much effort for me to try to figure out what's true and what isn't in this story. The only thing I know for sure is this—I scored the winning goal today.

We're 1–0.

[15]

When I get another text to sneak out, I don't say no.

First of all, it's from Rugger, not Jake, and second, I am feeling so jazzed about our win—about my goal—I can't focus on homework or fall asleep. My mom pissed me off with her bullshit tall tale-slash-warning and all I can think about is how Jake is one hundred percent wrong. He doesn't know me. I am not a milk-and-cookies person.

Not exclusively, anyway.

We meet at a park where, right above a small enclosed area that long ago housed a communal chicken coop, there's a big hill I used to sled down with Mallory the first snowfall of every winter. The exciting part of the sled ride was jumping off just before we hit the wooden fence. Watching our sleds smack into it and knowing we'd escaped getting hurt at the last minute is what made the whole endeavor worthwhile. We learned disaster was escapable. We learned we could survive based on our own quickness and guile.

Someone has moved a picnic table to the top of the hill and it's a known place for high school kids to get high after dark. We don't. Maybe Rugger got high before meeting me, but he doesn't smell like it, or even have a juicy smell like he vaped, and he doesn't break out a pipe while we're up there, or a Juul, or even suggest it. I call that respectful behavior.

We talk about our favorite movies from when we were kids and I tell him about how I never liked the Home Alone series. All I could think about was how lonely the kid was, and I didn't feel empowered when he outsmarted the villains and tricked them into pratfalls that broke their bones.

"That's deep," he says, which I think means he's not really listening, and I consider sprinting down the hill and escaping via the paths that wind through the old chicken coop and leaving him alone with the picnic table, but the paths are mostly overgrown and I don't want to twist my ankle and wind up on the sideline with Aaliyah.

"You know what I want to do one day?" he asks.

I don't think I care so I don't answer. Maybe I can go home soon.

He touches my wrist gently. Rubs his finger across the hair on my forearms. It feels, actually, wonderful.

"One day," he says, "I want to kiss someone as beautiful as you are."

"You are a cheeseball," I say, but also, I can't stop myself from smiling, and when we kiss, it's pretty decent. Not the best ever, not like a Chicago deep dish pizza that's flavorful and totally satisfying and that you think about afterward for days, but not horrible either, not like delivery from a franchise that brags about how fast it can process your order and that tastes the same as the box it's packed in. More like something you get at a mid-priced restaurant, passable and pleasant most of the time, pretty damn awesome when you're hungry.

He tries to go up my shirt, but I don't let him, and he doesn't get mad, he apologizes for trying, so then, at the very end, I put his hand there and let him, just for a little bit. He rubs where the bruise is and I like that, and when I get home, I drink milk but I don't eat cookies or do homework, and I don't feel guilty.

Not at all.

[16]

WE WIN our next four games no problem, 4–0, 6–0, 3–0, and 5–1, all at home. Coach is furious at us for letting up a goal. It happens against South Kensing with a minute left when our subs are in, including Aaliyah, whose ankle is finally recovered enough to let her see action on the field. She plays well but a fluke shot deflects off her stick and takes a lucky bounce past Marty Max, our goalie.

Marty looks at Aaliyah like she should remove herself from the planet and possibly the solar system and that pisses me off. What happened to Aaliyah could have happened to anyone and Marty knows that. Aaliyah was in the proper position and sometimes you just get unlucky.

Coach isn't having it though.

"The whole point," she says in her most disappointed voice, "is never to put ourselves in a situation where luck can hurt us. What's the ball even doing in our end against a team like that?"

Nobody answers because we feel like horrid, wretched children who have screwed up so tragically, we might get sent back to the workhouse.

"You do realize," Coach says, her voice an icicle now, sharp and jagged, "last year we gave up one goal. That's one goal *all season*, in twenty-two games, and that was in the state semifinals against a kid who was probably the best scorer in the Midwest. Now here we are, five games in, and we've already given up a goal. To a girl who hardly knows how to hold her stick. How do you feel about that? You OK with it? Nod your head if you're OK."

Nobody nods her head.

"All right, then, who's going to be on the field when we give up our next goal? Raise your hand right now if you'll be on the field when we let up our next goal. Anyone? Come on, it wasn't so bad, right? We still won by a ton. We're still undefeated. We're still ranked number one in the state. One lucky goal's not a big deal, right? Come on, raise your hand if you're OK with being on the field when we let up our next goal. You can do it, be brave. Anyone OK with it? Anyone?"

No one raises a hand.

Aaliyah looks real hard at her shoes.

"That's what I thought," Coach says. "You've now used up your quota for the season. I don't expect anyone else to score on us. Got it?"

"Got it," we say as one, so loud the whole city and the four cities next to us can hear us.

Then Coach sends us back to the workhouse.

Which means while the team we crushed boards its bus to go home for dinner and homework and boyfriends and Grand Theft Whatever They Do with a Joystick, we stay on the field to run.

It's a special kind of run Coach calls running murders, as in, "you guys got *five murders* before you hit the locker room." A murder is a lap around the field, except when you get to the fifty-yard line, which is twice during each lap, you have to dive to the ground and do ten push-ups. If you do two murders—forty push-ups—your arms will become that kind of spongy sea creature without a spine. If you do five murders, the sea creatures will drown and decompose and become fossil fuel for future generations.

There are no words to describe what happens to you if you run ten murders.

Coach makes us run twelve.

Mallory, of course, sprints out in front and won't cut corners. Not only on the running part. Every single push-up, from one to two hundred and forty, her nose hits the ground. I do my best to stay with her, but by lap eight I'm twenty yards behind. I figure I'll catch up with a kick at the end, but by lap twelve I'm fifty yards behind and there's no way.

She must be tired, but as I fall back her stride remains steady. She is running, as always, like an antelope. I'd say gazelle, but that's what everyone else would say, and gazelle is too delicate. She's more like an elk. The fastest, strongest elk that leads the stampede. When we ran track together in middle school, she'd run the anchor leg of the 4 x 100 relay and when I'd hand her the baton, it was like giving your teacher an essay that you knew was about to get an A. Just get the thing in her hand and the job would be done. Everyone running knew it and so did everyone in the stands. I remember her father up there in the middle of all the other parents—except mine, of course—not even cheering. Not clapping or smiling either, just tall with bigger shoulders than anyone else, quietly expecting his daughter to dominate.

No one is within seventy-five yards of me when I look back and Aaliyah is last, dragging her still-sore ankle but not giving up.

Marty Max, who, fortunately, is allowed to take off her pads to run murders, is running with Julie B. I see them look back at Aaliyah and then whisper to each other. I can't hear what they're saying but even the possibility that it might have to do with backs of buses makes me as furious as Coach and I sprint so hard to the end that I get much closer to Mallory than she expected and when I finish she is overjoyed and gives me the world's biggest hug and tells me I'm the best.

When I get home, I am so tired I don't do any homework or talk to my mom or even look at my phone when anyone—i.e., Rugger—texts.

[17]

When my alarm wakes me up—"I hopped off the plane at LAX / with a dream and my cardigan"—my shoulders and thighs are super sore. Mom has already gone to work and I wonder if I heard her retching in the middle of the night or if I just dreamed it. A text from Rugger he sent at one a.m. tells me he misses talking to me and wonders why I never texted back last night, and also, just in case, I should know there's nothing going on between him and Delaney.

The fact that he feels it's necessary to say that makes me think he's probably lying, and also I am flattered he thinks it's necessary to justify himself to me.

You can do whatever you want, I text back and leave it at that.

At school, I am sore in all my classes and can barely stay seated. It's a good kind of sore, and I'm proud of it. I can feel my muscles growing. Still, with my legs and arms groaning and weeping beneath my skin, I want to spend a half-hour stretching. Instead, I do my best not to squirm in my seat because I am playing catch-up all day, pretending I did homework when I didn't, and I don't want my teachers to notice me. I get away with it first and second hours, English and social studies, but get burned third hour in analysis when Mr. Martindale—what a name, it sounds like a bird married a puppy—hits us with a surprise quiz.

It's only a ten-minuter, two questions, but since I left the spine of my textbook uncracked last night, I can answer only about half of one of them. Clueless about how to proceed on the rest of the quiz, I do a different kind of math in my head.

> *1 goal allowed by substitute players = 12 murders (3 miles and 240 push-ups).*
> *4 out of 4 sore appendages plus 2 depleted lungs = 1 bad decision to do zero homework.*
> *A 25 percent on a math quiz combined with the 80 percent I got on the first quiz of the semester = my analysis grade is now 52.5 percent.*

Keep it up—or down, as it were—and I will be academically ineligible to play field hockey.

I try to text Mallory to tell her I can't eat lunch with her because I have to go to the media center—I can't stand that that's what it's supposed to be called now instead of the library, I go there for books, not *media*—to catch up on homework, but since I am not one of those kids who texts so much I can do it without looking at my screen, Mr. Bird-Puppy catches me and takes away my phone before I can send it. Instead of giving me a warning like normal teachers who are also human beings with hearts, he insists on interpreting the school's student handbook as if it's the Constitution and he's a literalist—see, I *do* pay attention in history—and informs me (or whomever it is he means when he says, "Ms. Allison the Academically Ill-prepared Athlete") I can pick it up in the main office after school.

Therefore, I now have to make a decision. Head to the media center and spend my only free forty-two minutes of the endless school day attempting to make up homework that probably won't be accepted late anyway and simultaneously blow off my best friend, who will be waiting for me at her locker and blowing up my phone with unreturnable texts while it vibrates hopelessly in the secretary's desk drawer in the main office, or go meet Mallory to explain, in which case, she will inform me to my face that she has to find Jake and eat lunch with him and that, as an academically ill-prepared athlete, I am setting a poor example as captain.

In which case, I will be upset and unable to concentrate and will waste eighteen to twenty-four minutes getting my head straight, thereby failing to complete my missed homework anyway or even to make much of a dent toward completing it.

School sucks and I choose life.

In which case, I will meet Mallory and not mention my shitty day and for forty-two blessed minutes I will forget concepts like media centers and homework even exist.

[18]

CREATIVE WRITING IS my last class of the day.

Makes the afternoon feel not quite as endless.

Julie B. is the best writer in the room and the teacher is a former hippy named Mr. Gowhatever. Really, that's his name —Gowhatever. Maybe it's his parents who were hippies. He's gray-haired and grape-shaped, but generally a nice person who wears ties with black backgrounds and stylized miniature vegetables printed on them, often of the root variety, and doesn't give a lot of homework. Seems like he's out of it half the time, like he's thinking about taking a vacation at a pastoral locale where he can spend several consecutive afternoons gazing through high-powered binoculars at stalks of wheat swaying in an uneventful breeze. However, when Gowhatever pays attention, he sometimes offers thoughtful comments about the work people are writing.

Today a lacrosse player named Brian, who's friends with Jake and Rugger—I'm not totally sure, but I think Delaney dated him at some point also—shares a rap he wrote, what Gowhatever would call a hip hop–styled piece, about smoking weed. He has a beat he made up for it, so he plugs his phone into the speakers and, like a lot of white boys at our school, he's pretty good at rapping and staying on tempo. He photocopied the lyrics for us, really so Mr. Gowhatever could understand what he was saying, and after he finishes his song and everyone applauds with fervor and he gets a bunch of high fives from the other boys in the class, most of them white too, but a trio of African Americans, an Asian, and a Latino as well, we talk about his refrain, where he says:

> *Friday night, rolling with the Rat Bros*
> *Spark it up, suck it down, got that fat dro*
> *Get so high I can fly, here I go, uh-oh, oh no*
> *Love my dudes and it's thick but no homo*
> *Find a ho, she sucks it down like it's Froyo*
> *Just another Friday night, end up running from the po-po*

The piece is in response to an exercise where Gowhatever told us to write about "you and your crew." He gave us a couple pretty cool model poems to look at before we wrote, one by a guy named Patrick Rosal about breakdancing on the streets of New Jersey with his buddies in the late eighties, and another by a younger poet named José Olivarez who wrote about playing basketball with his friends and what it was like when they found out one of their fathers—the only one in the neighborhood who still lived at home—had died. The poems were actually intriguing and really got to what the friendships meant to the writers and I appreciate that our erstwhile instructor with ugly ties took the time to find them. You can tell he sincerely loves poems and also that he wants to get the boys in our class more involved by picking examples he thinks they'll relate to, but the results have been predictable. At least a half-dozen boys wrote about who they smoke with, and all the hos they supposedly hook up with, and Julie B. is sick of it.

"I'm sorry," she says when we get to the part where we're offering suggestions to Brian about his piece, "except, let me take that back. I'm not sorry. Why do so many boys in here, especially the white ones, have to be such poseurs? I don't mean to pick on you, Brian, because you're not the only one, but have you ever heard of the phrase *emotional depth?*"

"Hold on," Mr. Gowhatever says. "I'm not sure I like your tone, Julie B. Remember, we are all emerging writers here, just starting to explore our voices. The goal is to encourage everyone."

"I *am* trying to encourage people, Mr. Gowhatever. Not just Brian, but all the boys in this class. Why are the expectations for them so low? They throw a few rhymes together, talk about weed, and everyone claps. They're not going to grow if no one encourages them to move beyond their comfort zones. He just used one of the stupidest phrases in the English language, *no homo*. He feels the need to declare he's not gay before he can say something as simple as he likes his friends? You're just going to let him get away with that without challenging it?"

This conversation could be interesting if all the boys were paying attention, but they're not. They've all heard Julie B. rant before in one context or another, so they're already tuned out, half of them playing on their phones beneath their desks, which makes me mad because my phone is still sitting in a drawer in the main office.

"I think a case can be made," Mr. Gowhatever says, even though he already looks bored and ready to go on his wheat-watching vacation, "that *no homo* represents progress in hip hop culture. First of all, it's recognizing that same-sex attractions exist and that they're visible, maybe even viable, and that's a big step in the hip hop world. Second, it does open the door to allow men to express affection toward other men. It might be an offensive on-ramp toward what you're calling emotional depth, but it is nonetheless an on-ramp. Because he used it as a disclaimer, you see, Brian was able to proclaim that he loves his dudes. That, however halting, is a step in the right direction, no?"

I am shaking my head, violently, and even think about raising my hand, but Julie B. is already talking, saying pretty much exactly what I would be saying.

"Why? *Why* does he love his dudes, though? Because they smoke together and get quote-unquote hos? Talk about clichés. I can turn on the radio right now and hear ten songs in the next hour that say the same thing. The only on-ramp he's driving on is the one to the homophobia highway and the global perpetuation of misogyny and rape culture."

Told you she was going to Princeton.

I do wonder though, how she can say everything she's saying and still be OK with what she said to Aaliyah.

"That's why I like country music," she says. "At least when white men perpetuate stereotypes about female behavior in country songs, they're not appropriating somebody else's culture in order to give themselves license to do it."

I'm not sure about that either.

I think maybe she likes country music because the ice hockey players, Jake and his friends, like it.

Then again, maybe I'm not giving her enough credit. Maybe I'm just perpetuating a stereotype.

Mr. Gowhatever is tired of arguing with her. He looks to the boys to see if they care enough to respond. They don't, so he uses me as his diversion.

"Allison, did you want to say something? I thought I saw your hand, almost, you know, kind of barely perceptibly, rise up."

I don't feel like being an on-ramp to calming things down and I'm pissed at the boys for playing with their phones when I don't have mine and I don't like Gowhatever teasing me, so, yeah, I do speak up and I say the one thing I know will get their attention.

"Brian, let me ask you something. *Who* are these hos you're talking about? Mr. Gowhatever's always talking about using specific details and avoiding generalities, so be specific. Are you talking about Delaney? Have the guts to call her out if that's who you mean. Because I'm friends with her and she has a laugh like the sunrise. The fact that she was willing to spend five minutes with you is probably the luckiest thing that ever happened in your life. Is *that* who you're calling a ho?"

Gowhatever waves his hands like a referee wanting to call time-out and Brian gets all red in his somewhat pimply face and a lot of the boys make an *oooh* sound like I got Brian good, which I did, but Derek, one of the African American guys who's mostly quiet and pretty much on his phone from the beginning to the end of class every day, says, "D-Crazy? Are you talking about D-Crazy?"

D-Crazy?

Then the fire alarm clangs and Gowhatever smiles as if his car just missed smashing into a lamppost and killing him.

"Grab your stuff," he tells the class. "We probably won't have time to come back before the period ends. You know where to go."

[19]

WE SHUFFLE down the stairs like obedient citizens, our backpacks creating one-foot buffer zones so we're not bumping into one another. When we get outside, the sun waves at us like a happy friend and I look for Mallory amongst the stream of student bodies but can't find her in the crowd. I don't see Jake either and it briefly occurs to me they may have disappeared together somewhere, but Mallory's not one to skip classes, so I doubt it.

I find myself walking next to Julie B. and she turns and thanks me for speaking up against Brian's piece.

"I understand Gowhatever wants to keep the boys from totally tuning out," I say, "but at some point, he has to call them on their bullshit."

Julie B. nods. "We didn't even get to talking about the Froyo part. Did he mean the so-called ho sucks down the smoke, or something else?"

"That's gross. But, yeah, I go with option two."

I squint through the glare.

Julie B. is silhouetted, a gorgeous, broad-shouldered Amazonian.

"My point," she says. "And the end might be the worst of all. With everything we've seen about people of color getting shot by police, do you think Mr. Brian Grand Imperial Wizard Jedi Master—or whatever he is—of the Fraternal Order of Rodents at all understands the privilege of bragging about being high and running from the cops as if it's some kind of joke?"

Fraternal Order of Rodents?

Why does she talk like that?

This would be an ideal moment for me to bring up Aaliyah and how I think what Julie B. said to her is just as bad as Brian's piece, maybe worse, but I don't because ahead of us at the soccer field, Brian and a bunch of the white boys from our class, plus another group that includes Robbie and Connor—and now I see Jake—have formed a circle—a cipher, they call it—and are bobbing their heads and trying to freestyle. It looks like Connor is the one making the beat with his mouth. I'm willing to bet less than ten seconds pass without someone making a reference to weed. Think of all the words they can use for rhymes—dro, blunt, chronic, blaze, pod, tree, pipe, herb—OK, I'll stop there because I'm ashamed to think of how much druggy slang I know.

And probably don't know.

"God," Julie B. says, "do you think they heard a single thing I said about appropriating culture? I swear, sometimes —no, a lot of times—I'm ashamed to be a white person."

Shame.

Guilt.

Intentional blindness.

Unintentional blindness?

I don't understand how Julie B. can be so political and race-conscious and, at the same time, so blatantly mean to Aaliyah. Maybe she's wrapped up in so many abstractions she can't see how her personal behavior hurts people. Or so focused on not giving an inch to the boys, she's oblivious to any other prejudices. I'm stumped and don't really want to think about it anymore because Julie B.'s my friend and my teammate, and also it's extremely sunny and, after the gloom of Gowhatever's room, this moment of fire-drill freedom feels delicious, like so much of an eye massage, I can't imagine stressing myself out with an argument.

Except I'm not being honest.

The truth is I don't respond to Julie B. because my attention is distracted. Drifting toward the edge of the circle to listen in and maybe wait for his chance to demonstrate his skill in weed-rhyming is Rugger.

And he's holding hands with Delaney.

I pretend not to look at them.

"Do you know what D-Crazy means?" I ask Julie B., my voice lazy and lilting. "Have you heard that before?"

[20]

SEEING Rugger hold hands with Delaney is a bit disconcerting because I guess I figured we were past that.

I've met him at the picnic table on a school night three times now.

Each time we've gone a little further than before.

I know what he feels like in my hand, but let's just say I don't know more than that.

To be honest, even without Delaney in the equation, I'm not sure I want to.

Our kissing hasn't really improved.

It's still that kind of restaurant I don't mind going to, like I won't turn it down if I don't have other plans, but it's not like I'd cancel plans for it either.

Last time, before we started making out, we were talking and he told me something I consider serious. He's afraid of dying before he falls in love. Sure, maybe it was just a line and he was only trying to make me let him do more when he said it—like, oh, I know there's no draft so it's unlikely he'll die in combat anytime soon but, who knows, he still could get hit by a car at any moment, so, you know, how tragic if he never experiences love, maybe I better step up and rectify that—but I still feel like he meant it, at least part of it. Like he knows there's something better than what he's currently committing himself to (with me), or what's currently being committed to him (by me), and I believe he has a fear, a true fear, it won't ever happen.

If I were a different person, with different parents, I might be able to soothe that fear, but I'm not, so I didn't. My father left when I was in preschool, but I can still remember all the yelling and how I hid in my closet when he was slamming doors and punching holes in the living room wall. My mother patched those holes in the wall. Now, you wouldn't even know they were ever there.

The holes my father made with his yelling?

The holes inside my mother and me?

Think we both still have them.

Sometimes I think the only way I can fill those holes is by breaking some defender's ankles on the field, passing the ball to Mallory, and watching her score.

Which is why, maybe, Rugger was holding Delaney's hand today.

Maybe my hand's too tough for holding.

That night, all I told him was, the way he's talking about love, how fully immersed and committed he wants to be one day, I have that already. That doesn't mean I'm ready to die now, but it does mean I won't die without experiencing total, unfiltered passion. It comes with a stick, a ball, and a surface that's usually artificial turf.

It's called field hockey.

[21]

AALIYAH TEARS it up in practice.

Her defense is fierce and fast and almost as good as Julie B.'s. Once, she even flies in to break up Mallory and me on a two-on-one, which happens approximately never. Granted, she was fortunate because I was a half-step late when I couldn't quite control the ball completely, but Julie B. gives her a huge high five and they smack sticks and look like they've been teammates and best friends forever.

So maybe it's good I didn't say anything deeper to Julie B. during the fire drill.

When we take a break and drink water from our respective bottles, I tell Aaliyah how great she's doing and she thanks me and says after she let up the goal, she has to prove to everyone that she still belongs on the field. She has to regain everyone's trust.

"That goal was lucky," I say. "It could have happened to anyone."

"Doesn't matter. I still have to prove I belong. I always do."

Her eyes tell me not to say anything else.

"I heard Julie B. went off in your creative writing class today," she says.

"You did?"

"Derek's my brother. You didn't know that?"

I didn't know that.

"He's older?"

"Yeah, a year."

"Who does better in school?"

She raises an eyebrow and smiles with the side of her face.

"That's what I thought."

"He could do well, he's really smart. Smarter than I am, actually, but he doesn't try."

"Why does that happen?" I say. "Why do so many boys seem to think it's OK not to try?"

Mallory stayed out on the field during the break, even though Coach has told her not to a hundred times, and she's working on smacking the ball into the goal. She hits a reverse chip high and hard into the upper corner, which is the kind of shot generally reserved for Olympians—starters, actually, on the Olympic team—and Aaliyah and I just stare.

"I think you're asking the question every teacher in this school wishes they had the answer to," Aaliyah says.

I nod, kind of helplessly, because making the boys try in class seems like such a lost cause, and I want to ask Aaliyah about D-Crazy since Derek was the one who said it, but instead I ask her if she knows who the Rat Bros are.

"That's the whole weed-smoking crew. There's like, fifty of them. If they weren't so idiotic, it would actually be kind of wondrous because it's so multiracial, but it's Derek and some of the other basketball players, and Jake and his boys, and Brian and Rugger. They started calling themselves that over the summer when the police broke up a bonfire and they said they had to scatter like rats."

Coach blows her whistle to bring us back to the middle of the field and I tell Aaliyah if she keeps playing the way she's playing she's going to be all-state next year.

"What about this year?" she says, sprinting past me toward Coach.

[22]

RUGGER TEXTS me at about ten o'clock.

I think about ignoring it because I am busy doing homework and hungry because we didn't go for burritos after practice. My mom cooked, sort of, a salad and grilled cheese sandwiches, but she barely touched hers so I felt guilty eating mine and didn't enjoy it. If I don't enjoy my food, it feels like I didn't eat it. Then I'm still hungry.

Just because we were holding hands doesn't mean we're more than friends, the text says.

I'm intrigued.

Not because I believe him, but because it'll be an interesting sociological case study to see what kind of BS he comes up with.

Really? I text back, and instantly feel like the stupidest fish in the lake for lunging at a plastic worm attached to a fat, inviting hook.

I'm not gonna lie, he says, *stuff has happened between us, but it's not like I really like her for real. It's just kind of a friends-with-benefits situation.*

Stuff?

Has happened and he *doesn't* really like her?

And he's telling me this as a way to convince me to hang out with him *more*?

And he says *for real* and *really* in the same sentence?

I don't text back.

Partially because, you know—guilt.

Shame.

Blindness, intentional or otherwise.

Is he saying he feels about Delaney pretty much the mediocre-restaurant way I feel about him?

Which would, more or less, mean he senses my ambivalence so, fair is fair, who am I to judge?

A few seconds later, he texts again.

I don't look at it for at least fifteen minutes until after I finish my math homework, but ultimately, I am the stupidest fish. Before starting my creative writing piece, which is the last thing I have to do before beginning my pre-sleep ablutions, I do look.

If you really think about it, the text says, *friends with benefits is not more than friends. It's actually less than friends because with your real friends, you don't want to do anything to mess up your friendship.*

I'll admit, there's a kind of twisted logic to what he's saying. It's definitely true that messing around with someone physically is not nearly as intimate, or as important, as an authentic friendship. I mean, boyfriends come and go, but Mallory doesn't, right?

There's also a kind of subtext happening—a subtext to a text, ha ha—that says, *We're both seniors and Delaney is just a sophomore and can't really understand what's going on. We can talk about it on higher-plane philosophical levels; she can only cluelessly participate.*

A.k.a.—*so what if I'm holding hands with a tenth grader during a fire drill or even if I've done stuff with her, you're the senior I want to go to homecoming with.*

Really.

For real.

Which is possible because homecoming is the day after the state championship final. If we make it that far, we'll be exhausted and (hopefully) happy and so ready to have a night where we can let loose that the dance will be super fun. We just have to be careful because, sometimes, as soon as the season is over, people get completely out of control. A few years ago, there was a goalie named Ashley, who had a scholarship to Virginia. After the dance, she tried to accomplish some kind of drunk version of parkour where she attempted to leap over a park bench and ended up shattering her kneecap and never playing college hockey.

So, what you're saying, I text back just to mess with him, *is that if we become closer friends, there's no way any "stuff" can continue to happen between us?*

I know I'm flirting and I feel bad about that because: A. It's stupid to flirt with a guy like Rugger who, despite his willingness to take care of his autistic brother and his yearning for a love greater than what he's currently party to, is also apparently something called a Rat Bro, and pretty much just admitted he uses girls and doesn't care if he hurts them, and B. Delaney actually *is* my friend in ceramics and she's probably already paranoid about dating a senior who won't take her seriously and here I am stabbing her in the back because if she knew about this conversation (let alone what happens at the picnic table), it would crush her.

So I tell myself it's just a sociological experiment. I'm mining material for my creative writing piece, which I've already decided will be titled "The Bogus Benefits of Friends with Benefits."

But the experiment is immediately over because Rugger is the kind of boy with laser eyes who can see right through my pretense, and he writes, *Totally different situation. I already know*

I want to be more than friends with you. With you, Allison, the concept of friends is just the base level. That's why I'm texting now. I've been thinking about you all night.

I am disgusted, but also, I can feel my mouth watering and the taste of the glowing, plastic worm—and the sharp, metal hook attached to it—already on my tongue.

[23]

IN OUR FIRST ROAD GAME, we crush. 8–0 against Ladywood Country Day, whom we barely beat 1–0 in the state quarterfinals last year. Afterward, Coach does not proudly tell us how last year's team never scored eight goals in a single game or made LCD look like a rec league team. On the other hand, she doesn't make us run twelve murder laps, and she also makes a point of saying that Aaliyah played amazing, which she did. She was on the field almost the entire second half and she and Julie B. built a citadel on defense almost as impenetrable as Rugger's theories about relationships. I don't think LCD crossed midfield once.

She was also adept at breaking the ball out, hitting me on at least three breakaways. Overall, Mallory had four goals and I had two, and three assists, and the mood on the way home is jubilant. I sit next to Aaliyah—in the middle of the bus—and we joke more about being Dauntless and congratulate each other on trying hard at everything we do, and I tell her making all-state this year maybe isn't unrealistic after all.

"What do you mean by *maybe*?" she says.

I don't elaborate because Julie B. has cranked up her

monster-sized, eighties-style radio, her *box*, she calls it, and we continue the tradition that's now two decades old of singing Prince's "Purple Rain" on the bus after every road win.

We are wearing our white-and-red visiting uniforms, which are not as intimidating as our red-and-purple home uniforms, which, let's face it are kind of a weird color combination. The school only added the purple part during the nineties when people did strange things like lust after Furbies and buy inflatable furniture that looked like giant Lifesavers. It was definitely an unfortunate era, but the purple also definitely turned out *not* to be an error. Shortly after it became part of our color-scheme, we began to dominate the state, thus initiating our purple reign. Even now, for our away games when our uniforms feature no purple, we all wear some kind of personal purple, purple sports bras under our jerseys, or purple hair ties, or stripes of purple face paint on our cheeks. Julie B., already 18, even has a purple-and-red W tattooed on her ankle. The Purple Reign lives on us and within us and we are purple-proud and we belt out the chorus of Prince's atmospheric ballad and my eyes tear up, as they always do, and I'm linking one elbow with Aaliyah and the other across the aisle with Mallory.

These are the moments I live for and I am smiling with all my face as we sing:

I only want to see you laughing in the purple rain

Purple rain, purple rain
Purple rain, purple rain
Purple rain, purple rain

I only want to see you bathing in the purple rain

I'm not sure what it means to bathe in purple rain, probably something creepy, but we don't analyze it too deeply. For us, it's reign anyway, not rain, and we are the Womack Warriors, the number-one dominant force in the state, and we have been for a long time, and we will be for a long time, and it doesn't matter whether our reign *rains* or our rain *reigns*, these moments on the bus are when we let loose, when we celebrate everything we've given to our team, and where it's just us and no boys to bring us down, and nobody can call us cocky or conceited.

Julie B. plays DJ and after Prince is over, we sing along to Taylor Swift, Katy Perry, and Beyoncé, and Aaliyah, like me, sings off-key and pretty much horribly, but nobody cares and just when we start losing a little steam Julie B. throws on the team's second favorite song, Joey Buckets's "Heartfire," and we all pretend we are from Tennessee or Alabama and the team goes crazy again and we belt out the chorus:

We are burnin'
Our hearts are flamin'
We are burnin'
We are all in, baby, all in
Ain't no going backward now

I am linking arms with Aaliyah and Mallory like I did earlier, but Aaliyah feels tense to me, her whole body rigid. She isn't actually singing either, just moving her lips but not even to the words of the song. I look at her, but she shakes her head as if she doesn't want me to see what she's doing, so I look the other way and keep singing and when the song is over and Julie B. puts on John Legend to chill everyone out, I ask Aaliyah if she doesn't like country music.

"Not really," she says.

"I didn't used to either, but it kind of grows on you after a while."

"It's actually not about the genre."

Mallory's sneaking a peek at her phone because she got a text and she's not supposed to be doing that because the rule is no phones on the bus—Coach wants us fully present with one another—but I look away from her and welcome her distracted attention because there's something about the stress on Aaliyah's face that tells me there's something serious happening, so I lower my voice to a whisper.

"What is it about?"

"Nothing."

"Aaliyah, you can trust me."

"Can I? Can I really?"

"Yes."

"No bullshit?"

"No bullshit."

"Then, when you get home, check out Joey Buckets's album covers. Every one of them."

[24]

I DON'T.

Not right away.

My mother isn't home when I pull in after dropping Mallory off and that's disconcerting. There's no note and she hasn't texted or left me a message. She's probably out with Harvard but it's unlike her not to tell me about it. Seems like she wants me to know when she's on a date because she wants me to think she's not a loser. I already don't think that, but that doesn't mean she shouldn't stop drinking.

Mallory and I didn't go for burritos because we can't do that every day—it's not in our respective no-job-because-we're-too-busy-playing budgets—and it's more of an after-practice thing than an after-game thing, and she said she had to get home anyway. Probably to meet Jake, but I didn't ask and she didn't volunteer any information or ask my advice. We haven't played the "That's not my boyfriend" game in, like, three weeks. Usually that's a sign one of us has a boyfriend she's potentially into in a serious way, and, with all due apologies to the Rugger-Rat, I know it's not me.

There's nothing microwaveable in our freezer because

there never is, so I pour myself a heaping bowl of cereal and start slurping. Part of me wants to turn on the television so I can hear sounds other than my own chewing, but I also don't want to give in to that urge. *I am not weak*, I tell myself. *Not weak*.

The house feels really big to me, like the opposite of walls closing in, as if the walls are moving outward and the space in the house keeps growing and feeling emptier and I am small and unprotected, but I am not weak. When I finish my cereal, I wash the bowl and spoon and then reuse them to eat grocery-store ice cream. A small amount. The flavor is vanilla with slim shavings of chocolate that on no planet could be accurately described as chips.

In my room, I look at the snakes in Rachel Dawson's forearms and mix my ice cream in the bowl, turning it into a coolish, chocolate-shavings soup. With the door shut, my room feels smaller than the house, but only for slightly less than a minute. Then the walls recede again and the bed I am lying on is attached only to a floor floating in darkness. I am unanchored and the air around me is vast. I shiver, even though it's not cold outside, so I stop eating the ice cream. My phone vibrates and I want it to be my mother, but it's Rugger.

Heard you guys crushed today. Congrats.

Who did he hear it from? It's not like we're on *SportsCenter*.

With no walls around my floating bed, and no word from my mother, I chew the insides of my cheeks and attempt to embark on the homework train. I usually start with what I least like first and save creative writing for last—a mirror of my actual day at school—but tonight I'm feeling salty about what happened when I shared my piece earlier, so I pull it from my backpack and stare at it.

My job—revision.

The boys in the room had no reaction when I read the poem. Half-hearted claps, then a million crickets. A bunch of them looked out the window, or at their expensive sneakers, or just got that vacant stare where they pretend they can't see anything, like the atmosphere in front of their faces turned into fog. I don't think they weren't paying attention either. I'm not trying to be cocky but even though it's true that the boys tune out from most people's pieces, when I share mine, they usually have something to say. I guess this time they didn't like someone calling out the idea of friends with benefits because they adore the concept too much. Julie B. wasn't in class—she had a therapy appointment—so most of the girls didn't say anything either. A lot of times it happens that way. If Julie B.'s not around because she has therapy, or is out getting another tattoo, or maybe flew to visit another school just in case she decides Princeton isn't good enough, and the boys don't respond to something, the other girls turn into mute statues with only their fingers moving so they can text under their desks.

After a few moments of awkwardness where Gowhatever sounded like a burned-out teacher in the movies—"Comments? Questions? Thoughts? Ideas?"—he finally decided to assume authority in his own classroom and expound.

"Well, I expect the problem here is we have a title that's too directive. If, as readers, we already know the author thinks the benefits from a quote-unquote friends-with-benefits relationship are bogus, what's the point of experiencing the poem? What's left for the reader to discover?"

A lot of the boys nodded their heads at that point, as if Gowhatever's wisdom were so much more profound than what I actually said about the bullshit idea of a healthy relationship in high school where you can have sex with someone and still get to say they're not more than a friend, which basically means it's OK also to be having sex with other people at the same time (not the same *exact* time, but you know, like, concurrently), which basically means you want a free pass to inflict emotional damage on your peers without any consequences.

Gowhatever was probably right though. The title was too directive. Still, I don't think that excuses the boys from refusing to engage in conversation.

Or refusing to be human beings with feelings.

When the automatic garage door squeaks on its hinges, I know my mom is home. I'm relieved but I don't want her to think I've been worried, so I stay in my room and act like I didn't hear anything. I try a new title for my poem: "A Cost-Benefits Analysis of Friends with Benefits." It sounds wordy and dry, like chalk in my mouth, when I read it aloud.

"Friends with Detriments?"

Awful.

It's been a couple minutes and Mom hasn't come into the house yet. It's crazy, I know, but I get this vision of her sitting in her car in the garage, in tears, engine still running, allowing the carbon monoxide to sweep her, and eventually me, to oblivion.

I'll say it, I panic.

Maybe Harvard broke up with her.

Were they even dating?

Or just coworkers with benefits?

Gross.

The house feels huge and even more open, like the tentacles of trees are reaching toward me and for some reason I get the image in my head of an abandoned amusement park, which has to be one of the loneliest and creepiest possible concepts. I am small, reaching to the soiled ground for an empty paper cone that once held blue-dyed cotton candy. Around me, the ruins of dead rollercoasters loom like desiccated skeletons, their severed tracks and bony frames spiking upward. Glass shards from a hall of a thousand broken mirrors litter the ground along with fake bashed-in skulls and jagged vampire teeth from what was once probably a not-very-scary haunted house.

My phone buzzes again.

Did I do something wrong? the text from Rugger says. *Why are you ignoring me?*

There are no walls.

Fumes from my mother's car float upward like steam.

I hesitate, then grab my phone and run downstairs to the garage.

[25]

I was right about the sitting in the car and crying part.

But the engine's not running.

I knock on the passenger window and my mother unlocks the door so I can sit next to her. We don't say anything for a few minutes. Her face is tear-streaked and she smells like she drank an entire boutique vineyard. I am happy she made it home without dying and terrified she drove after drinking so much.

"There's a moment," she finally says, "after you shut off the engine, when the energy of the day, all its driving force, seems to stop. It's a moment to slow down and take stock. You don't need to worry. That's all I was doing, taking stock."

I think about telling her I'm going to start a new political movement: Daughters Against Drunk Driving, but then I realize the acronym would be DADD and that doesn't seem like a fruitful place to initiate a discussion.

Plus, it probably already exists.

"You could've killed someone," I say.

"I didn't."

"You got lucky."

She smiles at me and takes my hand and squeezes it. "I know that."

It's odd sitting in a car that's not going anywhere inside your own garage. Seems like we should be moving backward, reversing into the driveway, and then looking both ways before backing into the street and heading to the pharmacy or the movies. But we're not headed anywhere. The car is pointed forward, toward the wall where the tools my mom uses to make birdhouses—that she used to use to rehabilitate broken furniture—still hang in organized fashion on a pegboard. I'm staring at two hammers—one with a yellow handle, one with a brown handle—that are next to each other, like a couple; a couple capable of building things, sticking them together for an enduring period of time, leading productive, sturdy lives.

Or, alternatively, smashing everything apart.

"He broke up with you?"

"No."

"You broke up with him?"

"No, but I should."

"How come?"

The one part of the garage that's not organized is the tangled pile of broken chairs. I can't see it from my perspective of staring at the hammers on the wall, but I know it's there, behind me to the right, looming.

"He's using me," my mother says. "I know it and I'm letting it happen."

She's venturing into too-much-information territory. I feel uncomfortable and when my phone buzzes, I look at it. Rugger.

I really miss talking to you. I think about you all the time.

Even when you're with Delaney? I text back in my head. But I'd never actually send something like that. It's mean and it's also flirty and the truth is I don't want to know the answer.

Or maybe I do. But not in real life. Plus, my mom would appreciate my being present in our inappropriate conversation.

I nod at her to go on even though I know it's a mistake.

"He has fun when we're together—we have fun, I should say—but he won't commit to anything more serious. He doesn't even want anyone at the office to know we're seeing each other. Physically, I know he likes being with me, it's pretty obvious, but he just keeps acting like it's so casual."

"Gross, Mom."

"What? You're old enough for me to talk like this."

I'm not. Not even close.

Then I start giggling because I can't help it.

"What? What's so funny?"

"It's like high school, Mom. It's exactly what I was thinking about earlier. What I'm writing a poem about. He wants to be friends with benefits."

"Now you're being gross."

"But it is. He wants no consequences for what he does, as if you've both mutually agreed to keep it fun and friendly and not hold any grudges when one of you finds someone else."

"God," my mother says, smacking the steering wheel with an open palm, "you're right. Don't they ever grow up?"

"I was kind of hoping you'd be the one who could reassure me about that. You know, give me the speech about how I just need to be patient, things will get better?"

"Yeah, well." My mother shakes her head. "Not happening. Not tonight anyway."

I don't say anything.

We gaze through the windshield at the tools on the wall.

My phone buzzes again but I don't look at it.

"Your father—" my mother begins, then stops. "Screw it," she says, and turns on the ignition. "Let's get some ice cream. You want to go get ice cream with your mom?"

Actually, I don't.

There's a lukewarm bowl of chocolate-shavings soup in my bedroom and I didn't want to finish that. Plus, she's probably still drunk. On the other hand, if my mother suggests an activity that includes her actively eating, that's hard for me to turn down. I check the new text from Rugger.

It's killing me that you won't text me back. All I do is think about you. How can I get back on your good side?

"You know what I'd really like to do right now?" I say to my mother.

"What?"

"Attack the pile of chairs. Can we keep the ones you actually might work on and get rid of the rest?"

My mother turns off the car.

"Let's do it," she says.

[26]

It's no easy task.

Cobwebs and dirt proliferate. The chairs are all broken and splintered and mold-ridden and there must be fifty of them. We work for at least an hour, but it's not tedious. I like the work because I always like physical work where you can see the results manifesting in front of your eyes. My mother does too. At one point, she untangles what looks like a metal stool from some kind of workstation. It's tall and sleek-looking but scratched all over, and there's a coffee stain on the seat.

"This one's in pretty good shape," she says. "I saw it sticking out of the dumpster behind the office one night. I was thinking I'd sand it down, paint and polish it, sew on some kind of cushion and give it to you for graduation. You could take it and use it in college."

Just in case there's a bar in my dorm room, I think. Either that or my desk would have to be five feet high.

"You dumpster-dive, Mom?"

"I prefer to think of it as recycling. And, no, I'm not ashamed."

I'm not either. I think it's cool my mom dumpster-dives.

"Speaking of college . . ." she says.

"I haven't heard. Or decided."

There are two D1 programs looking at me. Indiana University and Louisville. A couple of Ivies are also interested, and I guess they also count as D1, but with my garbagey grades right now, I doubt they're going to happen. Also, my mom won't say it, but she knows and I know we need a scholarship that pays for everything. Both Indiana and Louisville have offered partials. What I'm waiting for is to find out what's going to happen with Mallory. Louisville likes her too. But so does Notre Dame, and they're talking about offering her full. If they do, she'll go there and then I'll be on my own.

I get another text from Rugger and laugh when I see it. He can't be serious.

If you won't talk to me, will you at least send me a pic?

I text back because again I'm intrigued.

How can he possibly rationalize asking for a picture when he knows I'm pissed off at him? And, yes, it's true we've made out, even, you could argue, pretty strenuously, but a photo? That's next level.

Also, I text back because I'm stupid.

Seriously? Why would I send you a picture?

His response comes as quickly as if it's an auto-text, like he knew what I was going to ask and already had a little poem typed up and set to go.

> *Because all I do is think about you.*
> *Because I want to try to get more serious.*
> *Because I want to believe you trust me the way I want*
>   *to trust you.*
> *Because you're beautiful.*

> *Because I figure I have to take a shot or I'll regret it forever.*
> *Because you're so effin' beautiful.*
> *Because all I do is think about you.*

I feel my face getting red and can tell my mom is looking at me. I try not to think about that.

Tell me what D-Crazy means, I text, *and then I'll think about a picture.*

His response comes more slowly. I have time to untangle two more chairs from the pile before my phone buzzes.

Just that she's kind of wild, you know? That's all.

Bullshit, I text back. *You want me to trust you, trust me.*

Again, I have time to untangle a couple chairs.

OK, it means, you know, and I didn't make it up, but it means she's kind of crazy for The D.

That's what I thought it meant.

The D.

With an article.

Not just *his* D—which, let me say a bit too explicitly, is fine, but nothing particularly extraordinary—or D in general, but *The* D, like the way when Yale and Harvard play football, even though hundreds of other teams play on the same Saturday—most of whom are a lot better than they are—they call it *The* Game.

I'm furious and yank a chair so hard from the pile that a leg pulls loose, and I don't let go in time and get a nasty splinter in my thumb.

Ugh.

Does she know people call her that?

I don't think so.

That's disgusting. You're disgusting.

Hey, you asked for the truth and I told it to you because I didn't want to lie. I respect you too much to lie to you. Plus, like I told you, I didn't make it up.

Yeah, but did you tell your rat boys to stop saying it after you "did stuff" with her?

No response.

I get back to the chairs.

Or did you cite what you did with her as evidence the nickname applies, kind of like a quote in an essay? Is that what she is to you? An assignment to get done?

No response.

I look at the chairs but can't touch them.

Can't touch anything.

Think of Delaney's sweet, genuine laugh.

Want to hurl my phone against the pegboard, watch it hit a hammer and explode.

"Are you all right?" my mom says.

"Just got a splinter."

She drops the chair she's holding and walks over to me. I hold my hand out for her to look at and I'm a little kid again. She takes it and tries to dig the splinter out with her nail but can't, so she goes into the house and returns with one of her sewing needles.

When she takes my hand again, holding it palm upward, she can tell I've been crying.

"It hurts that much?"

I shake my head.

"The boy on the phone?"

I nod. She lightly presses the needle into my thumb and I grit my teeth. Bite my lip.

"Got it," she says, holding up something that looks so small between her thumb and forefinger it's almost impossible to believe it could hurt me.

"Tell me it gets better," I say. "Tell me the boys get better."

"I wish I could," she whispers into my ear and I can smell new wine on her breath, as if she fortified herself when she went into the house to get the needle. "I wish I could, honey, but I can't. Not tonight."

My phone buzzes again.

I almost don't look, but I can't help it.

Does this mean I don't get a pic?

I ask my mom to hand me a particularly dusty and dirty chair, one of the last ones left in the pile. She does and I smear the dust, dirt, and cobwebs all over my face and hair so I look like the grimiest pig in the pen. Then I make my wickedest, witchiest, meanest f-you face and snap a selfie and send it to him.

Cute, he texts, *but that's not what I had in mind.*

I don't respond.

[27]

It takes us another half hour to haul all the chairs my mother doesn't want to the curb and then we clean up and go for ice cream after all.

I drive.

We go to the dairy with the thick, frothy stuff, not the horrid place where Julie B.'s brother works. It's crowded, as always, and we have to wait in a long line, but the feeling is good, like we're at the favored sanctuary where the community gathers for fun and sugary fat, and my mother definitively eats.

A small vanilla cone.

Nothing fancy, but still.

I have chocolate chip with actual chips.

They rock.

By the time we get back it's past eleven and I'm totally exhausted.

But I have homework.

And I have to do it.

No excuses.

I slide my creative writing journal to the bottom of the

stack because I can't think of a good new title and I don't want to get stuck for an hour contemplating, so I start on math. About twenty minutes in, my phone rings.

Mallory.

I pick up because it has to be important. Otherwise, she'd text.

At first, I can't understand what she's saying because she's crying so much.

Then I do.

Something about a mistake.

A stupid, disgusting, terrible mistake.

"I need you, Allison," she says. "I need you right now."

[28]

When I get to her house, Mallory frantically ushers me upstairs to her room.

"I don't want my parents to know about this," she says. "Especially not my dad."

She's not crying anymore, but she's got no makeup on and her hair is piled above her head like a sloppy trash bag. She's wearing a T-shirt and sweats from the club team for indoor we played on two years ago. They are orange with green piping and I never liked them. Still, I think she's beautiful even though she'd never leave her house looking like this unless maybe we were going to practice and then definitely straight home.

We sit on her bed and without saying anything she shows me the picture on her phone. In the photo, she's got her cheeks sucked in and her lips pursed and her makeup hasn't been eviscerated by tears and she could be a model. She's bare-chested with her arms crossed below her breasts and even though I've seen her naked a million times, I'm startled because I've never seen her, I don't know, preening.

Except it's not a confident preening.

Her breasts are paler than her arms and shoulders and something about how she's holding her elbows, about the curve in her back, tells me she's self-conscious. In a way, it's a photograph that should be hanging in a museum or a gallery in a big city, a perfect portrait of the contemporary teenager, bold and vulnerable at the same time, proud of her blooming body, sensing its power, but also scared and anxious about the trouble that might be coming.

I'm transfixed and I look at the screen for too long and don't ask any questions because I already know what happened.

"You sent this to Jake," I finally say.

She won't look at me but nods her chin in the way she does on the field when she wants me to know she's going to break free and I should lead her with a pass. This isn't going to be that simple.

"How'd it happen?"

She shakes her head and her eyes tear up and she's ashamed. I have never before seen Mallory ashamed of anything. Shame is usually attached to me with my drunk mother, rollercoaster grades, and no father. Yet, it would be good to be in my room right now, not Mallory's, so we could stare at Rachel Dawson's forearms.

"Why am I so stupid?" she sputters, and makes a fist, but doesn't unmake it because she knows what she's mad about and pretends to punch the air instead. I flinch because if that fist happened to hit me it would hurt. A ton.

"Let me guess," I say. "He told you he thinks about you all the time. He told you you're beautiful. He asked you to trust him the way he wants to trust you."

"Oh my God, he asked you too? Tell me he's not that slimy."

She looks angry now. Anger's good. Better than shame.

"No," I say. "Not *that* slimy. Except . . . it might actually be worse."

"What do you mean?"

I want to tell her and I don't want to tell her.

"When did you send it to him?"

"Like an hour ago."

I walk over to her desk and pick up a framed picture of the two of us at Festival in Palm Springs last fall. We won our pool and have our arms around each other and she's about an inch taller, maybe two, and her hair is lighter and she's prettier. That's just an objective fact. Anyone would think it. What I remember most about that trip was how goofy she was. We were winning games and afterward, one night, we ate tuna salad sandwiches on whole wheat with pickles and they were the best ever, and then we went into a fancy clothing store and pretended to be mannequins in the window and made faces at passersby on the street and cracked them up.

"Rugger was texting me at the same time and asking for a photo. He said the same things. The same *exact* things."

"What are you saying?" she says, but I can tell she already knows because she's making her fist again.

"Those assholes were together, and probably some other boys too. Maybe the whole stupid rat crew. I bet they were playing some kind of game, texting as many girls as possible, seeing how many pictures they could get sent to them."

Mallory sucks in a breath and her shoulders shake.

"They'd stab their own girlfriends in the back like that?"

"Bros before hos. That's how they'd justify it."

"That's pathetic."

I give her the chin nod in agreement and look her in the eyes. She brings her fist over her mouth and holds it there. There's a question I want to ask, even though I already know the answer to it. If Mallory believed Jake wasn't sharing the picture, if she thought she made a mistake trusting him, but it was just limited to a mistake between him and her, and she just hated the idea of her being suckered and his having that photo of her forever, she'd be pissed, but I don't think she'd be as broken as she was when she first called me.

There's something else she's not telling me.

Because there's no way Jake, Mr. Frickin' Horror-show, hasn't shared the picture somewhere already.

If he were in this room right now, I'd punch his face so hard it would split in half.

I take her fist in my hands.

Then I pull her close and hug her and she puts her head on my shoulder. Her whole body is shaking and I'm hoping it's anger. But it's not. Maybe later it will be, but not yet.

I gaze at the wall behind her and smell her incredible, piled-up hair.

After maybe a couple minutes, she pulls away. It seems like she's gained some resolve. Her back is stiffer, but it might not last.

"There's a Dropbox," she says, her voice shaky.

"What?"

"I haven't seen it, but Julie B. called me. There's a Dropbox and it's called Womack Hos. It's been around for a couple years, apparently. When boys get pics from their girlfriends, they post them in it and there's an access code that, like, every d-bag boy in the school has, and they can all go look, download, do whatever. Julie B. didn't know about it either, but Aaliyah did because her brother goes on it. She called Julie B. and said I'm on there now."

Aaliyah called *Julie B.*?

Instead of me?

How does that work?

I try to push the question out of my mind and also the

thought that at least Mallory wanted me to help her deal with this nightmare instead of someone else.

"I'll kill him," I say. "I will. I'll go over to his house right now and bash his pretty face in with my stick. He deserves it and I will hit him so hard, his whole skull will break."

Mallory doesn't laugh or chuckle or smile or anything. Just waves away my suggestion with her hand, as if I'd had a bad idea for trying to score on a corner hit that won't work during a game.

"No, we're not doing that. How many people do you think have seen it already?"

"I don't know." I try to joke again. "Thousands? A few million? A billion?"

I still can't make her smile, but she sniffs in a tiny breath and almost smirks. Progress, I guess.

"Do you think I'm the only girl stupid enough to send a picture?"

"I doubt it."

"Did you send one to Rugger?"

I hesitate because I know I'm not better than Mallory, or smarter. I just got lucky. I was thinking about Delaney, and about Harvard being a jerk to my mom, and I don't like Rugger nearly as much as Mallory likes Jake. In a different moment, with a different boy, maybe even with Jake himself, I would've been just as stupid.

"Did you?" Mallory says.

I fish my phone from my pocket and pull up the selfie I took in the garage and show it to her.

I'm hoping she'll laugh.

She doesn't.

But she smiles.

"I hate you," she says. "And I love you so much."

[29]

OUR FIRST TASK is to contain the damage.

We need to find out if it's possible for Jake to unpost the picture and if the rat fuckheads have forwarded it all over the place. At least, that's the way I see it.

Mallory shakes her head.

"It's too late for that," she says. "It's been over an hour. That picture could be anywhere."

"But we can find out. Make Jake take it down."

"How?"

"We can tell him we'll tell his hockey coach what he did. Tell him he'll get kicked off the team for his senior year if he doesn't tell his friends to delete it. We probably can't get rid of it completely, but still."

Mallory makes a fist and thinks. Then she does something strange. She looks at the picture as if she's evaluating it, turns her phone so she can see it from different angles. For a moment, I wonder if she's proud of it. If she *wants* it out there. Then I feel like punching myself in the face for thinking that.

"No," she says. "Jake's a jerk and I'm done with him. For

real, I am. I'm going to tell him what a jerk he is, and how we, the two of us, will never again be a thing, and that I think he should take it down because it's wrong for him to share it with people, but I don't want to threaten him about hockey. *I sent him the picture. He didn't force me to.* I don't like what he's done with it, but that was my risk."

"Boys will be boys? Is that what you're saying? You should have known better than to trust him so it's your fault he's being an asshole? He gets to just laugh his ass off with his buddies at how gullible you are?"

"No, the consequences are he gets the picture, but that's *all* he gets. The real me is gone for him. Forever."

It's a good point.

Having a picture of Mallory is no substitute for having the actual Mallory, but I can't help feeling he's still getting away with much more than he deserves. And I'm not sure Mallory understands all the potential issues.

"What if Notre Dame sees it?"

"I thought about that," she says, "and it's not a what-if question. They'll see it, definitely. I'll be honest about it, tell them it was a mistake. They'll either still want me or they won't. It'll probably matter more whether we win states. If I can prove to them I'm still a leader, still reliable, then maybe they won't make a big deal out of it."

I don't say anything about Louisville. My fantasy of us going to school together, me passing to her for four more years.

I'm not sure how I feel.

I don't want Mallory to lose Notre Dame because she loves the coach there, and I definitely don't want her to lose it because of a reason like this, but if she does, and we wind up going to school together, playing D1 together—well, how is that a bad thing?

"What if your dad sees it?"

"That would suck." She kind of smirks, but not because the situation is funny. Because it's awful.

"So we should try to get rid of it. Minimize whatever damage we can."

Mallory shakes her head again. "Yeah, but we can't force Jake to delete it, or to tell his friends to. If we try to do that officially, like go through his hockey coach or the principal or a teacher, then my dad will definitely find out."

"True."

"Plus, I also don't want my father fighting this battle for me. I made the mistake. I was stupid enough to buy Jake's bullshit. I have to deal with it, not my dad."

In a way, her stubbornness seems to be giving her strength, so I feel myself falling in line with her. Then I remember how upset she was on the phone.

"Mallory, when you called me, you were crying so much, you could barely talk. I know you think you're the toughest girl in the universe, and you are, but you need some help here. Let me help you."

"Allison," she says, and reaches over to hold my wrist, "I was upset when I called you because . . ." She hesitates. Looks down instead of into my eyes. "Believe me, it's over with Jake. I can deal with Notre Dame. I can even handle my father if he finds out. I'll be embarrassed because I don't think he's seen me without a top in, like, five years, and certainly not without a top and *posing*, or whatever, and I'll be super embarrassed because he'll be embarrassed, but he's my dad, he loves me. He'll be disappointed, but he'll get over it. But the thing is, Allison, it's you. *You're* the one I let down the most."

Her eyes mist up again and I can almost see the steel drifting from her shoulders, as if her strength could just evaporate, blow away.

"After all that stuff I told you about what it means to be

captain," she says, and shakes her head to get rid of her tears. "Then I go ahead and do this. Like an idiot.

"I can't be perfect like you," she says. "I try, I try so hard, but I can't."

Me?

Perfect?

I'm the most un-perfect person I know.

I don't know what to say so I just stare until she finally looks up at me. Her eyes are full and the rich brown of fertile earth and I hope she knows there's no way she can ever let me down.

I show her the selfie I took of myself again with about a billion cobwebs in my hair. "This? This disgusting, filthy human is perfect?"

She laughs.

"Yeah," she says. "She is."

I pull back from her and extend my fist so she can give me a pound, the way she does on the field after either of us scores.

"It's the Mal and Al show forever," I say. "Nothing can stop us. Nothing."

[30]

It starts the next morning as soon as we get out of the car.

We turn from looking at the sunrise and a group of three freshman boys is staring at us.

At Mallory, I should say.

It's not clear if they even see me.

They are barely out of eighth grade and they carry musical instruments on their backs like backpacks that are way too heavy and they act like the parking lot is quicksand and they are stuck. Their eyes are round like doughnuts and radar-locked on Mallory's chest.

"Keep walking," she says. "Ignore them."

I can't.

I push the top of one of the boys' musical cases—maybe it's a cello—and he topples onto the asphalt.

"She can do more push-ups than all three of you combined," I say.

"Do you think that's how they got so firm?" we hear the boy say to his friends as he clambers to his feet. "From the push-ups?"

I can't actually tell if he's joking.

"Nice job ignoring them," Mallory says.

"Sorry."

"It's going to be like this for a while. You can't push down every boy who stares at me."

"Can too."

"Well, don't."

Every minute I'm with Mallory the rest of the morning, we navigate stares, whispers, titters. Between each class, the hallway is a minefield. Groups of girls hiss "ho" and "slut" to one another so the words build into a wave of sound. It curls and rolls and finally crashes into the shore of the collective female student body with the thud of a menacing question—if that's the way she respects herself, then what should *we* do?

Boys, like stalkers, trail us and breathe heavily.

The mass of their exhales is a too-warm wind and my body feels hot and red and lit-up and watched. I can't imagine how Mallory feels. At lunch, Julie B. sits down at our table, unwraps her peanut butter and honey sandwich and starts right in, "Let me first say, I hate them. The boys at this school are the worst. They have the group maturity of a caterpillar before it pupates. But you knew that, Mallory. I've heard you say it about Jake a hundred times. So yes, I have sympathy for you and I'm pissed and I hate all of them even more on your behalf but, can I also ask, what the fuck, Mal?"

Mallory almost loses it, puts down her bag of kale chips and drops her jaw, can't respond.

"Really, Julie B.?" I say. "Really? Aren't we supposed to stick by our teammates no matter what?"

"That's a questionable policy," she says. "What if our teammate gets someone drunk and rapes her? Hypothetically, I mean. Look at the college football quarterback who was accused of that. Were you applauding his teammates for sticking up for him, for calling her a liar, for erasing the videos they took from their phones before the cops could see them?"

The noise in the lunchroom is loud and whatever we say to one another usually gets lost in the sea of high school cacophony, but this time it doesn't. It seems like every teenager in America is watching Julie B. berate Mallory and me.

"You can't make that comparison. Mallory didn't hurt anyone except herself. She made the mistake of trusting her boyfriend. We all do that."

Right on cue, my phone buzzes and it's a text from Rugger.

I'm sorry. We were jerks. I'm so sorry, Allison. We were way too high to realize what we were doing. I didn't know all this would happen. I deleted everything from the Dropbox. Everything we put up, including Mal. I'm going to stop smoking. Don't hate me.

Lose my number, I text back.

"I know it's not the same," Julie B. says. "I'm just speaking theoretically. I'm sitting here with you guys, aren't I? You know I have your back, Mal. I'm just saying it's a distraction to the team. The Dropbox is out of control. Everyone's talking about it."

"I've been trying to tune everything out," Mallory says. "I don't know where the picture went and I don't really care."

I should leave it at that, but I'm built different than Mallory, who only wants to run harder, only wants to barrel through whatever's in her way. With me, it's like with my homework, none of which I ended up doing last night. I make piles, organize, have to know the extent of the struggle before I can attack it.

"It's not in the Dropbox anymore," I say. "Rugger texted me about it."

"Rugger still texts you?" Mallory says, looking as if I slapped her.

"I told him not to," I protest. "He said he deleted it."

"Yeah," Julie B. says, "it's gone now. He's probably worried about getting arrested. That's why he took it down. But by this morning, it already had thousands of views and hundreds of downloads. I think every boy in the school has seen it. Most of the girls too. Probably some teachers."

"Teachers?" I say.

"You know creepy Gowhatever has. Dude probably thinks it'll be something good to write about."

"That's disgusting and not funny."

"Was I the only girl on there?" Mallory asks.

"No, it was every girl they got pictures from last night. Eight of them, I think. Delaney, of course—"

"Wait, why *of course* for Delaney, Julie B.?" I say. "What's that mean?"

She gives me a look like I should already know the answer to my question and I kind of do, but I still don't like what she said.

"A few more sophomores," she continues, "that girl April who's a senior and was dating Connor for a while, but you're the star, Mal. Or you were."

"How? How am I the star?"

"Because you're you and you might make all-American and everyone knows who you are. Because all the girls want to be you. Because nobody can believe Jake is that big of an asshole to put your picture up like that. Believe it or not, that's what people are talking about the most. How you broke up with him. How much of a jerk he is. I heard he went home after first hour because people were talking so much shit and he couldn't take it."

"*He* went home?" Mallory says. "Because of what people

were saying about *him*? I feel like everyone's talking about *me*."

"They were, and they are," Julie B. says. "But not in the way you think. Shockingly, a huge number of people got seriously offended. I mean, we have freshmen, of course, boys and girls, who have no clue, but the vast majority of everyone else, they think Jake and his bros crossed a pretty severe line."

"And you know this how?" I'm skeptical.

"Well, I mean, everyone's talking about it. Jake is, like, insta-supervillain. I heard two girls arguing, sophomores, and one was saying it couldn't have been Jake because he's in her Spanish class and he's so nice and so cute and, whatever, all this bullshit. And this other girl just rips into her, says it was definitely Jake and he's a loser and not cute anyway, way too cocky, and if she saw him she'd spit in his face and a bunch of other people heard and joined in and were high-fiving and saying Jake sucks and using other foul insults about his lack of an appropriate level of humanity. I'm telling you, people hate him now. Three basketball players came up to me, *boy* basketball players, I mean, and *three* of them, I'm not just talking about one lone ranger, and they apologized on behalf of the population of rodent people. I mean, I'm sorry this happened, Mallory, I am, but it might be a watershed moment."

"For what?" Mallory says. "For what did they apologize?"

"I'm not sure exactly. Just for being boys, I think. For all the boys who are assholes. It was kind of sweet, actually."

"Kind of restores my faith in our generation," I say. "Kind of."

"Yeah, well, you haven't seen this yet," Julie B. says.

She pulls out her phone and shows us the Facebook page of a girl named Michelle Candle, the goalie for Brentwood East, whom we play against this afternoon. The picture of

Mallory's on her timeline and the caption says, "Homack's going down! That's all they DO is go down. Especially the all-American! Especially on the hockey players at their school!"

"See what I mean about the distraction?" Julie B. says.

It's quiet a moment and Mallory stares at the phone screen. I can't tell what she's feeling. Is she going to start crying again? Will I have to hold her, here in the cafeteria, and let her sob into my shoulder?

She turns away from the phone, pours her eyes into Julie B. and me.

"That's not a distraction," she says, and her back is straight and steel.

Something changes in the lunchroom. The air feels charged. I get, honestly, like, an electric shock in my forearms, like any snakes coiled there just got jolted out of hibernation. There's definitely no one else talking. The whole school is watching Mallory. At least it seems like that. I open my mouth slightly and I can feel my cheeks quivering. It's as if I'm about to bungee jump off a two-hundred-foot cliff and I'm excited about it. My blood's pumped.

I can't wait for what will happen next.

"They're dead," Mallory says. "So dead."

[31]

I FAIL another math quiz and am unprepared in creative writing.

"All I ask is that you write and revise one piece a week for this class," Gowhatever says. "That's it. That's all the homework you get. Would you like to enlighten me as to why you can't accomplish even that simple task?"

I'd like to see the internet history on your computer, I think. And show it to the school board. Enlighten *them*.

"Well, Allison?"

"I'm sorry, I was just super busy."

"Are you saying you can't handle your academics and playing a sport at the same time? Is that what you're saying? Because if you are, then I need to have a conversation with your coach."

"Whatever," I say under my breath.

"Did you just say *whatever*?"

Gowhatever, naturally, hates when people say whatever.

"I did. I'm sorry. I didn't mean it. I'm just tired. I care about this class, Mr. Gowhatever, I swear. I won't miss any more assignments, I promise."

He considers for a few moments whether I'm contrite enough, pretends to look at his gradebook to see if I've missed any pieces before, which I haven't.

"All right, Allison. Just don't let it happen again."

"Wait, that's all you're going to say?" Brian the weed-rapper-slash-lacrosse-player shouts out. "That's it? She doesn't get in trouble? If it was me, you'd be like, calling my parents or making me stay after. I swear, the field hockey players at this school get away with everything."

This is a remarkable statement.

Despite my academic screw ups, our team has a collective GPA of something like 3.8. I don't think anyone on our team has gotten suspended in at least a decade. Most of the teachers don't even know who we are. We can wear our game jerseys, our skirts, eye-black beneath our eyes, walk around holding our sticks, it doesn't matter, half of them think we're just dressing up for Halloween. Give Gowhatever credit. At least he has some small clue about what I'm involved in. Martindale too. At least they think it's possible for a girl to care enough about her sport that threatening her with losing it will motivate her. The truth is, even though we've won states five out of the last six years and the football team wins maybe half its games, they still get ten times the attention we do.

For Brian to say that though, means field hockey is on his radar for some reason, that what we've accomplished has created enough buzz to penetrate his brain to some degree, even if it's only to cause resentment. Does his sport, lacrosse, get as much attention as it deserves? Probably not. But the sport that gets the announcements over the PA, the front page of the sports section, the pep rally that urges everyone to show up for the big game wearing red-and-purple against our crosstown rivals, the cheerleaders, the homecoming dance, is the aforementioned football. That's who he should be mad at. Not us. Not our small slice of notoriety when we prove, over and over again, in front of pretty much just our parents in the stands—well, not mine—that we're the best team in the state.

But we're girls and we're good so the boys get mad at us.

Want to hurt us.

Why?

I have no idea. Ask them.

All I know is, Julie B. is about to go off.

"What are you talking about, Brian?' she says. "*What* do field hockey players get away with? I swear, if you're talking about Mallory, I will come over there right now and punch you in the face so hard, little pieces of your ugly, raccoon-fur eyebrows will be all over the floor."

Raccoon-fur eyebrows? Awesome.

"You see that, Mr. Gowhatever? You see that? She threatens me and you just sit there and don't do anything. That's exactly what I'm talking about."

"I suspect she's using hyperbole, Brian."

"No, I'm not," Julie B. says, her voice rising, the muscles in her neck looking like ropes. "Say it, Brian, say what you mean. This is an uncensored class. You're a dude. You're supposed to have balls, right? Man up and say what you mean."

Oh, boy.

"Hold on," Gowhatever says, and he's doing his waving-his-arms-like-a-referee thing again as if he'd like to stop play and give Julie B. a yellow card. "The no-censorship rule only applies to the art we're making, not the way we talk to one another. You know that, Ms. Bennett. You need to start demonstrating some civility in your discourse. Now."

"Fuck civility. The discourse in this class is sexist and ignorant. Tell the truth, Brian. You're mad because Mallory shared something private with her boyfriend and when Jake the Snake stabbed her in the back and you and your rat boy fuckheads blasted it all over the internet, nobody gave you props. It backfired and now everyone realizes what d-bags you are so you're crying about how unfair it is. You're wrong, Brian. Field hockey players don't get away with anything. We don't *need* to get away with anything because we're not assholes."

"You see that, Mr. Gowhatever? Now she's cursing. How come you're not kicking her out?"

"Ms. Bennett, I'm only going to say this one more—"

"What, Brian? Now Mr. Suck-on-it-ho-like-it's-Froyo is afraid of words? Is that it? Or maybe you're afraid of something else. Why don't you take your phone out now, Brian, and film this?"

Uh-oh.

She gets up from her desk.

The whole class is frozen, including Mr. Gowhatever.

She walks over to Brian and pulls her T-shirt over her head.

"Is this what you're afraid of, Brian? They're called mammary glands. Your mother probably nursed you on them when you were born. Why don't you take a picture now, Brian? Show all the rat fuckers?"

I have a feeling our team's no-suspensions streak is about to end.

"Ms. Bennett," Gowhatever warns, but it's too late.

Julie B. pulls off her sports bra and there are her breasts, right in the middle of the classroom, pointed like the prow of a battleship directly at Brian. He stares, open-mouthed, unable to say anything.

Her breasts, by the way, are not small.

"Where's your phone now, Brian? Aren't you thrilled? Don't you want to show your trophy to the rat boys?"

I don't know why, or maybe I do, but I feel like taking my shirt off too.

My body feels more mine than it's ever felt.

I stand up.

"Sit down, Allison," I hear Mr. Gowhatever say.

I won't. I'm terrified, but my feet keep moving.

To stand next to Julie B.

Then I hear, "Sit down, Jamie. Sit down, Melissa. Sit down, Ella. Sit down, Katie. Sit down . . ." and I know we are all up, every girl in the class. All ready to stand with Julie B.

To stand with Mallory and Delaney and April.

With one another.

But before we can pull our shirts off, Julie B. puts hers back on, still holding her bra in her hand. "That's what I thought," she says to Brian, whose face looks like she did punch him and break his eyebrows into pieces. "Don't you ever talk shit about my teammates again."

"Ms. Bennett," Gowhatever says, "in the hallway. *Now*."

[32]

I LEAD warm-ups across the big W at midfield while Coach talks to Mallory on the sideline. With Julie B. suspended—she got five days, so she'll miss this game and the road game against Beth Avery on Thursday—Aaliyah will have to step up and anchor the defense.

I'm not worried, and I don't think anyone else is either.

I lead us through high-knees, butt-kickers, side-squats, and lunges, and Coach is still talking to Mallory. Her back looks straight and strong and she's nodding at what Coach says, but she also looks down sometimes and makes her fist a lot, so I can tell she's embarrassed she put herself, and the team, in this position. When we finish Frankensteins—where we walk with both arms stretched out in front of us and alternate lifting our feet to touch our hands—Mallory runs up and tells me she'll take over. Coach wants to speak with me now.

"I got an email from your creative writing teacher," she says as soon as I run up to her. "I don't like getting emails from teachers, you know that. Especially right before a game."

"I was trying to support Julie B.," I say. "I couldn't leave her hanging out there."

Coach cocks an eyebrow and half smiles, and I realize what I just said.

"No pun intended," I say.

"None taken. I support that part of it, but that's not what Mr. Gowhatever, or whatever, is that really his name? That's not what he was talking about in his email."

"Oh."

"He says you missed a revision assignment that was due today. One of only two assignments you were supposed to complete."

"I'll make it up."

"That's not the only email I got. There's one from your math teacher too."

It's such a beautiful day to play field hockey. There's a breeze that feels like a massage. The sky is that forever blue that makes me want to build a house inside it and have lots of children. Leaves on the trees are just starting to turn gold. I've got a full water bottle and no injuries and I'm in big trouble. My cheeks feel paralyzed, like something cold crawled in and froze them.

"He says you have a 54 percent. If you don't get it up by the quarter-grade, you're going to be ineligible."

"I'll get it up."

"You're letting the team down, Allison. You're a captain."

"I know that."

"If I get another email, unless it's one telling me how well you're doing, I'm going to have to suspend that captaincy."

"Coach—"

"No excuses, Allison."

I want to tell her and I don't want to tell her.

"As it is, I'm going to sit you out for the first half today. I love you, Allison, you're a great kid, but you have to set a better example for your teammates. We've never had an ineligible player because of academics. Never. I don't want to start now."

"But I was with Mallory. She was upset. I was trying to—"

I stop talking because of the look Coach is giving me. Like I've cheapened myself and she's starting to love me a little less.

"I know you're a good friend, Allison. That's not the point. You have to manage your time better. It won't help anyone if you can't play because of your grades."

I nod.

On this incredible day to play hockey, I'll cheer from the sideline.

Loud.

[33]

BACK AT THE PURPLE-AND-RED W, Coach addresses the team.

She has no problem with what Mallory did, she says, everyone makes the mistake of trusting someone else too much. It'd be tragic if we got scared, if we all *stopped* trusting people. That'd be the worst thing. Sometimes we're going to get burned. Get used to it. Trust again. Get burned again. Live with it. Allow yourself to love. Be proud of who you are and be proud of your body. If you stop trusting other people, you might as well be dead.

"I don't have a problem with what Julie B. did either," Coach adds. "In fact, I'm proud of her. It's about time somebody made the boys in this school ashamed of themselves. Now, she might have gone a little over the top . . ." She pauses and lets us figure out it's OK to smile. ". . . pun definitely intended, but she was defending her teammate, picking her up for a mistake she made. Now it's up to us to pick up Julie B. Aaliyah, you're in charge back there. We need you to control the field. Can you do it?"

Aaliyah nods.

"Thought so. Unfortunately, we also have a bigger problem."

She pauses again and everyone waits.

My cheeks grow colder, zero degrees kelvin.

"We've got a player who's not completing her homework assignments and is putting her eligibility in jeopardy. This player is an important player and she's going to have to sit out the first half today. We're going to have to pick up for her too."

She doesn't say my name but everyone knows it's me. Who else was she talking to during warm-ups?

"A player who lets herself down academically also lets down the team. I want you to be great players, but I also want you to be great people. That means what you do in the classroom, the way you're engaged and actively learning, how you complete your assignments on time and to the best of your ability, all that matters more than what you do on this field. And you know how much I think *this* matters, so if I'm telling you schoolwork comes first, how much do you think *that* matters? A lot or a little?"

"A lot," we say.

"Am I making myself clear?"

"Clear," we say.

"Sydney, you're at center-mid. Can you control the field?"

Sydney nods.

"Thought so. Now . . ." She pauses again and gestures toward the stands, where a larger than normal crowd has accumulated. ". . . this isn't going to be pretty."

We all realize it at the same time.

We've been listening to Coach so intently we didn't hear it.

They're chanting, a cluster of about twenty students from Brentwood—"Ho-mack, Ho-mack, Ho-mack . . ."

They have signs too, four or five of them that say, "Homack Hos Know How to Go Down!"

"Here's what you need to know," Coach says. "The fact their parents didn't raise their kids right has nothing to do with us. They can chant all they want, make as many signs as they possibly can, what does it all mean? Mallory, what does it mean?"

"They're dead."

We count down and shout "Warriors!" and while we're heading to the sideline, Mallory scampers over and says she's sorry, it's her fault, she tried to tell Coach she made me come over even though it was late.

"It's not your fault," I say. "It's mine. My homework, my responsibility. Coach is right."

"I'm still sorry."

"Don't be sorry," I say. "Murder them."

"Oh my God," Mallory says. "Look at the stands."

I do.

And see my mother standing behind the group of Homack chanters.

She must have left work early. Either that or she got fired. But she looks sharp in her work clothes, and sober, and, despite the veil of sunscreen, beautiful.

And, for the first half, she's not going to see me play.

[34]

I STAND up with my team for the national anthem and hold hands with Aaliyah on one side and Mallory on the other. It's the first time I'm not in the starting line-up since that initial game when Mal and I were sixth graders playing with the eighth graders and I don't know how to handle it. I'm embarrassed and sad and I can't wait for the first half to be over. I try to focus on my teammates instead of myself. Aaliyah is sturdy and strong, her hand cool, her grip tight. Mal's hand feels like it's on fire, like if I breathed on it, flames would ignite and spread through her whole body.

Or mine.

I can hear her trying hard to control her breathing, keep it even.

"Are you OK?" I whisper.

She nods but doesn't say anything. I imagine smoke coming out of her nostrils. Maybe I'm not imagining it.

As soon as the anthem is over, Mallory bursts away and sprints toward the middle of the field to shake hands with the Brentwood captains and the officials. I stay on the sideline like Coach told me to and want to fall apart.

Aaliyah puts a hand on my shoulder.

"Do you need help in math?" she asks. "I'm really good at math."

I shake my head, touched by her offer, but, with me, it's not about the content. It's about the organization.

"When you do homework," I say, "do you have a plan? Like, do you make an order of stuff you like to do first and then what you hate to do last, or is it just attack whatever falls out of your backpack?"

She looks at me like I'm a bit odd, like she's thinking about whether it's too intimate to reveal her homework strategies just before a game's about to start.

"Why do you want to know that?"

"I don't know. Maybe I'm kind of a freak. I always have to do things a certain way."

"I guess I do too," she says. "I mean, my house is always noisy. Derrick has his music on all the time or is playing *Call of Duty* with my little brother."

"You have two brothers?"

"Three, actually. One's in college. He's a basketball player too, and when he comes home, it's even louder."

I think about how quiet my house is.

"I think I'd like that," I say. "I feel like I'd never get lonely with all those people around."

She looks at me thoughtfully again, as if she's considering whether she should say more, spill what's really on her mind.

"I'm the only girl with three boys and they treat me like I'm an alien," she says. "I'm always lonely."

It hits me then.

I want to be her friend. Her off-the-field and outside-of-school friend.

Because she needs one, but also because I like her, and I need one too.

"Do you feel lonely on the team?" I say, the question dry, like a rock in my mouth.

Something in her changes.

Her eyes harden.

She shakes her head.

"Did you check the album covers?"

Damn, I forgot.

"I'm sorry," I say. "Not yet. It's been crazy. I haven't had—"

She cuts me off. "It's OK. Game time."

I give her a fist pound. "Kick ass out there," I say. "Control the field."

"It's my field," she says. "The field is mine."

[35]

Actually, it isn't.
 The field is Mallory's.
 All Mallory's.
 It takes about thirty seconds.
 Brentwood starts with the ball but goes nowhere. Georgia, our center-forward, locks up their mid and the ball knocks free and Sydney's right there. She fakes like she's about to dribble right and arrows a pass to Mallory on the left wing. Mal pulls toward her backhand, then pokes the ball through the defender's legs and she's off. Another defender sprints toward her but she has no chance. Mallory's legs are V8 engines and they do not slow down. The girl on defense does everything right but it doesn't matter. Mallory blasts through her as if the girl's made of that wispy blue cotton candy, the kind that scares me.
 Only the goalie is left.
 Michelle Candle.
 She of the trash-talking Facebook page.
 Mallory grows taller. She's eight feet. Ten feet. Twelve feet. Fifty feet. Each stride she takes crosses the stadium. Her

muscles are locomotives. Her muscles are industrial factories. Her stick is a towering oak tree and the ball is a thundercloud.

Michelle Candle knows she has no chance.

It looks like she shrinks.

The Ho-mack chanters sound like shy butterflies trying to make some kind of noise in the face of a hurricane.

Mal goes into her backswing the way a bear opens its mouth to roar.

Michelle Candle flinches.

Actually flinches.

On the field of play, *flinches*.

In front of everyone.

But there's no rocket shot like we all expect. No glorious-sounding smack into the board. Somehow, Mallory stops the momentum of her swing and lifts the ball onto her stick for an aerial dribble as if she's going to carry the ball straight into the goal, as if she's a mother serving birthday cake and she's going to deposit it gently onto the tongue of a waiting, salivating five-year-old.

But she doesn't do that.

With Candle a helpless spectator, Mallory flips the ball into the air and she looks almost exactly like her father back in the day, about to hit us a fly ball on the softball field. Then she swings her stick and smacks a line drive into the upper right corner of the net.

The ref blows her whistle to signal the goal and the chanters don't know what to say. Nobody knows what to say. We've all heard of goals scored like this, rumors, but nobody —except maybe Coach—has ever seen it happen. You can google all day long and you won't find anything like it on YouTube.

It must be the kind of shot Mallory practices by herself in her basement after I've gone home to sleep.

On the sideline, after our moment of speechlessness, we erupt. Both my fists fly into the air and I am jumping up and down like a little kid and Sydney and Georgia are hugging on the W at midfield and even Aaliyah raises her stick high and thrusts it one, two, three times against the sky.

I look up into the stands and, yes, even Mal's dad is excited, high-fiving Sydney's dad next to him, who looks kind of afraid. My mother's mouth is open in shock, the same way Brian's was when Julie B. took off her shirt in creative writing. I want to run up to her and tell her, "Mom, now you understand."

This, this is why I love this game.

I am so glad Mallory gave her this gift.

Gave it to all of us.

When everyone calms down, Coach says something to herself, except she says it loud enough that I can hear it.

"You only get one like this, Mallory, one. No more hot-dogging. Don't embarrass anyone. Make the rest of them straight."

She does.

By halftime she's got five goals, the other four screaming cracks off the board. Sydney has four assists and a goal herself. It does not look like my team needs me.

"Don't kid yourself," Coach says as if she knows what I'm thinking. "We're going to face much tougher teams than this one. We're going to need every last ounce of you."

I nod, but I'm not sure I'm convinced.

The Ho-mack chanters keep it up for a few minutes after Mal's first goal, but when you're trying to taunt a team that's shoving it down your throat, after a while you just have to quit, and they do. They leave with ten minutes left in the half, trailing from the stands with their pathetic signs dragging behind them on the asphalt. The whole crew looks like a knot of sad wedding guests soaking in a slow, steady drizzle who just realized they've been waiting for a happy couple that's not actually as happy as they thought and is never going to show up.

I play fine in the second half.

It's me and the subs and I control the field and assist on some goals, even shoot one sweet bullet of a pass to a freshman on the post named Jessica who tips it in for our last goal of the game and her first on varsity. Mal cheers like crazy from the bench and I look up into the stands to see if my mother saw it too, but I can't find her.

She's gone.

[36]

AFTER THE GAME, when we get to the parking lot, Rugger's waiting at my car.

"Go away," I say.

"I just wanted to say I'm sorry," he says, but he's not saying it to me. He's talking to Mallory.

"It was my idea," he tells her. "Not Jake's. He didn't even want to do it. I convinced him."

"So, Jake's a follower now?" Mallory says. "I doubt it."

We are sweaty and hungry and want to go eat a burrito—even though it's game day and not practice, we deserve it after being harassed with the Ho-mack chant—and then get home and shower. I'm kind of intrigued to hear Rugger try to bullshit his—and Jake's—way out of what they did, but I also want to just get going so I can organize my homework and then carve into the monstrous pile.

"Leave us alone," I say.

He turns to me and his face looks legitimately crushed, bereft of any kind of cockiness. For a moment, I feel like I'm looking at the kid who stays home and plays with his autistic brother, hours of asking him the same trivia questions he's already memorized all the answers to.

"I know," he says. "We're idiots. We're jerks. I don't know why we did what we did. You don't have to forgive us. I just wanted you to know I'm the one who started it. We were all wrong, but I'm the worst one. I'm who you should be angry at the most."

There's something admirable about his wanting to take all the responsibility, but he's still not getting it.

"You don't get to decide that," I say, feeling as bold as Julie B. "Who we're mad at is *our* choice, *our* decision. You take the time to wait here at my car like some kind of creeper, but you didn't even come to our game? You didn't even watch us play? Do you know they called us whores? In public, they chanted it over and over. They had signs, Rugger, posters. Mallory's dad had to see that. My *mom* had to see that."

He looks like he's about to cry.

Good.

"All I can say is I'm sorry," he says, and his voice is faint. There are actual tears in his eyes. "There's no excuse for what we did. I wanted to come to the game, I swear, but I didn't want to be a distraction."

"We don't get distracted," Mallory says.

And it's true.

At least for her, and mostly for me.

Maybe this is the difference between the boys and us. Because we get no props, no social status for playing our sport, we only play because we love it. We don't care what people think about us when we're out there. We're just out there. We're being who we are. Responsible only to one another.

"Did you apologize to Delaney?" I ask Rugger.

"Not yet."

She wasn't in ceramics today. Nobody seemed to know where she was. I would've texted her, but I don't have her number.

I open the door to my car and climb in. Mallory gets in the other side.

"Tell Jake to fight his own battles," she says to Rugger.

"He says you won't talk to him."

"That's his problem."

"Don't talk to me either," I say. "Until you apologize to Delaney. Don't even try it."

I pull away and we leave him in the parking lot. He doesn't take his phone out, which would be the natural thing for him to do so he doesn't look stupid to anyone else who sees him. He just watches us drive away, then rubs the no-beard on his chin and looks up at the forever blue sky as if there might be salvation there and, if I'm being honest, I don't hate him.

Not that much.

Not really.

[37]

WHEN I GET HOME, my mother's in the backyard drinking.

She's not drunk but she's got a glass of wine next to her. She's out of her work clothes, just in a pair of jeans and a sweatshirt from the college she went to—where she met my dad who we don't talk about—and she's watching the birds.

"I would've cooked," she says.

"I know."

"How come you didn't tell me?"

I'm not sure if she means that I wasn't coming home for dinner, about Mallory, or that I have bad grades.

I choose Mallory.

"I don't know if she wanted you to know. I know she didn't want her dad to. *Does* he know?"

"Everybody in the stands knows. With all that ho stuff going on, it was hard not to. Who raised those kids?"

Alcoholic single parents, I think, but don't say aloud.

"Has her dad seen the picture?" I ask.

"I'm not sure."

"Have you?"

"Should I?"

I shake my head. What would be the point?

My mother takes a sip of her wine. A robin and a blue jay are at the feeder. Sharing. Not fighting.

"It was easier for us," she says. "I feel for kids now. When we made mistakes, no one recorded them. They weren't eternal. They couldn't go everywhere."

"We're not kids," I say.

"I know that, Allison."

We're quiet again. I almost feel like she's about to ask if I'm sexually active. I have no idea what I'll say if she does.

"I'm sorry," she says, the second person I love apologizing to me today. The third overall, counting Rugger, who's not someone I love.

"For what?"

"For not being a better mother. For not coming to more of your games. For not paying more attention to how you're doing in school. All of it."

My phone buzzes, but I don't look at it. I've been waiting for my mother to say what she's saying for a long time. Now that she's saying it, I'm not sure I'm interested.

"It's OK," she says. "You can check your phone."

"I don't want to."

"Just do it. I can tell you're distracted."

"I'm not distracted."

"Well, I am. Just check it."

It's a text, from Rugger.

Delaney's in the hospital.

[38]

Is she OK? I text back while my mother watches.

Not sure. I think so. She's alive.

Alive? WTF?

What happened?

I think she took pills or cut herself. Maybe both. She's in the psych ward.

Jesus.

My mother can see my expression, which probably looks like somebody snagged a fishhook in my chin and stretched my whole face downward, and mouths, "What's wrong?" but I shake my head.

Have you talked to her? I ask Rugger.

I can't.

Why not?

Allison, I'm so sorry for everything. I need someone to talk to. Can I call you?

I guess I'm proud of myself for not hesitating, for recognizing when someone, no matter how much of a jerk, needs help.

Yes.

"Mom, I'm about to get a phone call I need to take. Can we continue this conversation later? I'm sorry, I really want to continue it, is that OK?"

I get up before she finishes her slow nod. My phone rings as I open the screen door to go into the house.

[39]

"Rugger," I say, as I head up the stairs, my tired muscles moving quickly, pushing hard into each step. I want to go in my room and close the door. I have a feeling this conversation is going to need privacy. I also might need to be able to see Rachel's forearms.

"We messed up so bad," Rugger says.

"No kidding. Why can't you talk to Delaney?"

"Her parents might be pressing charges. They already went to the school. Me, Jake, Brian, and Connor all got suspended for two weeks."

"Can't say you don't deserve it."

Though, truthfully, two weeks might be a little harsh.

"They want to move toward expulsion proceedings. We could get totally kicked out."

"That sucks, Rugger, but I need to know something right now or I'm going to hang up."

"What?"

"Are you more worried about what's going to happen to you or about Delaney?"

"Delaney, that's why I called."

I'm not sure I believe that, but I guess I can hear him out for a few more minutes. I look at Rachel, the way her eyes are so focused on the ball she's about to hit, *only* focused on the ball she's about to hit, and that's what I want my life to be like. Something simple. Why do we get caught up in so much drama? Why can't we just live and have no homework and avoid hurting one another and try our hardest to be really good at something?

"I called the hospital and they said she's accepting visitors but it's only for the next few hours and I want to know how she's doing, but I can't go."

"Why not?"

"Her parents might kill me."

"Or they might really appreciate your showing up and apologizing and acting like you actually care about their daughter."

"My lawyer told me I can't talk to her."

"Your *lawyer*?"

"It wasn't my decision. My father made me get one."

That sounds about right, Rugger's parents looking to protect him while the girl he screwed over recovers from a suicide attempt. Meanwhile, he won't accept responsibility for any choices he makes.

I've had enough.

I've got assignments I need to make up.

He made his own bed. There's nothing I can do to help him.

"Rugger, I've got to go."

I head back downstairs to retrieve my backpack from the dining room table where I left it. I didn't notice the weight of it after the game because I guess I was still pumped up, but as soon as I see it, I know it's going to be absurdly heavy, that, with every fiber of my back and thighs, I'm going to hate lugging it up to my room.

"Allison, please, don't hang up. This is why I called. I want you to go visit Delaney and see if she's OK."

Me?

"Come on, Rugger. I'm barely friends with her. I hardly know her at all."

When I reach my backpack and sling it onto my shoulder, I realize how right I am about its heaviness. The damn monstrosity must weigh forty pounds. Five weeks into school and already it's filled with all kinds of garbage I don't need, a metaphor for my life really. If I can find some time, I'm definitely cleaning it out.

"That's the thing, Allison. She doesn't really have any friends. That's why—" He stops. I'm halfway up the stairs, feeling like the anti–Santa Claus, about to deliver an overstuffed sack of textbooks to my bedroom.

"That's why it was so easy for you to prey on her? Is that what you were going to say?"

"That's why, I was going to say, that's why—" His voice breaks like he's crying and I actually feel bad for him.

Damn it, I actually feel bad.

"That's why I called you," he blurts out. "I didn't know who else to call. She talks about you all the time. How much she likes being in class with you. She really admires you, Allison."

"Why? My pottery's atrocious."

Also, I sneak out sometimes to hook up with the guy she also "does stuff with."

If she knew that, she'd hate me.

I shotput my nine-hundred-pound backpack onto my bed and begin to pull out what I need to work on. Two days' worth of analysis, that's about two hours, another two hours of econ, maybe an hour of Spanish, an hour of physics, and then the creative writing piece.

Jesus, that's two in the morning at the earliest.

I put my head in my hands, feel the weight of my skull against my fingers.

"Delaney said that too."

"What?"

"That your pottery sucks."

"At least she's honest. Rugger, really, I hardly know her. If I showed up in her hospital room, she'd probably wonder what the hell I was doing there."

"I disagree," Rugger says. "She'd think she was important, that she matters. If someone like you visits, maybe she'll think she's not worthless."

"What are you talking about?"

"I don't think you understand how much people look up to you. Mallory too. Every girl in school worships you guys."

Which is why you wanted to bring us down.

It's the same thing as Brian thinking field hockey players get too much attention. The boys can't stand the idea that there are girls among them who don't live and die based on their smirks and text messages.

I pile the books in the order I'll attack them.

Math on top, then physics.

Get the numbers stuff out of the way, then switch to my computer for the econ, what a pain—all those notes—follow that with creative writing for a little break. Finish up with Spanish when I'm most tired, since that's the easiest.

"I can't do it, Rugger."

"Allison, Delaney's a good person. She doesn't deserve what happened to her. She needs you, Allison. Please."

Damn it.

"What were you thinking, Rugger? What did you expect was going to happen when you put her picture up like that for everyone to see?"

"We weren't thinking. We didn't expect. We were high and we were stupid. If I could take it back, I would, I swear, but all I can do now is help her any way I can. I'm not going to smoke anymore. I mean it. And I'm not going to hang out with those guys either. I'm going to try to be a better person, I promise."

Like that's worth anything.

My pile of books is growing larger.

It's a massive tower, threatening to push my bed straight through the floor.

"Please, Allison. There's no one else. She really needs a friend."

Coach's face looms over me like a giant hot air balloon, how disappointed she looked when she told me about the emails from my teachers. How she said she loved me. How she might strip my captaincy.

How Sydney was making passes I should have been making.

The Syd and Mal show.

No, I won't do it.

I won't.

"Please, Allison. I won't bother you anymore after this, I swear. She's all alone. She's not allowed to use her phone. She must be terrified. Please, Allison, please."

"OK," I hear myself say. "Tell me where I have to go."

[40]

WHEN I TELL my mother I have to go to the hospital, and why I have to go, she doesn't ask about my homework.

Instead, she insists on coming with me.

"What? Why?" I say.

"I think I might know something about what it feels like to be betrayed by someone you love. You might be a wise young woman, Allison, and I might be a not-so-wise older one, but pain is something I understand."

The Al and Mom show?

Why not?

When we get to the waiting area, Delaney's parents tell us we're the first people who have come to visit, and they're very thankful we came because Delaney seems to be growing sadder with each hour no one else has shown up. Chalk one up for Rugger, I guess.

They send us into her room and say they'll wait outside. "It'll be nice for Delaney to have some alone time with her friend."

I'm smart enough to resist saying we're not really friends.

"I don't want them all to get expelled," is the first thing Delaney says to us. "Then everyone will hate me even more."

"I don't think people hate you now," I say. "They just don't know you."

"They know my picture. Everyone knows my picture. I can't believe I was so stupid."

She's sitting up in her bed and she doesn't have makeup on but her hair looks brushed out and beautiful. There's a brush on the table next to her that she's probably been using for hours and that's where I put the books I brought for her to read since she's not allowed to have her phone. I open my mouth to say something about how Mallory felt stupid too, but my mom speaks before I can get the words out.

"You mean you did something foolish for a boy you like?" she says. "Welcome to being alive. Anyone who judges you for that is someone who's never been in love. Honey, you've got nothing to be ashamed of."

Did my mom just call her honey?

I think Delaney's a little shocked.

Maybe she figured my mom was only tagging along for moral support. That she just drove me like we're still in middle school, and now she's going to fade into the background, a mute, observing shadow. But my mom's not like that, and I'm not either. Delaney looks at me to gauge my response to my mother. I shrug. The room we're in is kind of sweet. It's quiet, the overhead light is dim and not fluorescent, and there's a soft glow from a light outside the window.

"What she said," I say.

"You don't think I'm an idiot?"

"Delaney," I say, pinching my fingers close together, "I was this close to sending a picture too." I don't say I almost sent it to Rugger because it might break her if she knew he asked me for one. I send imaginary vibes into her head that I have a non-imaginary relationship with some other jerky dumb-ass and I hope she doesn't ask any further questions. "I was just lucky and got distracted by something else. You know Mallory sent a picture, right?"

"Yeah, but Mallory's so gorgeous, it doesn't matter. No one's going to make fun of her."

I'm about to tell Delaney she's gorgeous too, or that Mallory did get made fun of, or something equally inane, but my mother starts talking again.

"Why, honey? Why do you think Mallory's gorgeous?"

Honey again.

My mother never even calls me that.

"She's tall. She's beautiful."

"A lot of people are tall. Some of them are damn ugly. What makes her beautiful?"

"She has amazing hair?"

"Honey, no one has more amazing hair than you do."

I'm a little puzzled by this conversation, not really sure where it's going, but Delaney seems engaged and not obsessed with how stupid she feels so maybe my mom knows what she's doing.

"Is it just the way she carries herself?"

"Are you asking me or telling me?"

"Telling you. It's the way she carries herself."

"How does she carry herself?"

Delaney thinks for a moment. Looks over at her hairbrush, makes what looks like an instinctive move to reach for it, then pulls back. I realize she doesn't have any bandages on her arms so she must not have cut her wrists. That's good, I guess.

"You brought me books, Allison?"

I nod. "Some of my favorites."

"Don't change the subject," my mother says. "How does Mallory carry herself?"

"Like a boss," Delaney says.

"What does that mean? I have a boss and most days I want to punch him in the ear with a full fist. Is that what you want to do to Mallory?"

Punch him in the ear with a full fist?

Who *is* this woman?

"I just mean she looks like she knows who she is. Like, she walks like she knows where she's going all the time. Allison does it too."

"I do?"

"Well, not in ceramics." She laughs. It's not loud, but it's an incredible, musical sound.

"Did you hear that?" my mother says.

"What?"

"Your laugh. I'm betting Rug Rat, or whatever his name is, when he hears you laugh, that makes his whole existence worthwhile."

"Well, he's not going to ever hear it again. Not up close."

"Then that kid just made the biggest mistake of his life."

"I still don't want him to get expelled."

"That's for later," my mother says. "We'll figure that out later. For now, what you said about Mallory, you're right. I saw her do something today with her field hockey stick that she can only do because she believes in herself one hundred percent. She believes in every part of herself. That's what made it beautiful. Everybody in the stands, we all saw it. She's dribbling the ball, and then she lifts the ball in the air—"

My mom tries to pretend she's Mallory and has a stick. It looks absolutely atrocious—she's about as athletic as a pregnant manatee with two broken flippers—but here in the hospital room, with the soft glow from the light outside the window washing over her, I still get chills.

"—then she balances the ball on the end of her stick which, let me tell you, looks impossible when you're on the dead run like she was, then she pops the ball into the air, still running, swings her stick like it's a baseball bat, and whacks the ball into the corner of the goal."

Delaney looks confused.

"All right, you had to be there, but trust me, it was phenomenal. You see my point? To even have the confidence to *try* something like that, she had to be fully committed, she had to believe she could do it. That's all you need, honey. You just need to believe."

"But in what? Mallory's special. I'm not. I can't do anything special like that."

"Yes, you can, sweetheart. You just don't know what it is yet."

We're quiet.

Nobody knows where the conversation goes from here.

My mother pulls a deck of cards from her pocket. "You like Crazy Eights?" she asks Delaney. "Let's play Crazy Eights."

And we do, the three of us sitting on the bed, for maybe two hours. Delaney laughs a lot. So does my mom. They both also beat me every single game. I'm mad, but not that much.

Finally, a nurse makes us leave.

In the hallway, Delaney's parents look at my mother and me like we're saints.

Maybe we are.

[41]

"You were pretty incredible up in that room," I tell my mother in the car on the way home.

"Maybe I was inspired by what I saw this afternoon."

"By Mallory, you mean?"

"By you too."

Mom's driving because I'm too tired, which doesn't bode well for the homework behemoth I still have to attack. It's a bit after 10:30, so not a ton of traffic, but it rained while we were with Delaney and the streets are wet and reflecting light everywhere and my head hurts and Mom has to squint hard and concentrate on the road and can't look at me, can't see me roll my eyes.

Too much has happened in the last twenty-four hours and I feel like I've yet to process any of it. I haven't even texted Mallory to see how she's doing and part of me wonders if she's already back to talking to Jake the way I'm talking to Rugger.

Am I talking to Rugger?

Or was I just willing to listen to him about Delaney?

"You saw me play?" I ask my mom.

"A little. I couldn't stay for much of the second half, but that's not what I'm talking about. What I mean, is I was inspired by how supportive you were of your teammates, even when you were on the bench. You weren't bitter or sulking. You were right in there, rooting for the other players, staying positive. Even Mal's dad said something to me about it, how you were showing everyone what it means to be a captain."

"Oh."

I mean, I guess that's good, but I really wanted my mother to see me play.

"It wasn't just that though. When I saw Mallory do that, what do you call that move, that crazy thing she did?"

"What you tried to imitate in Delaney's room?" I giggle.

"Don't mock me, please. I'm trying to be serious."

"Yeah, OK, there's not really a name for it. From now on, we'll probably just call it the Mallory."

We stop at a red light and my mother turns to me.

"All right then, well, when she did the Mallory, I saw you out there doing it too."

"But I can't do that. And I wasn't out there. I wasn't even the one who passed the ball to her."

She grabs my hand and I kind of want the light never to turn green, for us just to stay there at the intersection, and for my mother never to have any more wine or to smoke any more cigarettes or to pass out on the living room couch.

It would also be nice if my homework could evaporate.

"What I mean is," my mom says, "Mallory's a beautiful player to watch, what she did with that ball was something nobody who saw will ever forget, but she didn't get to where she is all by herself. All those hours you spent with her in her basement, all those years the two of you have hit to each other across that huge W in the middle of the field, she's the player she is because of you, and you're the player you are because of her. Her victories are your victories. Your victories are her victories. That's what I realized for the first time today while she was out there playing and you weren't. And, Allison, truly, that's the most beautiful thing of all. The two of you have built each other into these incredibly powerful human beings, and Delaney's right, there's no stopping either one of you."

The light must have turned green because I hear somebody honking his horn behind us, probably a really angry guy in a pickup truck with extra fog lights, but I can't see anything. My eyes are thick with tears and I am weeping, hiccupping hard, all of it, everything in the last twenty-four hours spilling down my face, and my mom turns around and gives the person behind us the finger and then accelerates through the intersection and I am crying and laughing and every definition of hysterical and she is still holding my hand.

I never thought of what she just said, but she's right.

Inside me and inside Mallory, inside both of us, are all those hours.

All those hits.

The Mal and Al show didn't just happen.

It wasn't luck. We built it.

We own it, and will own it, forever.

I can't really speak the rest of the ride home. When we pull into the now-much-neater garage without the tangled mountain of chairs, I take a deep breath and more or less compose myself.

"Thanks, Mom," I say, "for everything you did tonight. For what you said, for coming to my game, and for how you were with Delaney."

I don't say, "For not drinking too much," but I'm pretty sure she knows I mean that too.

"Are you OK, Allison? It's all right if you're not."

"Yeah," I say. "I'm OK. I just, God, Mom, I have so much

homework. I'm already exhausted but I'm drowning in it. I'm going to be up all night."

She looks at me, deep into me, with eyes that seem to understand exactly what I'm thinking. Why does it seem like all our big moments happen inside our car, inside our garage?

"Listen, Allison, last night you went to help your best friend get through something horrible. Tonight, you helped someone who wasn't even really your friend with something worse. That girl needed you there. Can you imagine what it would have been like if no one showed up to visit her? Good God, that poor girl. I hope you, and, well, Mallory too, I hope both of you reach out to her when she gets back to school, make her feel like people care about her. But either way, you shouldn't be penalized for helping your classmates."

"What are you saying?"

"Some things are more important than homework. Why don't I call you in sick tomorrow? You can stay home all day and catch up on your assignments and then go to practice after school."

I get an awful feeling in my stomach when my mother offers me this way out, this life preserver. She's right. I don't deserve to have Coach mad at me, or Gowhatever or Martindale, or anybody else. It's not like I've been wasting my time playing video games. Plus, half my teammates have done exactly what my mother is suggesting, taken a day off to catch up on homework. Julie B. even has a name for doing it —a self-care day.

But I've never taken one.

And I'm captain.

I'm center-mid.

It's my job to care about everyone, not just me.

It's my job to control the field.

Every field.

"No, Mom," I say, opening the passenger door and stepping into the garage. "I'll gut it out. I can do it."

"You sure?"

No. I'm not sure at all. The truth is I want to cry again. Even harder than before. My eyelids feel like they're four hundred pounds. I want to close them immediately and keep them closed for the next twelve to fifteen hours.

"Yeah," I say. "I'm sure."

[42]

.

I GET EXACTLY thirty-three minutes of sleep.
Close my eyes at 5:57 a.m.
Miley Cyrus blasts me awake at 6:30.
It's awful.
When I get up, I feel like throwing up. My head is a block of cement on top of my neck and my eyes are puffy like I got stung by an aggressive community of bees. My legs feel like overcooked spaghetti and they can't support me when I attempt to stagger to the bathroom. I have lost the human ability to stand erect or to do anything except be a blobby mess who wants to collapse back into bed and sleep for the next three weeks.
Other than that, I'm proud of myself.
It's my first all-nighter of senior year, after I vowed there would be no all-nighters senior year, especially not during the season. I have to admit though, I got into a groove.
People who pull a lot of all-nighters will tell you it's about the preparation. I don't mean Adderall-fueled all-nighters, that's cheating. I don't even mean energy-drink or coffee-fueled all-nighters either, that's cheating too. I'm talking

about the orchestra kids with four APs who stay up doing homework all night at least once a week, without pharmaceutical help of any kind, who have the process down. They'll tell you it's about the snacks you bring to your room, the granola bars and bananas, the carefully spaced-out and rigidly adhered to video game and social media breaks, the playlist in your headphones.

But that's not how it is for me.

Before I did anything else, I texted Mallory to see how she was doing and to tell her about Delaney. She was finishing up her own homework and getting ready for bed, and she'd had a long talk with her dad, who hadn't seen the picture and promised he'd never try to see it, and she was exhausted and cried-out and super grateful for the way Coach and Julie B. and the rest of the team supported her, and she hadn't talked to Jake but had heard about the suspensions, and she promised she'd come with me the next time I visit Delaney.

I said her first goal was sick and she said it was lucky and we both knew it wasn't and then we said we loved each other and always would, and she called it a night.

That's when I got started.

I like music, but on random shuffle so I can be surprised by stuff I really like, and also soft and in the background and not through headphones, and only for the first few hours. When it gets to be around two a.m., and I'm the only person awake in the house, and probably in the immediate neighborhood, I turn off the music and open the window.

Listen to the sounds of the night and try to feel their rhythm.

It's warm enough that there are still crickets, and a breeze through the trees, and far away the rush and swoosh of the occasional car. It's different than when I'm lonely and I want to sleep and my house feels huge and open and everything in the great outdoors is vast and echoey and anything can claw at me. When I'm up late and trying to do homework, it's like I go into a cocoon. I think of a drone, or a dirigible, really—I love that word, *dirigible*—some kind of aerial contraption that slowly hovers, and I imagine it looming above the world and using a camera to scan the area. Its view starts off encompassing hundreds of homes and buildings, the perimeter of the city, then it zooms down and narrows focus to my neighborhood, then my block, then my house, and then my small, enclosed room, and then it finds me, the only creature still stirring while everyone else is asleep. I am little and alone and immersed in my existential battle against the humongous Homework Death Star and most people would probably find that feeling of being watched creepy, especially by some kind of secret, government hovercraft, but I don't.

I find it validating.

Motivating.

I am alone, cooped up in my genius-lab—which is a genius-lab of effort because there's nothing organically super smart about me—and I am grooving to the night's natural music and working while everyone else isn't. That's what keeps me awake. That image: the effort-kid busting it, grinding, shoving her shoulder to the wheel while everyone else is conked out.

I rub my eyes and sit up straight.

The dark of the world slows down and I feel it.

I *am* it.

I am the pages turning and the ideas working their way into my brain, and the crickets chanting their mantras outside and when the train whistles through its tracks maybe a mile away, as it always does at 4:35 a.m., I know I am almost there, I'm going to make it.

I have become the night and it has fed me and we are friends.

I revised my original order of operations and finished my

Spanish around 5:15 and then went back to the latest draft of my poem, which ended up being pretty much a whole new creation. I finally just called it "Friends with Benefits" and, instead of trying to explain what wasn't beneficial when boys are assholes, I described Mallory's goal and how lucky I feel that my mother got to see it, and the hours we've spent in Mal's basement making the stick and ball appendages to our arms, and how I could feel the muscles in my wrists, and how I could trust them while I played cards in the hospital room with Delaney and my mom, and how round our laughter was.

I tried to paint the picture using specific sensory details like Gowhatever says, and when I put my computer to sleep at 5:55, and shut down my own system two minutes later, I knew I had described exactly what it means when friends are beneficial, and it was the best thing I'd ever written.

[43]

Everyone talks about the suspensions all day long.

Most people are on board with the punishments, including the one handed to Julie B., and even dudes who are part of the now hopefully defunct Rat Bros agree the boys crossed a line, but only a smattering of kids support the idea of expulsion. I'm not sure where I stand. It was a shitty thing to do, no question, but Rugger seems sincerely sorry about it. I guess, more than anything, I hope Delaney's OK. I also guess my head feels like ten bowling balls fused together and I can't really think clearly since it's all I can do to sit up straight and keep the giant mini-planet from lolling off my neck and smashing to the floor.

Amidst the churning of rusty machinery inside my bowling-ball skull, I do manage to hear a morning announcement proclaiming there will be an assembly about cyber-bullying on Friday, which occasions numerous exasperated sighs in my second hour because we suspect any kind of just-say-no-to-social-media campaign will be about as effective as the just-say-no-to-drugs one. Instead of paying attention while the overly cheerful college kids and their pseudo performance troupe try to enlighten us with role-playing skits, people will probably be tweeting, texting, and making memes.

I also feel like our particular instance of cyber-bullying is a symptom, not a cause. Our root problem is not social media. It's that it feels like the boys and girls at this school—basketball-playing apologizers aside—are in some kind of war, and not a goofy YA-novel, let's-stop-talking-to-one-another-in-the-cafeteria war. Not a straight-to-DVD movie with a smiley Zac Efron or other chiseled white boy as hero and can't-everybody-just-be-friends-in-the-courtyard war. I'm talking about a war that sends people to the psych ward, a war where it somehow seems acceptable to make hand-lettered signs and chant in public that twenty-two girls—who only want to defend their state title and play a game they love as hard as they can—are whores. And the casualties aren't just the girls who cut their wrists, or thighs, or swallow pills, or stop eating. It's the boys too, the ones who walk around in a daily cloud of weed smoke and memorize cheat codes for *Black Ops* and never become what they might be able to become, never want to look like they take anything seriously except for how expertly they can roll a blunt or how many pairs of colorful socks they have that match their Jordans or how many girls they can get to send them pictures.

Maybe I'm just overanalyzing.

Maybe I'm full of it.

My head hurts and my brain is a bowl of frozen Jell-O—*can* you freeze Jell-O?—and I want someone on the boy side of the world to step up and just be a decent person and also have a magic spell that can sweep up all the other boys and spin them around in a decent-person tornado and turn them into decent people too.

Instead of a lame assembly, what I really wish is that we could have class discussions—like, twice a week—where we talk about how we can build a better community, or maybe just play cards like my mom and I did with Delaney, and not have it be about the girls doing well in school and the boys goofing off and looking for ways to tear us down, even when half the time all we want is their attention.

I don't know how it happened like this.

Everyone used to be friends in elementary school, and the boys used to try in class, and I know some of them still do, but Jake, Connor, Brian, Rugger, they're not necessarily evil, not people who can never redeem themselves. Well, maybe Jake is beyond redemption, but otherwise, something's just wrong, something's broken, and I wish I knew how to make everything right for everybody, but I don't.

Other than that, high school happens the way high school happens, which means, of course, both Martindale and Gowhatever are absent so I get exactly zero credit for all the make-up work I did and, worse, the sub gives us a busywork assignment in creative writing—read an article and answer questions about what constitutes an allegory—so I don't get to share my poem in class.

I guess that's OK because suspended Brian isn't present to hear it anyway. In the hall, two hockey players, who I don't know the names of but they have mullets—the boys call it flow or, sometimes, lettuce—and I think they're sophomores, shoot me the meanest mugs they can muster as if it's my fault their captain got suspended for being an asshole. When I walk past them, they rapid-fire the words "bitch," "ho," "thot," "slut," and "slab," which is a mouthful of nasty vocabulary for two kids who can't even drive yet. I fantasize about doing a double drop-kick into their unprotected groin areas, but with Julie B. still unavailable and our road game tomorrow against Beth Avery Country Day—a pretty tough team—I manage to restrain myself.

In ceramics, the room is sad and heavy and when I put my hands into clay, it feels moist and cool and, for once, I like playing with it, even though when I try to get something going on the wheel, it turns into a mound of shapeless mush. I laugh at myself and think of Delaney and then I open my mouth.

"Can I make an announcement?" I ask Ms. Waldron, who is an incredible person who is short and barrel-shaped with a chest like an over-large luxury SUV and a pencil perpetually stuck in her hair, and she says, "Of course, dear," because she calls everyone dear.

I am shaking and my hands are gunked with clay, but I stand up and turn off the music on the ancient radio, which was playing Styx or Journey or something similar since Ms. Waldron has a fetish for eighties-rock bands that sing soapy ballads.

"Hey," someone says, but it's a half-hearted protest because the music kind of blows and everyone knows about Delaney, or at least has heard some kind of rumor, but no one wants to talk about it.

We just look at her vacant wheel and are sad.

"Hey, yourself," I say, my voice quivering. "I saw her last night."

"No, you didn't," says a boy from the back of the room. I think his name is Glenn and he's wearing a backward baseball hat that's the color of the water you see in commercials about resort hotels in the Caribbean. "I know for a fact she's in the hospital."

"That's true," I say, deciding not to start an argument. "And that's where I saw her."

"I hate hospitals," Glenn says, as if that's remotely relevant. He's actually really good at pottery, which sucks since I'm so bad at it.

"She's doing OK," I say, "but I think we should make her a card and, you know, everyone should sign it. I can bring it over tonight when I visit her again. Or we can wait until she comes back and give it to her. I think she'd really appreciate something like that."

"Is it true she tried to kill herself?" Glenn asks. "Because of the Dropbox? I heard she slashed her wrists."

"It's true she's in the hospital. She didn't slash her wrists. The rest you'll have to ask her about when she gets back."

"When will that be?"

"I think you have to be there at least three days and then the doctors evaluate."

"I'll make the card," a girl named Lillian says, who has like 150 percent out of 100 in the class. "My soup bowl's already done."

My soup bowl looks like a pile of ground beef.

"That would be wonderful, dear," Ms. Waldron says to Lillian. "Why don't you get started?"

And she does, arrows straight to the poster-board cabinet with a fistful of markers and before thirty seconds are over, she's got a third of the thing looking as colorful as the covers of Ms. Waldron's rock albums. I wonder if I could hire her to do my homework, or at least to life-coach me so I could be, I don't know, a tenth as efficient as she is.

"I have an idea," Glenn says, and I'm kind of terrified. I feel like he's about to say something about how girls get too emotional about meaningless fluff, how it was all just a joke and people are getting upset too easily, how our hyper-sensitivity is what's wrong with our way-too-politically-correct society.

"Why don't I make a vase?" he says. "And other people can help glaze it, well, maybe not Allison because she'll mess it up, but everyone else can help, and then we'll all carve our names in the bottom of it, and then the day Delaney comes back, I'll get some flowers and we'll have them waiting for her when she walks in?"

"You'll get *flowers*?"

"Yeah, good ones too. I'll pick them up during lunch. I work at Colby Florists."

"You work at a *florist*?"

"Is that impossible for you to imagine, Allison? Because I'm a boy? And we're all jerks? That's why I hate hospitals. I have to deliver to them like twenty times a day."

I nod my bowling-ball head, feel my face getting red.

"Dear, I think your idea is wonderful," Ms. Waldron says to Glenn, patting his clay-covered forearm. "Why don't you get started?"

And he walks over to my wheel, grabs the corpse of my soup bowl, and carries the mound of clay over to his wheel so he can start spinning.

"I'm sorry, Glenn," I say. "I guess I misjudged you."

"When you carve your name in the bottom," he says, "try not to be sloppy."

"I mean, I'll try to be neat."

"We're not all assholes," he says.

That's probably true, but I feel like I need more evidence. The stereo's back on and it's that weird, whiny song about breaking up being hard to do.

"Have you looked at the Dropbox?" I ask.

"No, and I'm not going to. My friends won't either."

"Delaney's going to love the flowers," I say. "That's really sweet of you."

"Go get some more clay," he says. "When I'm done with the vase, I'll help you make your soup bowl. You press on the clay too hard, that's your problem. You can't always be tough with everything."

That's bullshit, I think. Yes, I can.

[44]

AT PRACTICE, we stretch and then warm up with a relay race where we have to carry medicine balls back and forth to one another. We only have to run twenty yards with the ball and the ball is only sixteen pounds, but my body is so sore and exhausted, each step seems impossible, like my legs are encased in cement. I run hard and try not to let anyone see how horrible I feel, but I am even slower than Mallory than usual and that must be obvious to everyone.

Especially Coach.

Someday, I will have children, I tell myself.

I will have twins.

I will have two eight-pound newborns and our house will be on fire and a serial killer will be in it with a knife and a rifle and enormous, muddy boots and I will have to grab my babies and run faster than I ever have in my life. *That is what I am holding now*, I tell myself, *not a medicine ball but my twin babies*. They need me to run hard if we are going to escape the psycho. There is no pain in my arms. No pain in my spine. No cement legs or bowling-ball head.

This is the story I tell myself so I can catch up to Mallory.

I don't quite get there, but I almost do, and we are way faster than everyone else and Coach says, "Good work," and Mallory hugs me and I can tell already we will both be ready for Beth Avery.

In our next drill, we do one-on-ones off an inbound pass, and the best is when Mal and I face each other. I know all her moves and she knows mine and we go at it like two wrestlers who want to throw each other across the room and cause numerous bones to fracture. She is a hair quicker (a *hare* quicker!) than I am and beats me a hair more than I beat her, but I am sneakier and nastier, even though she is also sneaky and nasty, and my poke-checks annoy her like crazy. In our final battle, she spins and shuffles, pulls and feints, tries to go through my legs or over my stick, but I poke and poke, shuffle and move, block everything. The whole team is watching and Mallory won't let me steal the ball from her and I won't let her past me. We go at it for ten seconds. Twenty seconds. The team cheers. My body is a citadel and it doesn't matter how many cannonballs have already battered it. Thirty seconds. Mallory pulls left. I'm there. I jab at the ball. She won't let me knock it away. Forty seconds. She pulls right, then left, then right again. I am there, there, there. Fifty seconds. Coach blows the whistle.

"Enough," she says.

Everyone claps.

Someone, it's usually Julie B. but she's not here, starts the chant, a low, from-the-ground-up bass that builds higher, an echo from the seventies movie about street gangs in New York, the thing we say before the start of every game: *Warriors, come out to play . . . Warriors, come out to play . . .*

Mal and I smack our sticks together, the universal field hockey high-five, and I am ready to faint, but I don't. We hustle over to the sideline for water and then back to Coach so she can outline the next drill.

We maintain the intensity and it's our best practice of the year. Our passes are crisp and everyone receives them as if we're wearing softball gloves—smooth, with no bobble. When we shoot, we hit the fat part of the ball and send it rocketing toward the corners of the goal. We hustle from drill to drill and our feet pound the ground and our sticks click the ball in a rhythm that sounds like a well-rehearsed drumline. The autumn evening is flirty and sublime with brisk, smoky air and leaves blushing yellow and orange as the sun does its slow shimmy to the bottom of the sky. My homework is caught up and my body does not know tired.

My body knows only alive.

We finish with something we call target practice, where we make two lines on the twenty-five and everyone has a ball and we dribble for ten yards and then blast away at the goal. *Smack, smack, smack.* Not just Mallory and me nailing our shots, but Aaliyah too, and Georgia, Sydney, and Jess, all of us, the whole team except for suspended Julie B. *Smack, smack, smack.* A cavalcade of smacks.

Mal and I end up last. We look at each other and we know what we're going to do. I'm in the right-hand line and she's in the left. We dribble and at the fifteen we let loose our lasers. I aim toward the low left corner, she aims toward the low right. We make contact at the same time and our balls cross each other in a perfect X, then hit the board simultaneously. *SMACK!*

We turn, raise our arms high, and sprint to the W at midfield. The team joins us and we form a tight circle. Mallory starts the chant, low and steady, *Warriors, come out to play . . . Warriors, come out to play.* It builds in volume, speed, and intensity until we are shouting it, shouting it, the whole team shouting it, our sticks aloft and clacking, our words a verbal spear shooting upward, a tribute to the field hockey gods above, who smile and applaud, and cheer us from their magic bleachers made of clouds.

[45]

Coach tells us if we practice like that every day, we will be a team people remember for decades.

I want to lead a team people remember for decades.

Possibly centuries.

After we have retrieved all the balls and are packing our gear on the sideline, I am drinking water next to Aaliyah.

"Did you look?" she says.

"At what?"

"So you didn't."

"I don't know. I mean, I'm not sure. What are you—"

"It's OK," she says, her face impassive. "I didn't think you would."

Then I remember, the Joey Buckets album covers.

"I'm so sorry, Aaliyah. I meant to, I just, well, last night was insane." I gesture toward Mallory. "The whole Dropbox thing, and then I fell behind with my homework and Delaney in the hospital. I'm sorry, I guess, I don't know, I guess—"

She cuts me off.

"You guess it wasn't a high priority. I get it."

"That's not what I meant."

"But it's true."

"Look, I apologize, OK? I got caught up. I forgot. I'll look tonight. First thing when I get home, I promise."

"You promise?"

"Yes, I swear."

"Tomorrow's an away game," she says, stuffing her water bottle in her bag and walking toward the parking lot. "You're captain. Don't make me sit on that bus with the whole team singing that song."

[46]

WITH NO JULIE B. AROUND, no one suggests going for burritos and I'm grateful because I want to go home, look at the album covers, spend time with my mom, do my homework, and then see if Mallory wants to go visit Delaney.

We agree I will text her when I'm ready to go to the hospital, but as we walk to my car, we see there's someone waiting for us.

Not Rugger.

Jake.

When I realize it's him, all the exhaustion of my thirty-three minutes of sleep, the long school day, the hyper-intense practice, and Aaliyah's disappointment in me crash into my chest like a wave at the beach. I actually stagger backward and Mallory mouths, "Are you OK?"

I'm not.

I feel like the wave is snarling and ferocious, and the undertow is flipping me around, clogging my eyes and nose with salt and sand, sucking me downward into someplace frigid and dark. I hold my breath for a moment and see Mal looking concerned and I don't want her to worry about me so I gurgle upward, gasp for air, find my voice.

"You're not supposed to be on campus," I say.

"What are they going to do? Suspend me?" Jake chuckles at his joke even though it's not funny. I notice his dimples and that makes me feel like an idiot. He's wearing a faded black T-shirt that's taut across his muscles and there's a picture of a fat and colorful pheasant—a quail?—on it, as if he's a hunter who tramps through the woods and shoots things.

"Get away from us," Mallory says.

He shakes his head.

"I just want to talk to you, Mal."

"They could expel you," I offer.

"I don't care. I know what we did was awful. I just want to apologize. It was stupid and I won't ever do anything like that again."

Then he smirks, or smiles, it's hard to tell, as if he thinks he's said what he needed to say, the perfect thing to say, and now he can grin and flex his arms and puff up his slate-hard pecs beneath the pheasant (or quail) and everything will go back to how it was.

Unfortunately for him, Mallory is as angry as I've ever seen her. I think she would swing her stick into his forehead if it weren't packed and zipped in her bag.

"Get. Away. From. Us."

"Why won't you talk to me? Allison's talking to Rugger."

"I am not *talking* to Rugger," I explode. "I *talked* to him about helping Delaney. The girl who's in the hospital because of what you guys did. Remember her?"

He doesn't say anything.

I feel like my voice was big and harsh and echoed off all the cars in the lot and the four-story-high walls of the gymnasium, even the bleacher seats at the football stadium. I probably interrupted the repose of somebody under the ground in the cemetery across the street.

I look at Mallory and her eyes are misting, her lip quivering.

Two hundred feet away, seagulls squawk, pick at an overflowing garbage pail.

If Mallory goes back to him now, after I saw Delaney in the hospital—after how miserable her parents looked in the waiting area—I don't know if we can still be friends.

I wait.

The seagulls squawk.

"Jake," she says, a lot more quietly than my shout, but in a tone full of icicles, "it's so sad, I'm personally sad, because you have the potential to be such an awesome person, but you're not. Unfortunately, you've turned out to be a jerk and that means I'm going to say this one time and then I don't ever want to say it again."

Her voice is getting even quieter and I feel like punching him in the face so hard—no, not in the face, in the heart. Right where the eyes of the quail are.

"There is no forgiveness," Mal says, her voice barely above a whisper, but not quivering, just that kind of quiet, firm smoothness of a calm lake.

A calm, *cold* lake.

"I already gave you a second chance after you tried to hook up with my best friend behind my back. I probably shouldn't have, but I did. And then I gave you a personal picture, something that was supposed to be just for you—*only* between me and you—and you took it and showed it to your friends. You made my body into *entertainment*. You took who I am and treated me like a bunch of beers from a keg, or a joke you found on Twitter. Something you could share with your friends. Like a blunt you could just pass around the circle in somebody's garage. That's not a mistake, Jake. That's something wrong at the core of you. There is no sorry, no way for us to get over it. This body isn't yours to share with other people. It's mine, and you'll never touch it again."

Wow.

Jake opens his mouth as if he's about to say something, but what can he say?

The fact that Mallory wasn't screaming, that she could say it all so quiet and cold, he knows she's serious.

He tries to smirk again, but the grin gets stuck a quarter of the way across his face. For a moment, he looks super angry, like he might run toward us and grab Mallory's arm and twist it behind her back. If he does, I will take my stick—I have the kind of backpack where the stick ties to the outside instead of being zipped inside like Mal's—and swing it straight at his throat. But he doesn't come at us. Instead, he looks down at his luxury-item sneakers, as if the logos on their fat tongues can compensate for being excommunicated from the Church of Mallory. He breathes in and inflates his chest, but he doesn't look cute and strong, just bloated and probably full of steroids.

"So that's how it's going to be?" he says. "You won't even try to let me show you I'm sorry?"

"I don't care if you're sorry," Mallory says. "It's too late. I won't let you hurt me again."

"It might not matter if you let me," Jake says.

"What's that supposed to mean?" I shout and my hands are already untying my stick from my bag. I swear, I will hit him so hard, his whole body will break.

"Stop," Mallory says, and grabs my wrist. "Let's go. He's not worth it. He's not worth anything at all."

Jake smirks and smiles and I want to hit him so bad but I let Mallory drag me into the car and the big, strong hockey player doesn't stop us, just walks away, and I'm not scared of him, not even a little, can't believe I ever was.

Or attracted to him either.

He looks sad, trying to keep his back straight, a lonely high school boy without a high school, without a girlfriend, trying to act like he didn't just get told off by the best person he'll ever be lucky enough to spend time with.

Inside the car, Mallory's shoulders start to shake and I reach for her hand. It feels cool, not hot, as if she's not mad, just sad, resigned to the notion that Jake was never right for her.

"That's not your boyfriend walking away from you through the parking lot," I say. "Your boyfriend is beautiful and sweet and walking toward you in the future. And he'll never be a jerk, ever."

"Wrong," Mallory says, smiling. "My boyfriend won't be walking toward me. He'll be sprinting, and he'll be faster than both of us. And he'll run as hard as he can, and he still won't catch me. Not unless I want him to."

[47]

First thing when I get home, before I even talk to my mom, I run upstairs to my room and get on my computer and download all four of Joey Buckets's album covers.

Heartfire, with our team's favorite song, "Heartfire," is his third album. It came out about five years ago. His debut was *Day-old Biscuits* and his second album, which was the one that really made him blow up, was *Tennessee Summer*. His most recent album, which most people were disappointed in, is *Back Porch Holiday*. It has a song on it I like called "Don't Believe the Gossip (Rumors Can't Fly)," but the rest of it, to be honest, is super sappy.

I look at all four covers and try to figure out what Aaliyah's upset about, but I can't see anything massively offensive. He's leading a cow to a barn on the Biscuits album, and it looks like a happy, friendly cow, but I'm pretty sure Aaliyah's not a vegan or anything else connected to that genre—I mean, I sat right next to her when she ate a seasoned steak burrito—so that can't be it. On *Tennessee Summer*, he's up on a mountain, leaning against a rock, strumming his guitar, and looking ultra-sensitive. He doesn't appear to be littering or otherwise despoiling the landscape, so I'm not sure what the problem is there either. *Heartfire* puts him at the crossroads of a four-way intersection on a rural highway with one cowboy-booted foot up on the bumper of his pickup truck. His vest is silver and glossy and pretty damn ugly, looks like a cowboy suit of armor, so I can see his fashion sense being offensive to Aaliyah, who always dresses on point, but how would it make her mad enough to refuse to sing his song?

I know she's not upset about the environmental implications of his truck because her mom picks her up from practice in an SUV the size of my house.

Back Porch Holiday, matching the songs inside, has the cheesiest cover art. Joey's on the porch swing of a chalk-white farmhouse with a woman who looks like Daisy Duke from the old *Dukes of Hazzard* show. She's got pornstar breasts tied together by a flannel shirt above her tan, flat stomach with a pierced bellybutton, and cutoff shorts that barely cover her crotch, and legs as long as Mallory's. She definitely has too much makeup on her cheeks and luminescent blood-red lipstick, so yeah, major ditz, and the two of them appear to be toasting each other with homemade moonshine so, no doubt, silly, but insulting? Hurtful?

I don't get it.

Is it because the farmhouse somehow could be interpreted as the "big house," the master's house, of a plantation?

Is it because the woman is too close a doppelganger to Daisy Duke, and her brothers drove a car called the General Lee, which had a Confederate flag on its roof?

Oh.

Wait.

I go back to the first album.

It's small, but it's there.

Joey's kind of in profile while he's leading the cow, but if you look closely, you can see it. He's wearing a Confederate flag belt buckle.

Once I know what I'm searching for, it's easy to find.

On his second album, there are a lot of stickers on his guitar case. Various beer labels, a faux Tennessee license plate, a silhouette of a busty woman like one might see on a trucker's mudflaps, a lightning bolt, a toad or frog of some sort, a snake with fangs too large for its mouth, a crucifix, and a Confederate flag.

On *Heartfire*, there's a bumper sticker plastered to the rear window of his truck.

On the porch swing, Daisy's glass has the flag printed on it. It's glass-on-glass and the image is transparent so it's hard to see, but if you know to look for it, you can't miss it.

Obviously, these flags are not a coincidence.

They were carefully placed on each album.

I call Mallory.

[48]

WE MEET FOR ICE CREAM.

Is my homework done?

No.

Do I still want to visit Delaney?

Yes.

The plan is both of us will go to the hospital after we talk.

It's a serious conversation so we get serious ice cream at the dairy. Mine's strawberry and the strawberries might even be fresh and not frozen. Mallory has a double scoop of Moose Tracks. My eyes are drooping and I wonder if I should have ordered coffee-flavored, but I don't like coffee and even if I did, I don't know if coffee-flavored ice cream contains caffeine so, no.

"You don't think she's overreacting?" Mallory says.

I lick my spoon slowly, wanting the ice cream to last. I wish I could eat as much as Mallory does. I'm not complaining, I mean, my metabolism's pretty fast, but Mal has the Usain Bolt of metabolisms. She eats twice as much as I do and never gains a fraction of an ounce. Of course, she also burns energy like a furnace.

"I'm not sure we can think about it like that," I say. "We're not African American. I don't think we can judge whether someone who is, who's the only person of color on our team, feels a certain way. You know what I mean?"

"I hate that expression—people of color. Why does anyone have to be *of* anything? What are we? People of non-color?"

I lick my spoon again.

I don't think Mallory really means what she's saying, that she hates that particular expression. It's her way of telling me not to lecture her. Which is something I definitely don't want to do. I'm not wise enough to be lecturing anybody. The jukebox here always seems to play ice-skating songs from my parents' past lives, like Frankie Valli and the Four Seasons, or Nancy Sinatra. I kind of like that stuff. My mom plays it sometimes when she's in a good mood.

"Think about it, Mallory, would you want to be the only white person on a team of not-white people? And then have them sing a song made famous by a guy who displays a symbol that makes you feel unsafe?"

"Allison, this is what I think. If you can hit the ball, if you can play defense, if you run hard, pass the ball, that's what I want out of a teammate. I don't care what anyone's color is. If you can help us win, I want you on the team."

"Why are you getting mad?"

"Because this is going to come down to us versus Julie B. Personally, I say yeah, let's get rid of the song, who cares? We'll sing something else. I like Aaliyah and I hear what you're saying. The dude's flag fetish pisses her off. Fine, ditch the song. But you know Julie B.'s going to be upset. When she didn't make captain, that's the first thing she said, remember? Right after the banquet last year she came up to us and asked if she could be DJ on the bus. It was the one thing she really wanted to do. Now it's going to be like, she gets suspended, and as soon as she's not on the bus with us, not only do we get rid of a tradition that all of our teams, our *state championship winning teams*, have been doing for, what, the past four years, since before we even got here, but it's like we take away the one thing she really cared about because we don't think she was doing a good job with it. Actually, it's worse. We cut a song from her playlist because we think it's racist. And she's not even here to defend herself. That's not going to go over well."

"She's smart. She'll understand."

"She won't."

I want to say something loud, but a mom and her two kids are next to us and I don't want to scare them. They're already out late on a school night, probably because something bad happened at home. The mom's clothing is sloppy, her shirt buttoned wrong, and she's been on her phone the whole time, listening and nodding, and the boy and girl look like they don't even want the chocolate sundaes in front of them. I'm betting the kids' dad did something awful, came home drunk and yelled a bunch of curses or hit someone. It's horrible that the first thing I think when I see unhappy children is "alcoholic parent," but that's my reality. My mother has never hit me, but she's come close, and she's yelled. She's called me a slut. She's called me a bitch and a drama queen. Maybe she's getting better, I don't know. I just get really afraid when she passes out. And when I think about her driving after she's been at a bar.

"I don't get it," I say, trying to keep my voice low. "It's like Julie B. is this soldier when it comes to standing up for how the boys treat us, but it seems like she has some kind of blind spot when it comes to race."

"Yeah, and she doesn't know she has it."

"And she won't listen to anyone who brings it up."

"So, is it worth it?" Mal says. "We've got, what, eight

games left before playoffs? Do we really want to set her off, maybe divide the team for the rest of the season, just because one player feels uncomfortable? I mean, he never says anything racist in his songs, right? It's all that corny love stuff. Maybe it's like people say. It's just a heritage thing. He's just proud to be a country guy from the south."

I don't say anything.

The kids next to us don't eat their ice cream.

"All right, yeah, that's bullshit," Mal says, "but next year, Julie B. will be gone. We'll be gone. Aaliyah can lead the team and do whatever she wants."

"So that's our strategy? Do nothing and wait for the racist white people to go away? That's the kind of captains we're going to be?"

Mallory's quiet. The mom and her kids head for the door. She's still on the phone and she stumbles and almost falls, nearly dragging her daughter down with her. The little boy laughs.

A guy I think is named Dion is on the jukebox singing a song called "Runaround Sue."

"Why can't we just be a normal team," Mallory says, "and worry about which parents are going to bring snacks and what we should get for our Secret Sisters?"

I raise an eyebrow.

"You mean, and not send nudes to our boyfriends?"

"OK, I deserved that. But that's the thing. Julie B. stood up so hard for me. I feel like I'm stabbing her in the back if I call her out for racist DJing."

I nod because what Mallory's saying makes sense. Julie B. took a big hit for all of us, made every boy in our school think twice about being an unthinking bro-jerk. She had all our backs, even Aaliyah's. If we change the one thing she gets to make decisions about with our team, how's she going to feel? Like we didn't appreciate what she did for us? Would she think we like Aaliyah better than her? That we think Aaliyah's a better defender? That she got suspended on our behalf and we just moved on without her?

"Should we ask Coach what to do?"

Mallory shakes her head emphatically.

"We're captains. This is on us."

"The thing is, Mal, it's not just that the flag pisses Aaliyah off. It *hurts* her. When we were singing, there was pain in her eyes. Her whole body was tense. I think if we don't get rid of the song, she'll never trust us. She'll never trust anyone on the team."

"I think you're right."

"So, we talk to Julie B.? Meet with her before she gets back on the field so it's not like we're springing it on her?"

Dion sings, *Ask any fool that she ever knew, they'll say / Keep away from Runaround Sue.*

"Yeah," Mallory says. "We talk to Julie B."

"Should we do it tonight?"

"Why?"

"Away game tomorrow."

"Do you still want to go to the hospital?"

"Yes."

"Did you finish your homework?"

"Not even close."

"So how are we going to do it tonight?"

"I don't know, but we should."

Mallory digs into her ice cream and finishes it in two quick gulps.

"We can go," she says, wiping the back of her hand across her face. "We can get moving now, hit the hospital, then meet with Julie B., but honestly, you look exhausted already. You slept less than an hour last night. I know you want to be everyone's savior, but if you burn yourself out, you're not going to be good for anyone. I mean, even right now, before we do anything else, you think you're going to be OK for the game tomorrow? You think you're going to be able to control the field? Beth Avery's no joke."

Truthfully, I feel horrible.

I have no idea what I'll be capable of doing against Beth Avery.

Or how I'll finish my homework.

I raise my eyebrow again, try to conjure my own half-smirk.

"Don't worry. I'll be ready."

"Warriors," Mal says offering me her fist.

"Come out to play," I say, giving her mine.

[49]

When we walk into Delaney's room, her face lights up like we're the birthday present she always wanted.

I immediately feel uncomfortable.

My mom's not with us and I don't know if I can handle the responsibility of trying to say the right thing, or if we can even stay long enough to make Delaney feel better in any tangible way. We ask her how she is and she shrugs and says she'll be back in school in a couple days. Then she thanks me for the books I left because she actually read them and liked them, and then there's an awkward silence until Mallory asks if she can talk to Delaney by herself for a few minutes.

I'm relieved because I've already run out of things to say, but I also feel weird about it. Mallory hardly knows Delaney.

She wouldn't be here if I didn't ask her to come and now she wants to talk to Delaney without me?

"Uh, OK," I say.

"It's only because, well, you weren't dumb enough and we're the ones who were so stupid we—"

"I get it," I say, and leave the room, but still feel kind of jealous. I understand Mallory and Delaney have a shared experience, but part of me feels Mal's also saying the reason they sent the pictures and I didn't is because they're more willing to take risks than I am, more willing to fully let go of themselves in a relationship, and that pisses me off because it might be true. Maybe I'm more like Rugger than I want to admit, except with a different twist.

He's worried about no one ever loving him fully. Maybe with me, I'm worried I'll die without ever loving another person as deeply as I love my sport.

Delaney's parents took off to get coffee when we showed up, so I guess it's just me and my way-too-weary self in the hallway. I sit down in what's actually a pretty comfortable chair and I don't know if I've ever felt more tired. I wish I'd brought my math book so at least I could crank out a few problems while I'm waiting. I guess I could play with my phone, but I don't feel like it. The whole sexting episode makes me want to use my phone significantly less than I've been using it. I kind of don't want it at all anymore, like I'd get rid of it if I weren't afraid I still need it to check the weather sometimes and for the GPS. I can tell I'm making a face thinking about it and I don't want to bum out any sick or injured patients who might wander past, so I force myself to look across the hall at a painting on the wall of a giant cargo ship. It's of the variety we learned about in second grade that used to carry freight across the Great Lakes. That's what I feel like right now, a giant cargo ship, overloaded and carrying too much ballast, stuck in water that's threatening to drown me.

Then again, those ships had steel hulls, or iron hulls, some kind of metal that was strong and thick but still managed to avoid sinking, and that's me too. I'm carrying a lot of cargo because I'm *capable* of carrying a lot of cargo. I get out of the chair, which is difficult because it's so comfortable and the whole ship of my body feels like it got rammed by the hull of a different ship, a mean and nasty bully ship, but I get up anyway, and crack the door so I can peek into Delaney's room, hopefully, without bothering them.

What I see is astounding.

I don't know what I was expecting, but it definitely wasn't Mallory—stately, superhero, I-can-score-on-anybody Mallory—kneeling next to the hospital bed, holding both Delaney's hands while the two of them cry their eyes out and whisper to each other. I can't hear what they're saying, but I know it's not my moment and I back away from the door, try to close it without making a sound.

Back in my chair, I'm not jealous anymore.

My whole body wants to smile.

It's exhausted, that body, still wrung out, but now in a satisfied way, like it's full after a mongo weekend brunch at the diner, an omelet with spinach, veggie bacon, and feta. In just that brief glimpse, I saw Mallory and Delaney sharing their grief, a loss they'd let happen because they trusted someone they cared about, and they both knew what it felt like to have their bodies in private moments out in the cyberworld for everyone to see. It's a raw pain they're experiencing, but they're experiencing it together, not shrugging it off like it's no big deal, but allowing themselves to be unhappy about it, each allowing the other to see she's not the only one who was hurt.

I don't feel excluded at all.

I'm so glad Mallory wanted to come with me.

And I'm also glad I know both of them.

Now they each have someone new they can trust.

I look at the painting of the ship again, at its sturdy, heavy skin, and think about how, no matter what, it floats.

No matter what, it floats.

[50]

Mallory shakes me awake.

"Come on," she says, "we have to go meet Julie B."

"Wha—? What? I barely talked to Delaney."

"It's OK, she gets that you're exhausted. We came out here and started cracking up because you were so zonked. You were snoring and it sounded like a bullfrog. Delaney thought it was hilarious. She appreciates you, don't worry."

My eyes are blurry and I try to make them focus.

My head spins for a few seconds but the cargo ship is still hanging on the wall, solid and defiant amidst the roiling waves. Mallory's face is sharp, all smooth angles, like she's never cried in her life. Did I imagine what I saw in Delaney's room? Dream it?

"How long have I been asleep?"

She checks her phone.

"About forty-five minutes."

"God, it feels like it was four seconds."

"You sure you're up for this?"

"Maybe not. This chair's so comfortable I'm not sure I understand how to disembark from it."

"Disembark? You're weird."

"Just saying. You have to try this chair, Mal. It's like a spiritual journey, just being in it."

"Stay here then. I'll go talk to Julie B. and come back and pick you up."

The offer's tempting.

Me and the hallway and the cargo ship and the most incredible chair ever designed by human ingenuity. But Mal and I are a team, co-captains. No way I can let her face the defensive specialist by herself. I shake my head, extend my hand, and she pulls me up.

"How's Delaney doing?" I ask when we get into the car.

"You want me to drive?"

"Nah, I'm all right," I say, even though I barely avoid bumping into a pylon as I back out of the parking spot.

"She's struggling, but I think, eventually, she'll be OK. She was really into Rugger."

"Maybe there's something redeemable about him."

Mallory scrunches her eyebrows together.

At least I think she does.

I can only look at her out of the side of my eye because I don't want to scrape the front of my car against the curvy exit ramp as we circle down it.

"You sure you don't want me to drive?"

"I'm good."

"Not in ceramics, according to Delaney. She's really nice, by the way."

"That's what you talked about? How terrible I am in ceramics?"

"Only for a little while." She laughs.

"What else?"

Mallory doesn't say anything for a minute. I successfully navigate the rest of the exit ramp, then fish a dollar and eighty cents from the pile of change in my cup holder to pay the attendant in the cashier's booth, who smiles at us. She's wearing a blue golf shirt with the parking garage logo and her hair, dyed black, is piled at least two feet above her head. It's like a gorgeous, licorice-flavored Christmas tree sprouting from her skull. An old-school radio in her booth plays the Black Eyed Peas.

"Is it OK if I keep that just between her and me?" Mallory says. "I think when we were talking, she was kind of assuming I wouldn't tell anyone else what she was saying. She really opened up."

"Definitely, no problem."

I have to admit though, I'm feeling kind of hurt again about being locked out of the conversation, as if they were glad I conveniently fell asleep in the hallway, but I can't tell if I'm jealous that Mallory has a new friend or that Delaney does.

"You really think you might forgive Rugger?" Mal says.

"No, probably not."

"You ready to talk to Julie B.?"

"I'm ready for it to be the weekend so I can sleep fifty hours straight."

"You need to work on your math."

"I left my book at home."

"No, I mean there are only forty-eight hours in the weekend."

"Oh."

We're stopped at a red light.

I feel for Rugger because he knows he screwed up. Jake knows he screwed up too, but I'm not sure he cares about how that screw-up affects anyone except himself. Rugger does care, I'm pretty sure, but it's not enough. Delaney's in the hospital and the hurt in her eyes when she was talking to Mallory was real. There's no forgiving somebody who caused that.

"It's green," Mallory says about the light. "You sure you're ready to do this?"

"Guess we'll find out."

[51]

JULIE B.'S house is twice the size of mine and nearly empty since her brother's working at the faux ice cream parlor and her two sisters are away at school. Isabel plays field hockey at Berkeley and Hannah is in law school somewhere on the east coast. I want to say NYU, but I'm not sure. There's a field hockey room in the basement too, but not as big as the one at Mallory's. It's basically just a laundry room with a small square of turf and a kind of soccer goal with a thinner net. It'll work though, and both Mal and I bring our gear so we can do about a half-hour of drills with Julie B. since she can't practice with the team while she's suspended.

My body does not feel like playing, but I play anyway, and after a few minutes of quick passes and drag-flicks into the net, I'm into it and we're going at one another, trying to steal the ball and inventing slick moves to get past the defender and we're sweating and it feels like a real workout. When we're done, we go upstairs to the kitchen and Julie B. plays DJ and puts Jessica Simpson on the digital music system on the counter beneath the microwave and we drink iced tea from a space-age refrigerator.

"Jessica Simpson?" Mallory says with a level of disgust equivalent to watching someone in front of you in the cafeteria sneeze directly into the salad bar.

"See, I know what happened," Julie B. says. "I know why you guys were late getting here."

I bite. "Why?"

"Because Mallory had to stop for a four-course meal at the Hatred Café."

Oh, boy.

"Actually," Mallory says, "since we're on the topic of music, can you turn that off? We have something we want to talk about."

Julie B. mutes Jessica via remote control and we're quiet for a moment. The sub-zero refrigerator hums. My shoulders feel heavy, like somebody mammoth is sitting on them, a hairy and massive boy-man with muscles like truck tires who wants to push me down and bury me in the ground. Mallory and I didn't plan for how to talk about Aaliyah—like who would take the lead or who would be good cop—so we look at each other, and since I'm too tired to do anything with my body, including lift my glass to sip the arctic iced tea, Mallory shrugs.

Guess it's up to me to talk.

"We've got a road game tomorrow," I say, "so, you know, without you, we're not sure what to do about the DJ situation."

"We need to turn off the music so we can talk about how to turn on music? I don't get it. I'll just give you my iPod and the box. It's got the playlist on it. Stick it into the aux plug and you're good."

Mallory shakes her head.

"Well, but," I say, sounding like I'm applying for a job I don't really want, "we're thinking about not playing everything on the list."

I'm not sure if we expected Julie B. to get mad and start shouting or baring her breasts at us, but she doesn't. Her face falls apart and her shoulders slump, as if the truck-tire man-boy shifted from sitting on top of me to sitting on top of her. The refrigerator makes a weird clunking sound and then ups the volume of its hum. The clock on the microwave reads 10:47 p.m. and I haven't started my homework. We can't draw this out.

"You don't want to use my playlist?"

It looks like Julie B. is about to cry.

The only other time I've seen her like this is when the team chose Mallory and me to be captains and not her.

"We do want to use your playlist," I say. "There's just one song we might not play."

"Might not or won't?"

"Probably won't."

This is the key moment.

Mallory's nervous too, I can feel it.

More nervous than she's ever been on the field.

More nervous than she was in the cafeteria with everyone watching.

More nervous than when Jake confronted us in the parking lot.

Both of us are terrified.

Will Julie B.'s shoulders slump more and will her head fall to the table, meaning she's destroyed and she'll never again be the impenetrable stalwart who shuts down half the field and is going to Princeton to make the rich(er) kids from the east coast shudder?

Or will she erupt upward and flip over the table (even though it's a marble-topped island cemented to the ceramic floor), causing frigid iced tea to spatter our faces?

Mallory and I shake some more.

Julie B., I think, sees us shaking.

She opens her mouth, tilts her head back, breathes slowly.

Then her shoulders gain strength.

Not flip-over-the-table strength, but I'm-your-teammate-and-have-your-back-no-matter-what strength, and she gives us a tender half-smile.

"It better not be *Purple Rain*," she says.

All three of us shiver. Just the possibility of not playing *Purple Rain* after a win, just that somebody would conceive of a future like that, is unimaginable.

"No, no way. It's the Joey Buckets," Mallory says.

Julie B. nods her head as if she understands.

"Because of the Confederate flags?"

"You knew about it?" I ask, pissed off. It's a whole different deal if she knew about the flags beforehand and still put the song on the playlist, still wanted the whole team to sing along and be blithely happy as if the flags didn't matter. "You knew about it and you still let Aaliyah be on the bus and pretend—"

Julie B. waves her hands in the air, Gowhatever style.

"No, I didn't know. Not before I got suspended. I've had nothing to do the past few days so I've been looking for new songs. I saw his album covers and realized. I swear, I didn't know. I really didn't."

"So you don't mind us getting rid of it?" Mallory asks. "Because Aaliyah's really upset."

"Honestly, I was thinking about telling you guys to get rid of it anyway. Like I said, being home all day, I've had a lot of time for thinking. It's not just about Aaliyah feeling bad either. When I saw those flags, *I* felt bad. I was thinking about that intellectual debate, can you separate the art from the artist, right? And I'm sure there are a lot of people who say you can. Like, was Hemingway a good guy? J. D. Salinger? I mean, Charlie Sheen? R. Kelly? Michael Jackson?

So what, right? It doesn't matter what they do in their personal lives, if they produce something awesome, then the *thing* is still awesome regardless. I think I thought that was true, maybe part of me still does, but this guy is putting a symbol of oppression on the cover of every album he makes. That's *part* of his art. It doesn't matter if his songs aren't explicitly racist. He's proudly claiming that symbol and I don't need Aaliyah to tell me I can't stomach that."

Mallory's nodding her head and I am too and the refrigerator's humming along, but there's something about this new song, this sans-Jessica Simpson music we're creating in the kitchen, that's still not satisfying me.

I look at Julie B.

Lock eyes with her.

Don't waver.

I'm so tired. My eyes want to close so much, but I don't let them.

The refrigerator hums.

Julie B. starts talking, almost too quietly to hear.

"Allison," she says, "there's something else. I owe you an apology too. Like I said, I've been thinking, and I should never have said that thing about the back of the bus to Aaliyah. You were right and I should have apologized right then. I knew it too, as soon as the words came out of my mouth. I knew it, but I just didn't want to admit it. So, I'm sorry for being a dick. And don't worry, I know it's Aaliyah I really need to apologize to, not you, and I will. I want to do it face-to-face, next time I see her, I promise."

I want to turn Jessica Simpson back on and dance around the kitchen.

I want to open the refrigerator door and stand in the midst of the icy blast so my smile will be forever frozen on my face.

I want to hug Julie B. and I do. So does Mallory. We get

up from our seats around the marble-topped island and swarm her as if she just dove into the crease and smacked away what would have been the game-losing goal after Marty Max had been beaten and was helplessly out of position and we hug in the kitchen and feel the muscles in one another's broad backs.

"You're the best, Julie B.," I say. "You should have been captain."

"No," she says, backing away from the group hug and re-radar-locking onto my eyes. "The team got it right."

"Warriors," Mallory says.

"Come out to play," Julie B. and I respond.

Then we're all saying it, chanting it again and again, and we don't need the refrigerator to hum, or Jessica Simpson to sing, or the clock on the microwave to do anything but watch us make our noise.

[52]

But it's not enough.

I feel it as soon as we leave Julie B.'s house.

I let Mallory drive. My eyes can barely stay open and all I want is to lean my head against the seatbelt strap, let it hold me up like the way those huge rescue belts hold up whales marooned in too-shallow water so I can drift off, wake up in about twelve days.

But I can't.

Something's not right.

Julie B.'s willing to change the song, it's all love, that's good.

She says she'll apologize to Aaliyah, that's good too.

And yet.

And yet.

Mallory's bopping along to some ancient Backstreet Boys. Where that girl gets her energy, I have no damn idea, but she's driving safely, stopping at yellow lights, trying to avoid clunking the car through potholes. She knows my body's a ratty beach towel ready to shred, but I can't sleep yet.

My jaw hurts.

My whole face hurts. Something's wrong.

And the truth is, I know what it is. Have known all night. The thing is, we just spent the better part of two hours worrying about not hurting Julie B.'s feelings when, really, who was the person who was hurt?

Not Julie B.

Mallory brakes for another yellow light. Turns down the Backstreet Boys, leans her head back against the seat, sighs.

Turns to look at me.

"We messed up, didn't we?"

My answer is slow, drowsy, like I'm talking through a wine glass full of maple syrup.

"Yeah."

"There's more for us to do, isn't there?"

"Yeah."

"But what?"

I think.

What are we talking about here?

I mean, what are we *really* talking about here?

We're quiet again as the light turns green and we don't talk until we're at Mallory's driveway. Light glows through the living room window, warm and hazy. Maybe her dad's still awake, watching *SportsCenter* or reading a detective story, waiting to make sure his daughter gets back safely. Maybe my dad is still awake too, who the hell knows where, doing who the hell knows what. We unlatch our seatbelts so Mallory can head inside and I can scurry around the front of the car, if I'm even capable of scurrying right now, then squeeze into the driver's seat and power through the last mile and a half, the final mile and a half, until I'm home, home, finally, home.

"Mal," I say, looking at her warm living room, "be honest. Have you ever had a Black person in your house?"

"What?"

"Think about it. Have you ever had a non-white person

inside your home? I'm not sure I have. Like, maybe a plumber or the cable TV guy, something like that, or maybe when my mom invited people, but me, personally, a friend, a teammate who isn't white, I can't remember it ever happening."

"Honestly, me neither."

"Talk is talk," I say. "Getting rid of a song on playlist? Actually not that big a deal." I nod toward her house. "I think we both know what needs to happen."

Mallory peers at me, hard. She's that single inch taller and I feel it now, her looking down at me. She understands that what I'm suggesting means breaking a tradition we've spent hundreds of hours building, something we've owned for basically half our lives. It means sharing something sacred.

I peer back at her, up at her, unwavering.

"You sure?" she says.

"Yeah," I say.

"Let's do it."

[53]

ON THE BUS to the game against Beth Avery, I do one of the hardest things I've ever done.

We pass a church on the way out of town, but I don't think it's what makes me want to confess because I'd already been thinking about speaking up. We also pass a Dairy Queen so, you know, no real significance, and the sky is slightly murky and my head feels extremely murky and I tell Coach she should sit me out again for the first half, maybe the whole game.

"Am I about to get more emails from your teachers?" she asks. "Is this a preemptive strike so I don't get surprised?"

"No," I say in a voice that sounds horribly delicate, like flimsy paper. "I'm all caught up on my assignments, but I had to stay up until four o'clock last night in order to do that. And the night before, I was up until almost six. I'm exhausted and I don't want to hurt the team. Sydney can do better than I can right now."

Coach nods, squints her eyes, and I can see the barely visible scar on her forehead where she once got hit by the sharp edge of a stick and needed two dozen stitches. She has another scar on her chin, smaller and almost impossible to notice, and others she says she used to have on both cheeks that you can't see at all. I know because when I got hit in the mouth last year in a tournament and had to go to the emergency room, she made me examine her face. "Here," she said, touching one cheek, then the other. "And here, and here, and here too. I got stitches in all these places. Look at me. I'm married to the person I love. You'll be fine."

And I am.

"Are you saying you can't play at all?"

"I don't know. I think I might be able to be at my best for a short stretch if you need me, but I'm not sure. It's my fault. I put myself in this position and I don't want the team to suffer because of it."

"Hmm," she says, nodding again.

We're on the highway now and there's a billboard for a business-based university that promises I can get a degree in a couple of years and a job where my management skills will be utilized immediately. That sounds awful. My management skills, at least my *time* management ones, would probably, immediately, put the business out of business. I glance backward into the middle of the bus and Aaliyah is sitting by herself, looking grim. She might just be readying her game face, but I'm still going back to sit with her after Coach and I are done talking.

"All right," Coach says, "I have three things I want to say to you. First, I'm glad you're being honest with me. I'll sit you the first half, but if it's close and I need you second half, you're going in. Second, don't ever let this happen again. If you want to play D1, you're going to practice twice as much as you do now, and your homework is going to be twice as hard. You can't let yourself fall behind with your schoolwork, period. You've got to learn how to prioritize your time better."

"I know. I'm working on it."

"Work harder."

I nod.

"Here's the last thing. Allison, look at me."

I pick my eyes off the floor and look into hers.

"What I'm going to say now stays between you and me. It is not for the ears of any third party, including Mallory, you understand?"

I nod again.

"You need to know Sydney is an outstanding field hockey player. When you graduate, she will step right into your position and the team will be fine. But, Allison, and please take this seriously, you are the best center-mid I have ever coached and I will be shocked if I ever coach another one as good as you. When you're at your best, it's your field and everyone in the stadium knows it. It's a beautiful, astonishing thing to watch. Be at your best, Allison. Give us that beauty."

I want to nod some more, and sort of do, at least with the top of my head. My eyes are full and I don't want Coach to see that.

"Look up, Allison. Look at me."

I look up.

"It's all right for you to be emotional. You care about the game so much. And you're so good at it. It's OK to let it get to you. Now, I have one more thing I want to say and then I want you to go back to your team and get yourself mentally prepared to play. You understand what I'm saying?"

I manage to nod. My face is wet.

"Speak, Allison, I need to hear your voice. You get what I'm saying to you?"

"Yes, Coach."

"Good. Now, I know your grade in this particular class is fine because you must get credit for trying, and apparently the teacher is some kind of saint, either that or a total pushover, but I keep hearing horrible stuff, I mean, absolutely nightmarish descriptions about what happens when you put your hands into clay. For goodness sakes, can't you get a tutor or something for ceramics?"

I laugh.

It's soft, but it's a real laugh.

Coach smiles.

"Thanks," I say.

"Just be ready when I need you," she says.

[54]

SHE NEEDS ME.

With six minutes left in the game, it's a scoreless tie. We're dominating, keeping the ball down in their end, and Sydney's playing solid, but Mallory's a little off. Her shots are just wide, or too close to the center of the goal so the goalie can make the save. And the goalie is phenomenal. She transferred to Beth Avery from somewhere in Pennsylvania and she's big and quick and aggressive and a wall.

At first it looks like she has no weakness, but Coach tells me to keep watching.

"Everyone has a weakness," she says.

I look, try to sharpen my focus through the head-fog.

Imagine my eyes are the scope of a rifle zooming in on the goalie, watching how she moves, how she stands, where she looks.

I zoom in some more.

Sharpen.

Zoom in further.

Sharpen.

Finally, finally, I see it.

When the ball's coming in from the left side—her right—and she steps out to square up for a shot, she's so worried about anything that might get over her shoulder into the upper right corner that she shifts her hips a hair too much and leaves a small opening in the lower left. It would be an almost impossible shot, but there's room.

There's room.

"I can beat her, Coach," I say when there's a stoppage of play because the ball's out of bounds.

"You sure?"

I stand as tall and straight as I can, look Coach dead in the eye.

"Put me in."

"I don't want a tie, Allison. Marty Max is great, but if we have to go to strokes, this girl's so good, it's going to be tough."

"There won't be a tie," I say.

"Get in there," she says.

"Sydney!" I yell across the field. "When you can!"

The ball rolls out of bounds again with fifty-two seconds left and Sydney sprints to the sideline. I clack sticks with her and take off for the middle.

Mallory rolls the ball to me so I can take the hit and says, "About time."

"I'm going to get it to you in the circle," I tell her, "but don't shoot. Make a move that'll get us a corner, OK?"

Mallory looks puzzled. Nobody ever tells her not to shoot.

I hold her gaze.

She nods.

I insert back to Aaliyah and snake free in the middle. She passes it to the edge of my stick and I dribble around their mid and push-pass to Mal just as she breaks into the shooting area. Two defenders rush at her and she blasts a shot into the foot of one of them and the ref blows the whistle.

Corner.

Twenty-nine seconds left.

I look toward the sideline to see if Coach will call a play, but she doesn't shout anything, doesn't hold up any fingers, just watches me as if she's interested to see what I'll do. I feel a fire rising from my hips and into my chest. Coach trusts me to call the play and I will.

I agree, we have to end this game in regulation.

As long as we're playing the full field, Beth Avery can't get the ball into our end, but if we go to strokes and they get to shoot as many shots at Marty Max as we get to shoot at Goalie Wall, their chances at beating us grow a lot higher.

Time to end this now.

Aaliyah runs from the center of the field so she can insert.

"Here's the deal," I say. "Bring it in from the left. Mal, you take the center of the circle. Aaliyah, get it to Mallory. Mal, no fakes, just take the pass and reverse it back to me on the left side. Do it as quickly as you can. When the goalie rushes out to square up the shot, I'm going to try to squeeze it through on the near side. Aaliyah, be ready for a rebound if I miss."

"You won't miss," Mallory says.

"Warriors," Aaliyah says.

Mal and I click sticks with her. "Come out to play," we say.

[55]

AALIYAH'S INSERT IS PERFECT, not too slow, not too fast, not jumpy so it bounces over Mal's stick. Beth Avery's fly runs out at Mallory and she's quick, almost fast enough to get there before Mal can backhand the ball to me, but not quite.

Two defenders sprint in my direction but they angle the wrong way because there's no chance they think I'll shoot short side. Out of the corner of my eye, I see another defender slashing across to cover Aaliyah so she can't get to the post. There won't be a chance for a rebound. It's all on me. The mammoth goalie moves into position and, just like before, her hip's open a splinter too much. I've got maybe a half-second before the defense closes and I'll have no shot.

I almost have no shot anyway.

The distance between the goalie's right pad and the corner of the goal is the width of a ball and, maybe, another two inches. The short-side angle I have to shoot from is ridiculous, comical, some deity's bad idea of a cosmic joke, but it's there. The opening is there.

Everything seems to slow down.

It's like I'm back in Mallory's basement and my body's doing something it's done thousands of times.

I don't think about my backswing, but it happens, short, quick, and choppy.

I don't think about making contact, I just do it.

Flush.

The defender nearest to me lunges and tries to smack the ball out of the air with her stick, but the shot is already past her. The goalie slides her pad to the corner, but it's too late. The ball cracks against the board and the ref blows his whistle and the clock ticks to zero. The horn blows and it's all over. No more scoreless tie.

I look at our sideline and Sydney and Jess and everyone else are jumping up and down and hugging. Everyone except Coach, who's already shoving her clipboard into her gear bag, packing up as if what just happened was exactly what she thought would happen.

No big deal.

Time to board the bus.

That's why she's the best, I think, before all my thoughts are swallowed by Mallory and Aaliyah tackling me and my body falling backward to the ground and the whole team, including Marty Max and everyone on the bench, sprinting over, joining in, jumping onto one big pile of unstoppable Warrior love.

[56]

THE BUS RIDE back is boisterous.

I sit next to Aaliyah and Mal and we link arms and sing *Purple Rain* and it feels like our bus is a mythic spaceship traveling through time. We are not afraid of asteroids or black holes or evil galactic empires. We just careen. We are just loud. Our noise and our light spark the formation of many new planets and subsequent new civilizations. When we swing our sticks, the ball hits the board and we tackle one another and when we sing our voices bend the properties of physics.

We sing many Motown favorites like *Please Mr. Postman* and *My Guy* and *My Girl* and *Build Me Up Buttercup* and nothing at all written by, performed by, or otherwise connected to the country-pop sensation known as Joey Buckets. No one protests and when we disembark in the parking lot at school, Aaliyah looks me the question she won't ask out loud and I gaze at her in what I imagine is the way Coach looked at me when she wanted me to stop staring at the floor. I don't think I nod, but maybe I do, just a little.

Aaliyah nods back, or just nods of her own volition, I

guess I'm still not sure. A slow smile spreads across her face. Then she extends her fist for a pound and I accept the offer.

I wish I could say the night ends like that, or at least the part before I shower, gently breeze through my homework, and fall asleep perfectly content ends like that, with the molecules of the bus still vibrating with our music and the molecules of us still glowing with our victory, but it doesn't.

Mal and I head to my car and there's no Rugger or Jake waiting to ambush us so that part's satisfactory. We are too tired to talk, our voices verging on hoarse, so we chill through a comfortable silence during the drive and when I drop her off, she says, "Sweet goal, Al."

I say, "Sweet corner, Mal," and we laugh and I'm exhausted and I want nothing more than maybe a slice of sourdough bread with some butter, a glass of cold water, and a spell to make my homework disappear, but when I get home I find my mother passed out on the kitchen floor.

[57]

Maybe I've been watching too many CSI shows, though truthfully, since school started, the television and I have been more like camp friends who don't really keep in touch with each other after the summer ends, but the way my mother's body is splayed out, face on the floor, one leg folded beneath her, skirt rumpled and hiked up nearly to her hips, my first thought is that she's dead.

It doesn't help either when she doesn't respond after I scream, *"Mom! Mom!"* ten times and the result is no movement from her at all. I try to remember what I learned in health class as a freshman. I know I'm supposed to call 911, but what am I supposed to do before that? Something about checking for a pulse and making sure the airway's not blocked?

I kind of wish I were more of an emotional person and less coldly clinical, someone who would have rushed straight to her mother and shook her shoulders like they do in the movies, or poured cold water on her face to snap her awake. But I'm not, which is also why I was able to recognize the mammoth goalie's weakness and aim right for it, so I guess I have to take the athletically good with the emotionally sucky. The truth is, I am kind of grossed out by my mom because I can see what looks like a mixture of drool and puke on the floor near her mouth and it's not very nice but I have to admit I'm thinking, God, Mom, I just did maybe the greatest thing I've ever done on a hockey field and I have to come home to this?

Honestly, I didn't think she was dead.

I thought *about* it, true, but I've seen her passed out on the couch enough to know she looks dead then too.

I take a deep breath and try to ignore any feelings of panic. Bending down to the floor, I put two fingers on her wrist. Her skin is warm and her pulse is steady. I lean in close to her mouth, trying not to inhale the smell of puke and vodka, and hear her warm breath pushing outward.

Alive, clearly.

Part of me wants to leave her like that, let her sleep off her drunkenness on the floor and roll her hair through her own secretions. Then I could go upstairs, bang through my homework, get to sleep before midnight. When she wakes on the floor and realizes I went straight to bed without trying to help her in any way, maybe she'll understand how much she hurts me.

I can't do it though.

I might be cold and clinical, but it's still not remotely within me to step over my mother like she's a wasted frat boy at a party and move on with my life.

Gently, I cradle her head and lift it off the floor.

"Mom," I whisper. "Mom, are you OK?"

No response.

Slowly, I rotate her head from side to side, make it seem like I'm asking her if I can go to Cancun with Mallory for spring break and she's saying *no, no, no*.

"Wha—?" she mumbles. "Stop it."

"Wake up, Mom." I try to pull her into a sitting position, but her dead weight is heavier than I thought it would be. "Come on, let's go upstairs. You can't sleep here on the floor."

"Sleep here? What? Allison, what?"

"You're drunk, Mom. You passed out."

She makes an effort to sit up by herself, then rubs her wrist against her forehead and groans as if she has a massive headache.

I hope she does.

I hope it lasts for two days.

She puts her hand on the floor, right in the middle of the drool-puke oil spill, to support herself, so I let go of her head. She turns around to face me, seeming not to notice the yuck her hand is soaked in.

"Allison," she says, "I'm sorry. I'm so sorry. I'm a terrible mother."

[58]

"I DON'T HAVE time for this conversation," I say to my mom. "I've got math and physics and Spanish, and I want to go to sleep."

We're sitting at the kitchen table. She's drinking coffee. She offered to make tea for me but I refused.

"I know I need to get help."

"Yeah, you do."

She looks down at her coffee as if the help she needs is swirling amidst the cream and sugar.

"God, my head hurts."

I wish I felt sympathy, but I don't. I'm the one who cleaned the floor, not her. She was making coffee.

"Mom, do you have any idea what this week has been like for me?"

"The sexting stuff and your friend in the hospital?"

"Her name's Delaney and no, not just that. I've been swamped with homework too. I pulled basically two all-nighters, had to sit out most of two games, have Coach be disappointed with me, and had to figure out how to deal with potentially pretty serious drama on our team. You know what I need right now?"

"A break?"

"No, a mother."

"You don't mean that."

"I do," I say, getting up from the table. "I need for you to be for me what you were for Delaney when we visited her. I know I'm almost going to college and I'm smart and tough and independent and all that, but I still need for you to take care of me, not for me to take care of you. I can't handle it, Mom. Not when I have so much other stuff I have to deal with. It isn't fair, and I don't want to talk about it anymore. I want to go do my homework so I can get some sleep and get good grades and get a goddamn scholarship so you won't have to pay for my college. Please don't let me find you on the floor anymore. Just don't."

She doesn't say anything, and I don't know that I want her to.

What can she say? She's sorry?

I know that already.

[59]

Before I can get started, my phone blows up.

It's the team group chat.

One text after another flies across the screen.

So much buzzing, it sounds like somebody smashed a beehive in my bedroom like a piñata.

At first, I try to ignore what's happening, attempt to focus on my analysis, but the buzzing doesn't stop. Finally, I can't resist. I grab the phone and scroll backward to see what sparked the flurry.

It's Sydney.

The basketball team just called us a bunch of racists. Check Derek's Instagram.

Marty Max is next.

I took a screenshot. Here's what it says, "Those white bitches told my sister to go to the back of the bus. Captain Thot who put her picture all over the internet didn't say shit about it either."

Then Julie B.

What? That's not what happened.

Except, it kind of is, except for the Mallory-as-thot part,

and the part where she was the one who viralized her own picture.

Aaliyah told her brother about it?

That's from Georgia.

Does it matter how he found out?

From Mal.

Aaliyah chimes in.

I didn't tell him about it. Derek doesn't need to know my business.

Then who?

I have a feeling Mallory knows.

Who said it in the first place? Georgia asks. *Nobody really said something that foul to Aaliyah, right?*

Uh-oh, Marty Max says. *My friend on the girls basketball team just texted me. She said their whole group chat is hating on us, calling us the field hocKKKey team, that everyone should boycott our games and we should all be suspended like Jake and them. They want to go to the principal tomorrow and tell her Aaliyah's getting bullied.*

Boycott our games? Sydney says. *Nobody comes anyway.*

I'm NOT getting bullied, Aaliyah says.

Mallory calls me.

"It's Jake," I say. "You told him?"

"Yeah," she says. "This is how he's trying to hurt me."

[60]

"I WAS UPSET," Mallory says, "after we argued that day when you dropped me off. Jake was there to listen. I told him how horrible a captain I am since you stood up for Aaliyah and I didn't. He was actually kind of cool about it, like he didn't bullshit me. He didn't say, oh, I did the right thing because I didn't want to divide the team. He said I needed to step up if I want to be a leader. He was honest and I appreciated it. Of course, he also said he'd never tell anyone."

I'm so mad I could throw my phone out the window.

How could Mallory trust Jake with something about our team like that?

I mean, her body's her business, but telling Jake what she and I talk about—the inner workings of our team—that's a betrayal.

My phone keeps buzzing, sounding like a swarm of locusts, while I'm considering how to respond to Mallory.

I'm the one who said the thing about the back of the bus, Julie B. texts the team. *I didn't mean it like that, but it was horrible to say anyway. I'm sorry to everyone for this mess.*

What the fuck's wrong with you, Julie B.? From Georgia.

Shut up, Georgia! From Marty Max.

Don't tell her to shut up! From Sydney.

Everybody already thinks we're uptight rich white girls, Georgia says. *Thinks we're basic. This is just going to make it worse.*

I'm not white, Aaliyah texts. *Don't throw me in with everyone else.*

"Mal," I say, trying to control the rage in my voice. "We need to handle this. We need to shut this down. Right now."

Mallory doesn't say anything, but I can practically hear her thumbs moving. A few seconds later, the text comes through.

None of this is Aaliyah's fault. I'm the one who told Jake, and he told Derek. Everybody needs to stop texting. Mandatory team meeting in the school parking lot, by the bus stop. Be there in a half hour. Everyone. Nobody text anyone else between now and then. See you in thirty minutes.

[61]

I pick Mallory up, but we don't talk much in the car.

I'm still seething and most of me wants her to clean up her own damn mess. I'm trying to temper that rage but she can sense how I feel, and anything either of us could say right now would only make everything worse.

I still have homework and this better not take all night.

When we park, Mallory grabs my hand.

"I'm sorry," she says. "This is our senior year. I'm such a disaster."

Maybe it'd be nice if I felt sympathy for her, but I don't.

My mother apologized to me tonight too and that didn't work either.

Right now, I just hate everybody.

I lean back in the driver's seat, close my eyes, blow out a breath.

Then another one.

Mallory's my best friend.

And let's face it, I'm no saint. I made out with a boy—I touched the most intimate part of a boy—who I knew was also seeing a girl who was in a class with me. A girl who admires me. A girl who—let's face this too—I already knew was emotionally vulnerable.

I squeeze Mal's hand.

"Warriors," I say.

"Come out to play," she says.

[62]

WE TELL Julie B. to speak first and she agrees.

"This is all my fault," she says.

We're gathered around my car. The night is cool and we're all wrapped in heavy coats. People look smaller like this, huddled up in their almost-winter clothes, and I'm uncomfortable, impatient. Everyone's got homework, not just me.

"I said something horrible to Aaliyah," Julie B. starts. "I was being mean and obnoxious and a stupid senior who thinks she knows everything, and I never should have said it. But it's worse than that. I said something racist. It's hard for me to admit something like that could come out of my mouth, but it did, and I can't take it back. Aaliyah, I owe you the biggest apology, but I'm sorry to the whole team too. I'll never say anything like that again and I'm going to try as hard as I can not to even think it."

I look at Aaliyah, who looks embarrassed, as if she wishes all this would just go away and I feel like I want to take charge and say something that gets her off the hook so she doesn't have to forgive Julie B. if she doesn't want to. I can feel Mallory also itching to talk.

I touch her wrist.

We can't talk.

Not now.

If Aaliyah doesn't want to say anything, she doesn't have to. But if she does want to, I think it's time for the white girls to shut up.

It's quiet for a few seconds.

The air gets colder. We huddle in our big coats.

Georgia looks like she wants to fight Julie B.

Mallory makes a fist, then unmakes it.

I feel like, right now, we could lose the state championship. Right here, we could blow the whole thing, in this cold, damn parking lot.

"All right," Aaliyah says. "There's only one thing everyone needs to know. I've been wanting to play on this team since I was little, just like you guys. I came to all the games when I was in middle school and had the same dreams everyone else had. Last year when I was on JV, I looked up to Mallory and Allison and Julie B. and wanted to be who they were, wanted to play on the same field as them and have them respect me. All I want is to hold up that trophy and know we did it. Julie B.'s my partner. We own the back half of the field. Nobody scores. Nobody gets a good shot on Marty either. I got love for her and yeah, she said something stupid, but on the turf, she has my back. I know she does. Racist shit happens every day at this school. Please, please don't let it happen on this team anymore. Just don't."

There's, like, a group exhale and a bunch of solemn nods.

We don't know what to do next. Maybe Aaliyah wants to say more. We wait. The air's cold. I so want to go home.

"OK, I'm just going to say it," she says, "and I'm sorry if this hurts some of you, but it's how I feel. It's not a coincidence that I'm the only Black girl on the team. You think I'm the only Black girl in this school who could play good hockey if she had the chance? The truth is, some of y'all wouldn't even be on this team if this sport was the kind of sport that made it easy for everybody who wanted to play to play it. Think about all the travel teams you played on with only white girls. What if Black girls had been playing since we were all ten years old? Be honest, some of y'all might lose your spots. Maybe the truth is that what Julie B. said came from a place that's comfortable with how things are, comfortable with a sport that's a 95 percent white world. I believe Julie B. when she says she's sorry, like I said before, I know she has my back, but you all need to ask yourselves something. When we play a game and there's almost fifty athletes out there and there's maybe only one or two Black people, are you OK with that? Seriously, does it bother you? You don't have to answer now. You can think about it, and maybe you should, maybe you should think about it *a lot*. Because the truth is, it bothers the fuck out of me."

Huh.

Aaliyah's words do hurt.

Because I know they're true.

Maybe Mallory and I shouldn't be captains anymore. When we talked about what we wanted to do with the team this year, the tone we wanted to set, did we even consider any of what Aaliyah just said?

No, we did not.

But if we quit now, what would that say about us? That as soon as we realize we messed up, we just give up?

Without really thinking about it, I grab Mal's hand and tug her gently with me into the center of the circle. She doesn't resist and that means she trusts me.

"Aaliyah," I say, and my voice shakes less than I thought it would, "you're right. The whole team, really our whole sport, is messed up. An apology isn't enough. I can't speak for anyone else, but I promise you, from this moment on, I will try to be a better captain. I won't ignore what you're saying. The team needs to know it wasn't a coincidence that we didn't play any Joey Buckets songs on the bus yesterday. He has Confederate flags on every one of his album covers. Every one. It took Aaliyah to make me look at that and I didn't even look right away when she asked me to. That's unacceptable. I screwed up. It won't happen again. From now on, I will be looking, *before* anyone asks me. I will keep my eyes open, Aaliyah, and I won't be perfect, I'm sure, I'll mess up, but I'm going to try. I mean it, I'm going to try."

Aaliyah stares at me, doesn't nod or smile, just looks into me hard as if to say, *We'll see, Allison, we'll see.*

Yeah, we will.

"I agree with Allison," Mallory says. "We have to be better captains and we all have to be better teammates."

She begins to apologize about how she should have spoken up when Julie B. first made the comment, but before she can finish, we hear a rumble and Jake's fat, blue pickup slants sideways next to my car with a roar.

He turns off the engine and he and Derek and Connor and Robby and three basketball players tumble out and stand facing us with their arms crossed as if they represent the military wing of the United Forces of Rat Bros and they arrived just in time to rumble us. I'm confused by the basketball players. I thought some of them apologized to us for the picture thing, but now, here they are, pissed off, I guess, because they think we're racist, and I suppose that means no more sympathy.

Thankfully, Rugger's not there, but, honestly, the whole setup makes me giggle. I can't help it. It's like we're Sharks and they're Jets and it's about to go down. Who thought this was a good idea?

"What is this? The Annual Convention of Basic White Girls?" Jake says with his signature smirk. "It's the twenty-first century, maybe you should figure out how to join the multicultural bandwagon."

I look at Aaliyah.

She looks frozen, rigid, the way she was on the bus when the team was singing the Buckets song.

I stop giggling.

"Go away, Jake," Mallory says. "You're trying to hurt me, but it isn't going to work. My team has my back. We have *one another's* backs. You mean nothing."

"We'll see," Jake says, turning to Julie B. "Why don't you take off your shirt now? Or do you only do that when you can show off for your creepy creative writing teacher?"

I can't help it, I laugh. It's a bitter laugh, but the idea of anyone showing off anything for Gowhatever is so ridiculous, there's no other rational response.

Actually, I'm wrong.

There might not be a more rational response, but there is a better one, and Julie B. offers it.

"Is that what you've learned, Jake?" she says. "After all this, you're still trying to get girls to take their shirts off for you?"

It's the perfect thing to say because it makes the basketball players uncomfortable, makes them remember the guy they're riding with is not exactly a role model for how human beings should relate to one another.

"What are you doing here, Derek?" Aaliyah says to her brother. "Go home, you look foolish."

Derek does look foolish, and chastened, like he'd like nothing better than to go home.

Why doesn't he?

Don't tell me he's afraid of Jake.

Who looks enormous, by the way, as if he's done nothing during his suspension but eat more steroids.

"No," Derek says. "Tell me something first. Are you even

Black anymore? How are you going to let yourself hang out with a racist team?"

"Black enough to tell you I can handle my own business," Aaliyah says, her voice a bolt through the night. "We're trying to figure it out. We don't need you to help us." She looks at Jake. "You've got your own problems to work on."

What I think, and what I'm betting the rest of the team thinks, is that's next year's captain talking right now.

Derek nods. Knows better than to challenge his sister.

"Oh, so now everything's all rainbows and butterflies?" Jake says, his voice so filled with sneer he might be about to steal Christmas. "What's next? Look at your pathetic secret meeting. Are you all going to hold hands and start singing *Kumbaya?*"

I get an idea.

And I'm not the only one who gets it.

Mallory's eyes are lit up. She has it too.

So does Aaliyah.

And Julie B.

Everybody on our team, actually.

We space out our circle, surrounding the boys and their over-compensating truck.

We reach for one another's hands.

"You think this is a joke?" Jake says. "You're going to ruin our hockey season and it's a fucking joke?"

We don't respond. Mallory's hand feels warm in mine. So does Aaliyah's.

My whole face is a smile.

We start to sing.

I never meant to cause you any sorrow
I never meant to cause you any pain

Jake keeps shouting, but our voices rise in unison and his ugly sounds disappear into the night.

I only wanted to see you one time laughing
I only wanted to see you
Laughing in the purple rain

Derek unfolds his arms and climbs into the truck. Jake is cursing loudly now.

Purple rain, purple rain
Purple rain, purple rain
Purple rain, purple rain

The rest of the boys join Derek in the truck. Jake stops shouting. Walks toward Mallory. We keep singing, but more quietly. I'm ready to punch Jake, but Mal pushes me back. "I got this," she whispers.

I never wanted to be your weekend lover
I only wanted to be some kind of friend

Jake puts his chin in Mallory's face. She puts her chin in his. "Why are you such a bitch?" he says.

Baby, I could never steal you from another
It's such a shame our friendship had to end

"Don't talk to me," Mallory says, "until you win a state championship. In fact, until you win one multiple times."

Purple rain, purple rain
Purple rain, purple rain
Purple rain, purple rain

[63]

It's my job to wait in the hallway for Delaney before ceramics.

Glenn has it all planned out. He already has the flowers and the vase set up where Delaney usually sits and I'm supposed to stall her while everyone else in the class signs the card Lilly made. The vase is gorgeous. It's slender and hipster-looking and glazed a dark purple shade that looks like a cross between the bottom of the ocean and grape jelly. The flowers are a fall wildflower mix, bright oranges and yellows. I have to give Glenn credit.

Dude came through.

After I sign Lilly's card, I slip back into the hallway. Delaney's always the last person to get to class because she has to come all the way across the building from PE. I have a few minutes before she gets here so I look through the room's open door at Ms. Waldron. She's seated behind her desk and smiling like a proud parent whose elementary school child just got awarded a blue ribbon at a science fair. I used to love science back then when we were charting the daily temperature in the playground and waiting for chick eggs to hatch from the incubator. I think I'm still OK with science, I don't mind it really, and it's not as much homework as math or Spanish, but it's a lot of repetitive data gathering, then I guess we put the data in a different kind of incubator and see what hatches, but it just doesn't seem to answer questions, or even ask them, the way it did when I was little.

Or maybe I'm preoccupied with other questions now.

I'm unprepared for how happy I feel when I see Delaney.

Instead of the tight, short skirt and heels she typically wears, she's got on an oversized red hoodie and baggy gray sweatpants tucked into basketball sneakers. Her hair is an incredible, messy nest on top of her head, and she's not makeup-less, but her facial adornment is definitely less pronounced than normal. To tell the truth, she looks absolutely adorable and I won't say I'm as psyched as when I scored the goal against Beth Avery, put it's pretty close, and I also know it's not fleeting.

I do something I never do to anyone except my teammates, which is run to her and hug her.

Her sweatshirt smells freshly laundered and she feels sort of frail inside my hug, and I tell her she looks great.

"Oh, please," she says, but she's smiling when she says it.

Two freshman girls approach in tights and UGGs.

They look like 70 percent of the rest of the female freshman population, bored and slightly anxious. They're both gazing at their phones and not each other. I want to shake their shoulders and tell them never to take their best friends for granted, to, instead, walk with them down the halls as if they own the building and couldn't care less about what anyone else says or thinks.

Also, not to fall behind in their homework.

"I'm serious," I tell Delaney. "It's awesome to see you back. How's the day been?"

"Hard. I'm glad it's almost over."

"Me too."

I probably should have made plans to eat lunch with her, but my new program for staying sane—at least until Julie B. gets back to school, if not beyond—includes eating lunch in the media center and working on math problems. I convinced Mallory to join me and we feel like nerds doing it, but at the same time we'll be able to get more sleep at home, which means we'll play better and hopefully win states and get scholarships so, nerds or not, it's a strategy we're sticking with.

Delaney looks backward over her shoulder, checking, it looks like, to see if anyone's within earshot.

More freshman girls approach, a clump of five or six, also all playing with their phones, but Delaney doesn't seem to see them.

I want her to see them.

Or maybe more than that, I want them to see *her*, how dazzling she looks in her sweats, how she's back in school and standing up straight and not just the girl in the psych ward because her naked picture went viral.

"I talked to the principal at lunch," she says in a low voice.

My immediate reaction is relief. I'm glad she had something to do at lunch besides get depressed about not being able to hang out with Rugger. Maybe it's ungenerous of me to think she'd be sad about something like that, but I wonder if I should invite her to study with Mal and me. It's hard to imagine her spending lunch in the media center but, then again, it was hard to imagine her showing up to school in sweats before today, so who knows?

The next thing I wonder is if someone's bothering her, if she went down there because some shithead was teasing her about her picture. If that's the case, I feel like Mallory and I might have to break somebody's face bones.

"She call you in?" I ask.

"No, I went on my own. I told her not to expel Rugger and Jake and everybody."

"You did?"

"Yeah." She picks at the glorious sand dune of her hair and looks around again, as if she's not sure if she should be ashamed of what she's saying. "My parents don't agree with me, but I think my dad's just humiliated, like it's his body on the internet, but it's not. It's mine and I feel like I should decide and it's, like, they made a mistake, but so did I and, yeah, they should be punished, but they don't need to get kicked out of school forever."

"You're OK with their coming back here?"

"I don't know."

"But?"

"But I'm also not sure my feelings are the only thing that matters."

I don't know what to say.

Part of me wants to call serious bullshit to what Delaney just said. Her feelings *do* matter. Her feelings are the whole damn point. It's like women have been told forever our feelings don't matter, that we need to get over it, whatever *it* is, but we *don't* need to get over it. Just like Aaliyah said about racism, we need for *it* to go away.

Do Rugger and Jake and the rest of them deserve to come back to school?

I don't know.

I do think Rugger is sincerely remorseful.

Do I believe him when he says he won't hang out with Jake or smoke anymore?

I doubt it.

He might have good intentions but sticking to them is a

whole different story. What's going to happen when he feels like school is boring, and he hasn't been studying and the tests and assignments pile up and Jake texts him and says he has a dime bag and it's a beautiful day at High Oak?

It's then I realize something.

Maybe it's the lack of sleep over the past week, maybe it's seeing Delaney back in school looking goofy but adorable in her sweats, maybe it's scoring the goal, but I'm seeing both of them differently. Jake is technically handsome, no question, he's got those model looks, but, after that trash he pulled last night, I feel no attraction to him whatsoever. Picturing him, with his muscles and his gleaming teeth, does exactly nothing for me.

Same with Rugger.

Who cares if we had a few conversations via text and he was clever and fun?

If we made out while sitting on a splintered picnic table?

I'm trying not to think a whole lot about my mother right now, but there's something she likes to tell me. People can become less or more physically attractive based on how they act, on the kind of person they are. I don't think I ever believed her until just this moment.

You know who's attractive?

Delaney.

Mallory.

Julie B.

Aaliyah.

They're people I want to spend time with and be around.

Glenn too.

I have to say he was looking pretty damn cute putting those flowers in that vase he made.

Of course, if I had to guess, he's not doing all that solely because he's nice.

He's probably got a thing for Delaney.

"I'm with you," I say. "Personally, I'm done talking to those guys, but however you want to handle it for yourself, I'll support you. Mal will too. I mean, I can't speak for her, but that's what I'd bet on."

Delaney nods.

A couple strolls down the hall. Something we rarely see, a boy and a girl holding hands, talking to each other instead of examining their respective phones. How sad that I'm surprised to see something like that. They look older than freshmen, but not by much. He's got on a hooded sweatshirt like Delaney's, red, but it says *Warriors Lacrosse* in purple. Delaney's, I realize, only says *Warriors* and is generic, not affiliated with any specific team. That gives me an idea. I'll talk to Mallory and Coach about it later. The girl-half of the couple is holding a spiral notebook. She opens it and shows it to the boy. He stops walking to examine what she's showing him, peers at the page with concentrating eyes, as if whatever she's written is more important than the next class he has to get to, or the pocket on the back of her pants he'd like to stick his hand in.

"Look," I say to Delaney, but she's already watching.

The boy nods his head repeatedly, as if what he's reading has a hip hop beat, then hands the notebook back to the girl. "Getting there," he says.

Wow.

Not *perfect* or *beautiful* or any other lie designed to get her to worship him, but something honest.

Getting there.

The girl nods and pinches her lips together and looks a little perturbed, not at him, but at herself, then nods again as if she's glad he told her the truth.

"That gives me hope," Delaney says.

I want to tell her I agree, but the bell interrupts and she heads into class. As soon as she enters the room, everyone bursts into applause. "Delaney, dear," Ms. Waldron says. "Welcome back. Please head to your seat now, the bell has already rung."

Delaney, blushing because of the applause, turns toward her seat.

Sees the flowers, the card.

Covers her mouth with her hand in surprise.

Her shoulders shake and I can tell she's crying. The class moves toward her as if she's the goalie at the end of the game and it's time for a group hug. I hang back, so does Glenn. I've had my hug from Delaney already. He looks like he wants his to be a solo endeavor.

Or maybe he's just worried any physical contact with a male, any male, might make her uncomfortable right now.

Even the possibility he might be worrying about something like that also gives me hope.

[64]

WE HEAD down the stairs into Mallory's basement, my legs shaking.

When we reach the doorway to the field hockey room, it feels like there's a kind of force field, one of those electric-eye, laser-red lines you see in movies that surround the famous diamond someone's trying to steal. My breath is coming quickly, raspy. I kind of want to throw up. Something like this has never ever happened, the sacred temple of me and Mal being breached by someone else, a third party, a stranger.

I'm betting Mallory feels it too, or, I guess I hope she's feeling it, but whatever she feels—trepidation, excitement, guilt, whatever—she's hiding it well. "It's not much," she jokes to Aaliyah, "but it's where we put in extra work. We've been practicing here since we were in sixth grade."

Aaliyah stops to look at the room, the worn-down turf, the beat-up net, the shaft of evening light that drifts through the cobwebbed window. One corner holds a collection of our sticks, about a dozen of them, ones we've cracked or grown out of since sixth grade. I like looking at them. They make me remember all the goals I've set up and scored, all the tryouts, every practice where Mal and I made the boards sing. We had a light walk-through after school today—Coach wants us to make sure we're on top of our homework as playoffs approach—so we skipped burritos and brought Aaliyah here, with the promise of Thai food later. She loves Thai food. She wrote that on an index card at the beginning of the season when Mal and I ran icebreaker activities. Good thing we kept those cards.

"You sure you want me here?" Aaliyah says. "This feels like your secret cave or something."

"Yeah," I say, "we do. And we were thinking about it before what you said the other night. We wanted you down here, without the team, without Coach or Julie B., because we want to see how good you really want to be."

"Allison told me you want to be all-state," Mal says before Aaliyah can respond. "Well, we're the best two-on-one combo you'll ever run into. We want to see if you can stop us."

"What? You're testing me?"

"Yup," I say. "But we're testing ourselves too. We want to see if we're good enough to beat you."

We're still wearing our practice clothes and have our sticks and water bottles. We just need to stretch a bit, warm up, then go at it.

Aaliyah looks around the room again, fixes her gaze on the sticks in the corner.

"This isn't going to be a walk-through, is it?"

"Nope," Mallory says. "It's not."

[65]

WE GO HARD for about an hour.

I will not repeat the language we hurl against the cinderblock walls when one of us messes up.

At first, Mal and I pretty much dominate, moving Aaliyah from side to side, getting her off-balance, flipping the ball past her into the net. But the sweat pours and she curses a lot and she doesn't give up.

And we don't let up.

There are no subtle signals between Mallory and me, one urging the other to back off a bit, give the poor girl a chance. Screw that. She wants to be great? We'll push her to be great.

Slowly, she begins to figure it out, tracks our moves, doesn't get fooled as easily. We take a break, drink some water, and then, it becomes much harder for us to score. It's me and Mal who curse when Aaliyah jabs her stick so quick we can't keep the ball away from her, when she reads a pass and picks it off. We go through a stretch where she stops us every other time, then she stops us twice in a row. All three of us breathe hard. A lot of female muscle heaves and stretches.

"OK," Mallory says, "one more. Nobody's beaten us three times in a row in, like, five years. It just doesn't happen."

We back up to the far wall, eighteen feet from the net.

Aaliyah sets her feet, bends her knees, waits.

I slide the ball to Mal and she takes two quick jab steps to her right. Aaliyah, patient, doesn't bite. Mal pulls left, jumps back right, fires the ball to me. I wind up to shoot for the left corner, Aaliyah moves to block and I scoot a quick pass to Mal for the tip-in on the right post—goal.

Except it's not.

Aaliyah dives full-out across the crease, extends her stick-arm as far as she possibly can and somehow manages to deflect Mal's tip off-target just as she lands on her elbow and somersaults across the floor, barely avoiding crashing into the wall.

"Fuck yeah!" Mallory yells, pulling Aaliyah up and into a mammoth bear hug. "Forget all-state! That's all-American right there!"

Aaliyah looks sheepish, and exhausted, drains her water bottle and still looks thirsty, so I offer her mine. She drinks, then squirts me in the face and I laugh.

"That's for faking me out and making me dive," she says, then hugs me.

"Y'all ready for some pad Thai?" Mallory says.

"With tofu?" asks Aaliyah.

"No doubt," Mal and I say at the same time.

[66]

THE MATH TEST IS AN ADVENTURE.

I don't mean that in a sarcastic way.

It's a difficult test, but I adventure through it. I am a real-estate magnate and the properties of calculus become properties owned by me. I follow the dips and turns of equations like an intrepid hiker on a shadowy trail that becomes easier to identify with each step forward. I have been doing my homework during lunch in the media center. I have, despite the fog in my head that is only slowly receding, been trying to pay maximum attention in class. People say math sucks. People say girls suck at it. People say, *When will I ever use this in real life?*

I encounter none of those thoughts during my adventure.

I bop my head to Hannah Montana refrains and my pencil architects the solutions to story problems one at a time, starting with a stable, solid foundation. My eyes are lances, piercing the questions, rooting for their heart. When I find the heart, I take it apart, labor to figure out what goes where, open the valves to each ventricle, watch numbers flow through the blood-river like sailboats in a regatta, each majestic and aspiring. I am mixing a plethora of metaphors, I know—I am making a metaphorical mathematical meatloaf—but everything seems to make sense and the fifty-three-minute test feels like a momentary breeze, a dip in a perfect-temperature lake. When I finish it, seconds before the bell, I lie back on a noonday dock and let the sun bake me warm. I may not get a hundred percent, may miss a point or two, but I know when I have triumphed.

I have *triumphed*.

Today is the day Julie B. is back in school.

It feels like her warrior spirit has infused the hallways.

Even the freshman girls are standing a little straighter, paying a little less attention to their phones. When I take my math test, I am taking it for her, for them, taking it for all women. I will not be intimidated by stereotypes. I will mix and match metaphors and equations and variables and I will not be ashamed and I will solve everything that needs solving. That is the power I feel with Julie B. back in the building and that is how I handle the test. It is an adventure and I am an adventurer. I triumph.

I wish I could say the same thing about ceramics, but, sorry, my soup bowl—Ms. Waldron calls it a tureen—still belongs on the please-take-this-for-free table at a garage sale. Delaney has been back three days and continues mostly to wear sweatshirts. She and Glenn have been working together on a large flowerpot, the kind you find on somebody's expansive front porch or in the lobby of a museum. It's a project I'm sure I could make look exactly like the corpse of a sheep. They are laughing and joking and having their own adventure and all is momentarily right with the universe of the Great American High School.

My mom did not come home last night.

[67]

I stayed up late doing homework and ignoring texts from Rugger and she still wasn't back.

She'd left me a note saying she was seeing Harvard—it was make or break time—and she didn't know when she'd be home.

Fair enough.

She's often up and out before me in the morning so it's not unusual for me not to see her at all, but I never heard her come in—no car, no garage door, no retching sounds in the bathroom, no glass breaking—and when I woke up, the house had that huge empty feel like no one except me had been in it for a significant chunk of time.

Her bed didn't look slept in, but she always makes it neatly before work so that didn't tell me much.

But there was no remnant of coffee smell from the kitchen, no shower heat emanating from the bathroom, no hint of shampoo.

Everything felt too undisturbed from the night before.

Make or break time.

Which would be worse, if the relationship with Harvard broke, or if it somehow made it?

If it didn't break, then maybe she stayed over with him. Which would mean she'd forsaken one of her cardinal rules and left me, her only daughter, home alone for the entire night. That makes me feel horrible, but at least she'd be safe.

If it broke, who knows?

She could be passed out in a bar somewhere, or arrested, or dead with her car in a ditch.

Or maybe there was some combination of all of the above. Maybe she stayed most of the night and then they woke up, broke up, and then she got drunk, and then the bar, the car, the ditch.

I didn't want to panic.

I didn't want to give her the satisfaction of acting like I needed my mommy.

So I didn't text her.

Didn't call her.

Instead, I did what I always do, which is block her out of my mind, pick up Mallory and go to school.

Then I took a math test.

Killed it.

Thrilled to the energy of the return of Julie B.

Molded something unrecognizable out of clay.

And when I got to Mr. Gowhatever's class, he said the one thing I absolutely did not want to hear.

"I got a message, Allison. You need to go to the office right away."

[68]

It was the same hospital Delaney was in, but a different part.

I drove there myself even though the principal insisted she'd take me if I wanted. I didn't want.

What if I felt like leaving and going somewhere else? Plus, I couldn't imagine sitting in a car with the principal. She might be nice, might even be a good person, but who wants to sit in a car with a high school administrator?

Gross.

Mallory came with me.

I asked if I could get her out of class so she could come.

The principal said yes. She was being terrifically understanding. That made me think my mom had to be in worse condition than what she suggested. She told me there was an accident. She used the phrase *Intensive Care Unit*. She never suggested my mother wouldn't eventually be all right.

Turns out I was wrong about the ditch.

My mom slammed into a telephone pole.

She didn't wrap herself around it the way people sometimes describe but hit it almost dead on. I guess there was a slight enough angle so she could survive. She was wearing her seatbelt, thank God, and suffered broken ribs and a leg fractured in two places. She smashed her head against the airbag and the doctors induced a coma so they could perform emergency surgery and drain fluid from her brain, but she was alive and they were pretty sure she'd ultimately stay that way.

They tested her blood for alcohol and found it, but wouldn't tell me how much, what level. A police matter, they insisted, but they let Mal and me into the room so we could see her. She looked awful. Tubes attached to her wrist and up her nose. Her leg in traction, the top of her head heavily bandaged. Black bruises under both eyes. *That's my mother*, I was thinking.

My mother.

Mine.

"Are you OK?" Mallory said, rubbing my arm.

I wasn't, but I nodded.

Listened to the beep of the heart monitor.

The *steady* beep of the heart monitor.

My stomach gurgled and part of me felt like I was going to puke right there, in the post-surgery recovery room where everything was supposed to be sterile. The rest of me felt calm though, relieved. My mother was alive. Half her head shaved but breathing. I went to her, moving slowly, as if my feet were dragging through shallow water on a beach, and touched her hand. It felt warm. I let the warmth funnel into me, heat my blood, the bones in my face. I pressed her hand to my lips, kissed it and held it there, tried to send my own warmth, my youth and strength, back into her. I must have stood there for a long time, the heart monitor burping its metronomic meter, because Mallory came over and put her hand on my shoulder. We stood like that for a while, Mal's power flowing into me, mine and hers combined flowing into my mom.

"OK, girls," the doctor said. "I have to let a nurse in to do some tests."

"How long will she be unconscious?" I said.

The doctor pursed her lips. Peered down at the clipboard. She was small and slender, and had a face that was kind and firm, like a science teacher who would help you on your lab report if you came in at lunch but wouldn't accept any excuses if you didn't finish on time. Mallory and I towered over her.

"We'll wake her probably about nine o'clock, get her talking, check on her motor responses, then sedate her again, let her sleep through the night."

"Motor responses? Does she, is it possible that, I don't know, is there—?"

I couldn't make the words happen in my mouth, but the doctor understood.

She didn't nod her head or shake it, but her eyes looked soft and liquid.

"We're doing what we can. Any time there's a traumatic injury to the head, there's the possibility of neural damage, but the surgery went well, your mother's strong. I can't tell you anything for sure, and either way she's going to be different for a significant period of time, going to need help with some basic tasks like washing dishes or sweeping the floor. She might not remember some things, and no driving for a while, obviously, but her chances for a full recovery are better than her chances for anything else."

I guess that's good news.

"You two can wait in the waiting area if you want," the doctor said. "Or you can go out and get food or coffee. Nothing's going to change until we wake her. We have your cell phone number if we need to contact you."

Mallory sent me a question with her eyes.

"Yeah," I said. "Let's go to practice."

[69]

On the field, I am wild.

I not only hang with Mallory on the run, I actually finish ahead of her, my breath heaving with strain. Maybe she lets me beat her, maybe she understands what I need as much as I do, but I doubt it.

She knows it wouldn't mean anything if it's not legit.

We have two more regular-season games and then it's time for states. If we win our last two, and we should—we're playing Holbrook and Chesley-Durham and they're both generally mediocre—then we'll go in as top seed and play all our games at home, including, if we make it, the championship. That's a good goal but, also, we just don't want to lose.

Ever.

When the drills start, I don't hold anything back. On defense, I rush anybody with the ball as if I'm an army and it's one last suicidal charge up the hill where the machine gun spits fire and I don't care how many times I get shot. I run over Sydney and leave her on the turf. I run over Georgia and Jesse and leave them on the turf. Mallory tries to pull past me and I pick the ball clean and smack it a hundred yards straight down the field and let out a roar that feels primal and loud and everyone looks at me like I'm insane. I feel a little embarrassed but not much, and I lower my center of gravity into a defensive stance, spacing my feet shoulder-width apart like I've been taught since I was ten, and stare at the rest of my teammates, like *come on, who wants next, I'm just getting started, come on.*

When it's time to be on offense, I run over more people.

Aaliyah goes down.

Julie B., her first day back on the field and fired up to be there, topples like a soda bottle from the edge of the marble-topped island in her kitchen.

The next time I dribble toward her she hisses at me like a pit bull and digs her feet into the turf, the muscles in her thighs tense and centered.

I truck through her like a drug dealer running a roadblock in a tricked-out action movie and she hits the ground hard and Coach blows her whistle in three sharp angry bleats and when I reach my hand down to Julie B. to help her up, I see something in her eyes I've never seen before.

Fear.

Julie B., who is afraid of no one, is afraid of me.

"What's wrong with you?" she says. "You need to chill."

She must be talking to someone else.

I do *not* need to chill.

I take the ball and sprint toward the goal and unleash a swing as if I am wielding a scythe and cutting every wine bottle in the world in half. The ball flies high over the goal and bounds into the parking lot and barely misses denting a car that's not mine.

Coach blows her whistle again.

"Two laps around the field," she says. "Take it slow. Make

it a relaxed team jog. Drop your sticks at midfield and go. Everyone. Except Allison."

Uh-oh.

I jog over to Coach, try to look sheepish, but nothing about my body feels sheepish. I'm going to sound like Ernest Hemingway or someone else who wants to be a bastion of male macho, but I don't know how else to say it, I am full with the blood of a bull. I feel twenty feet taller than Coach even though she is taller than I am and I would not want to try to out-run or out-tough her.

"Allison, what's the problem?" she says.

I say nothing. Stare. Try to look composed, as if I'm at a job interview for something corporate. I'm a graduate from that billboard business college. Valedictorian, in fact, but I don't want to make a graduation speech. I don't want to talk at all. I want to run over Julie B. again. Want to roar so the whole city shakes.

"You're going to hurt someone. I need you to dial it back."

"I can't."

"Why not?"

My composure breaks.

My shoulders tremble.

My face is wet.

I want to tell her I don't know why not, but I can't tell her that because I do know and I won't lie to Coach.

But I still don't want to talk about it.

Coach looks concerned, not mad.

There's nothing she can do. If my mom doesn't want to help herself, no one can help her. If she has brain damage and will never be the same, it's her fault. All I can do is rail against the universe.

"I just can't," I say, and shake my head.

Coach grabs both my shoulders, makes me look her in the

eye. It's hard for me to see. Everything is blurry. The team has begun its second lap. The air feels still, but ominous, like a million crows are about to invade the trees across the street and start cawing at us, demanding we abandon the land they think belongs to them.

"Go to the other side of the field," she says. "Take a dozen balls with you. We'll work on this side. You shoot. Swing that stick as hard as you can. Swing until it's out of you, Allison. Whatever it is. I don't care if you have to shoot five hundred times, you keep shooting until it's out of you. I don't care if it makes you a better player, it's going to eat you alive if you don't get rid of it. I don't care if you break the backboard, keep shooting until it's out of you, Allison. Keep shooting until it's gone."

[70]

I DO.

I shoot through the rest of practice.

I shoot from far out on the edge of the circle, and I shoot from in close.

I shoot for corners from straight on and I shoot from impossible angles.

I pull my stick back and focus on hitting the fat part of the ball and try not to think.

Just shoot.

Shoot it out of me.

My thighs feel pain first.

I bend lower, try to shoot with more power.

I aim for high corners, top shelf, so far up any canned goods would grow cobwebs.

I drag-flick and try to burn a hole through the boards.

I reverse-chip and reverse-chip and reverse-chip until I can do it without looking and still make the flush kind of contact that feels like a boxer's fist to the jaw.

I shoot darts at low corners.

My wrists feel like someone ran them over with a steamroller.

I shake them loose, keep shooting.

Practice must be over because there's no noise at the other end of the field.

The air grows cold.

I shoot.

Cars rev up and leave the parking lot, or maybe I just imagine that.

I can't see the goal.

My face is wet, streaked with sweat and dirt and whatever else is flowing from inside me.

I shoot.

My lower back burns.

Then my shoulders, as if a tattoo gun is writing a florid script, spiderwebbing in, out, and through the skin of every inch of my upper body.

I shoot.

I can't feel my thighs anymore.

Or the breath in my throat.

I sense someone next to me.

It's Mallory.

I shoot. She shoots.

Julie B. shoots.

Sydney shoots.

Georgia shoots.

Jesse shoots.

I shoot.

Aaliyah shoots.

Balls pepper the boards like a hailstorm.

The whole team is surrounding me.

I am in the center.

We shoot. We shoot. We shoot.

Coach blows her whistle. "Enough."

CENTER-MID

I can barely stand up.

My body feels like it got thrown off a horse. I am in the middle. The team surrounds me. I stagger toward Coach and fall into her chest. She catches me. I sob. My breath coughs, hiccups out.

The circle tightens.

I am in the center.

Everyone is close.

I want to roar, but nothing comes out of my throat but cries. I hiccup. I shake. I heave. The circle tightens more. We are one body with a lot of sweaty arms and legs. I chuckle at my lame joke.

"It's my mom," I say to Coach. "She might not be my same mom anymore. She might not be my same mom ever again."

[71]

When we get to the hospital, my mom still looks dead.

Her hair, the part that isn't shaved off, looks brittle, as if she hasn't washed it for weeks, which I know is untrue because she washes her hair every day. Too much, actually, in my opinion. The bruises around her eyes are growing, turning yellow and a swampy shade of green. It's like her face found a new disease and it's almost impossible for me to look at it without throwing up the sandwich Coach bought for me on the way here. She bought one for Mallory too, both of them basically salad on a kind of oaty whole grain, and no sodas either, and made us take our backpacks full of homework into the hospital.

The doctor won't wake my mother for another hour and a half, so after the initial look at her, we retreat to the waiting area. Mal and I start with physics, but it's hard to concentrate. Some kids are watching *SpongeBob SquarePants* and there's a smiling starfish who looks a little like Rugger if Rugger weren't such a scum-sucker and it all happens in a surreal-looking under-the-sea environment and I'm finding that a lot more compelling than the oscillations of sound waves so I get up and wander and don't focus on anything and scuff my feet on the synthetic carpet—brown with green and blue stripes—and wish I had my stick and a ball so I could shoot it through the window and hear a lot of glass break.

"I'll write a note for you," Coach says. "Let your teachers know what's happening so they can ease up a little."

I shake my head.

"I can handle it."

"I know you can. I'll write it anyway."

What she's doing is subtly reminding me I should use my time wisely and not create more problems for myself by wandering around on ugly carpet and wanting to break things while simultaneously avoiding my homework. I sit back down and try to write equations about sound waves.

It's kind of interesting actually. How many oscillations ensued when my mother's car hit the pole? Did she scream? How sharp was the oscillation then? What does the wave look like when Mal swings and cracks the ball into the board? How round was the shape of the crest when those kids were chanting *Ho-mack, Ho-mack, Ho-mack*?

It's strange, but we are kind of moving into a life with fewer sounds. We are learning to text instead of talk and how to signal our laughter with an emoji instead of a deep bellow. I don't know if I have any equations for lack of sound. What if my mom can't talk anymore? If she can't make words with her mouth? I'm not crying right now, not howling loud enough to drown out the cartoon undersea creatures, but it feels like there's a giant wave inside my chest, oscillating against my ribs, pinging like a Richter scale. Maybe, on top of the tsunami, there's an earthquake in there too.

When I look up from my textbook, Coach is behind me, her hands kneading my shoulders.

"I know one thing," she says. "Your mother is proud of you."

"How do you know that?"

"Because she's a mother and you're you."

I want to say thanks, but I also don't want to.

I know Coach is trying to make me feel better, but I'm not in the mood to be told how great I am. On the TV screen the starfish is dancing like it's the 1970s, doing something he must have learned from John Travolta.

It's not charming.

"You know," Coach says, "there was a time when my own drinking was out of control."

Mallory looks up from her book, eyes wide. I make a face where I scrunch my lips together. The idea of Coach not being in control of anything is ridiculous. I try to imagine her throwing up in the bathroom of a fraternity house or dancing with wild abandon, tripping over somebody's lawn gnome in the high heels she's wearing. Can't see it.

"It's true," she says. "My first semester of college. The season wasn't going well and I wasn't playing much."

"Bullshit," Mallory says.

"Feel free to stick your nose back in that textbook, forward. I'm not writing any notes on your behalf, just so you know."

I smile.

It's funny when Coach calls Mallory "forward," as if she doesn't respect the position, as if she's saying, *You just finish what the midfielder starts so don't get too excited over there*. I know she doesn't really think that, but she played midfield and she'll never be able to stop talking trash at least a little.

"When were you ever not playing much, Coach? Weren't you on the national team?"

"Didn't matter. We had a bunch of seniors and they were tough and confident and better than me. I was used to being in the middle of everything, like you are, and when I wasn't, I didn't know who I was. I tried to find new places to get in the thick of—parties, bars, anywhere where I could be the person everyone was paying attention to. It's where I thought I deserved to be. It's where I thought I needed to be."

Is she talking about field hockey or something else?

Mallory's pretending to be studying, but I know she isn't. Coach never tells us about her personal life. For some reason, maybe because of my mom's broken face, she's telling us now. The sponge and the starfish are doing push-ups in the sand. A lobster or a crab, something with claws and eyes like ping-pong balls, barks at them through a bullhorn made from a seashell. I try to block that out, focus on what Coach is saying, but it's hard when I can't see her face, when her hands, which feel like clamps, are still working on the knots in my shoulders.

"It was the worst, but also the most important thing I ever had to do, learn how to support my teammates without losing confidence in myself. Learn how to be on the sidelines, like I am now, like I am with you two, and watch the action happen without being able to do anything about it. But it wasn't just the watching. It was feeling helpless when we were getting beat. It was making sure I didn't quit on myself out of frustration, making sure I didn't lose more than just a game I wasn't playing in."

The physics textbook on my knees feels like it weighs a thousand pounds.

Like I'd need my whole team to lug it off me if I wanted to walk anywhere.

"Are you talking about my mom?"

"It's her battle, Allison. You can't fight it for her."

There's a stain on the ugly carpet. It's probably been there for months but I make it expand, grow it large and deep enough so I can dive into it, first the tips of my fingers, then my arms up to my elbows, then my head. Inside, it's warm and dark.

Quiet.

Safe.

My mother giggles. We're at a waterpark. I'm seven years old. It's winter but we're indoors, cheating the ice. The water is warm—eighty-four degrees, a sign says—and we're in the Lazy River. She's sitting in a plastic inner tube and I'm pushing her, standing in the water up to my collarbone. She's giggling because the lifeguard, a teenager with her hair dyed pink, is giving us dirty looks. I'm not supposed to try to push the tube upward and tip my mom over, but my mother whispers, "Do it again."

I haven't been able to do it yet even though I've tried my hardest. My mother loves to make me use my little muscles and she wants me to be proud of how visible they already are.

They just mean you're strong. Celebrate them.

I duck underwater and crouch as low as I can, keeping my hands above me in contact with the tube. The muscles in my legs coil and I am a sea serpent ready to erupt from the ocean depths and crash through the massive hull of a fishing boat. I push off the floor with my feet and feel my power funnel upward through my hips and into my chest and arms. I have always known how to do this—find all my strength and use it. When my face breaks the surface, the lifeguard is already blowing her whistle, my mom is laughing, and the tube is lifting, nearing the point where it cannot fall back down. The whistle is shrill but I push, push, push and my mom laughs, laughs, laughs and the tube flips, flips, flips until she splashes down and I am standing, tall and straight and alone, king of the Lazy River.

"Allison," Mallory says from somewhere above the rug, "the doctor."

[72]

It's not the same doctor.

This one is also slender, but much taller, and his fingers are branchy and thin, like wicked witch fingers. His face is kind though, and crinkles when he smiles, and I wish he were my father.

"Dr. Lowder," he says, extending his hand for me to shake. "We're going to wake your mother now, Allison. It might be nice for you to be there when she opens her eyes."

His skinny fingers are strong and I look him in the eye like I am strong too and nod. I'm pretending though. I'm terrified of what will happen when my mom wakes up.

What if she doesn't recognize me?

What if her eyes don't work right and she can't focus them?

What if she can't speak?

Coach and Mallory come with me and we follow the doctor down the hall. I wish it were a longer hall, like ten miles long. I wish the carpet in it were stained too, and I could make the stain a pothole and we could sink into it until we were stuck and my mom was back to how she was before the accident, except that she forgot how much she loved wine and isn't interested in it anymore.

The closer we get to her room, the more afraid I become. My legs shake and it's hard for me to keep moving. In moments, my whole life could change. Maybe I won't go anywhere to college. Maybe I'll have to stay home and take care of her if she can't regain her regular functions. Maybe these last few games with Mallory will be the only ones I'll ever get to play.

There are no portraits of cargo ships in this part of the hospital, and the rug has been purged of stains. We are fifteen steps from my mother's room and I wish the floor could swallow me, that the earthquake in my chest—that's definitely what it is now—would tremor out of my body and shake the entire hospital to the ground. Gently, of course, so no one else gets hurt. I'd like my mother's bed to land on a soft cloud of leaves and marsh grass so she keeps sleeping, so her brain keeps recovering, so she wakes up with no black eyes, no broken legs, and no desire to drink or smoke or be anything but the mother who's proud of me and my muscles.

Ten steps.

Mallory squeezes my hand.

I will be strong. No matter what happens in that room, I will handle it. I do not have to fight my mother's battles, but if the rest of my life ends up being a war against fate, I will wage it. I will stay home from college and bathe my mother and feed her with a spoon if that's what it takes. Field hockey is important and it has built me stronger, but I was already strong before I met it and I will be strong after I leave it.

Five steps.

Coach kneads my shoulders with her iron-vise fingers.

Three steps.

"Are you ready?" the doctor says.

"Yes," I say, and my voice sounds like it belongs to me.

I am not afraid I am not afraid I am not afraid I am not afraid I am not afraid.

When we enter the room, a nurse is tenderly nudging my mother, trying to wake her. She opens her eyes and her lips move as if she's pleased to have air to breathe in, happily surprised by it.

"A good sign," the doctor whispers.

But my mother's eyes can't focus.

Her head is stabilized so she can't move it and she blinks twice, then two more times, then twice again, as if the light hurts her. Or maybe it does, she's not sure, she can't decide. She moves her jaw quickly from side to side and, for a moment, I think her brain must be too messed up to slow down, that she'll be a twitchy rabbit the rest of her days.

Nobody prods me but I move directly into her field of vision. She blinks two more times, then three times. Then, I think, she sees me. Her lips purse again as if to take the happy breath.

"Allison," she says.

I'm so overjoyed I don't know what to do. I lean in closer and everything wet on my face makes her face wet when I kiss her cheek. "Mom," I say, barely croaking it out.

"Did you bring a deck of cards?" she asks.

"What?"

"Didn't you learn anything from your mother? Whenever you visit someone in the hospital, bring a deck of cards."

[73]

IN THE STATE SEMIFINALS, it's déja vu all over again—the Warriors versus Westgate, me banging ribs with the Elbow.

She pushes into me and I push into her and we are two bruised combatants, each of us trying to break the other. Midway through the first period, my body already feels like the middle layer of lasagna, half-chewed. I know what the Elbow knows, and what she remembers, and I don't want to wait for a scoreless second period before making something happen.

Last time I pulled the chair on her and she'll be wary, won't let me do that again, so when Julie B. wins a battle on the sideline and sends the ball to midfield, and the Elbow and I both sprint for it, we run shoulder to shoulder and I know she's thinking I'm going to ease back like I did last time, use her momentum against her, wrestle the ball free, and send it up to Mallory.

I don't.

I fake like I'm going to do it just when we reach the ball, just a twitch as if I'm going to pull away, so she pulls away, and I slam right through her and I'm gone. The ball's out in front of me and I tip it forward even more and she falls two steps behind and I feel hungry. I want to eat the rest of the field in five quick strides and I do. At the edge of the scoring circle, a defender rushes at me but she's got no chance. Mal's to my right, and the defender has to watch her too. It's like her body's being drawn and quartered, pulled in opposite directions by two massive horses. If she leans toward me, I pass to Mal and then the goalie's got to deal with her rocket dead on. If she leans toward Mal, I'm open and the goalie's got to face my shot. Another defender tries to run over to help out, but it's too late. I hear the goalie yell, "I got ball!" but she doesn't. The defender drifts toward Mal so I wrist-flick the ball top-shelf right side. I don't even think about it. I've been shooting so much, my body knows what to do. Nothing but net. The crowd erupts, or I imagine it does, I can't hear because I block it out. Mal clicks her stick against mine. Without excessive celebration, we head back to midfield. Business as usual. That's the message we want to send and it sinks in.

For both teams.

A minute later, thanks to a steal and a drive upfield from Aaliyah, we are back in their circle and Mal feints a defender, who then hacks her, and we get a corner. Julie B. inserts to Mal who, before the fly can reach her, clocks the board low left.

Two-nothing.

With forty seconds before halftime, we're up four-zip and Westgate's got a wait-till-next-year look in their eyes. The Elbow's still beating on me, but it's just for the sake of beating on me. She's not trying to make field hockey plays anymore. She's trying to hurt me—not a lot, just enough so I'll remember—and she knocks me down with her hip and earns herself a yellow card and a trip to the penalty chair.

Before she leaves the field, she extends her hand and pulls me up from the ground and I say thanks and she grunts and smiles and tells me I suck and we're friends again, which is good because, in a month, we'll play together on the state elite team for indoor.

At the half, Delaney, who is loving working as our manager—that was my big idea and Mallory and Coach said hell yes so now this is her third game working with us and she's awesome—hands me a water bottle and asks me how the Elbow can try to hurt me if she's my friend.

"She doesn't really want to hurt me, but she wants me to know she's not giving up. She's still going to play me tough. She's showing me respect."

"I don't get that."

Delaney is wearing a proper sweatshirt that says *Warriors Field Hockey* on it with a quotation from Coach on the back: "Dreams don't make teams, hard work does." I'm glad Delaney feels like she's part of ours.

"If she doesn't try to beat on me, it means she doesn't consider me a rival anymore, doesn't consider me someone who can push her to be better. When she goes after me, it means she admires the way I play. She wants to prove she can play as well as I do. I do the same to her. Mallory and I do it to each other in practice, and to Julie B. and Sydney and Aaliyah too."

"So, you challenge each other?"

"It's also how we challenge ourselves. Coach always says she wants the toughest people we'll face all year to be our teammates. It's true. The reason I can beat the Elbow is because I've been facing Mallory and Julie B. and Aaliyah all year. If I can get past them, I can get past anyone."

"You call that girl *the Elbow*?"

"She calls me *the Shoulder*."

"Is that respect too?"

"Definitely."

Around us, the air clutches our necks and the backs of our legs with its first truly cold claws of the season, at least cold during the daytime. It hits me hard that I only have this game left, and the final if we make it, and then I won't be a high school field hockey player anymore. I won't have this kind of halftime where our parents (well, not mine) are in the stands and we've all been little kids and middle school kids and adolescents together in this same city and Delaney and her gorgeous floppy curls will bounce against the hood of her oversized sweatshirt and I will be playing on this field I've grown up on. I want to slow down this moment, feel like I'll always have another half left of a game we're winning, another half to play on this field with the W in the middle.

"I don't really want to do this," Delaney says, and I'm crushed.

"You don't like being our manager?"

"I do like it, but I want to *play*. Next year, I know I'll be a junior and I might not even be good enough to make JV, but I want to try out. I want to be out there on the field like you guys."

I can't help it. The smile on my face seems like it's so big it's stretching my cheeks like taffy. I feel like my whole body got microwaved with warmth. I get a vision of Mallory's basement. It'll be tight in there, but it'll be a quartet smacking balls all winter instead of just the usual dynamic duo. Mal and me, and Aaliyah and Delaney.

"Not make *JV*?" I say. "No chance of that. Me and Mallory have a year with you. A year, Delaney. We're going to work you so hard, you're going to hate us."

"I could never hate you guys," she says, then looks down at the ground as if she's embarrassed she said that and wants to change the subject. She tells me Glenn asked her to homecoming.

Was it just a few weeks ago I was thinking homecoming was something important, that I was imagining Mal and me in tight dresses and heels showing everyone the muscles in our legs, wondering if I'd go with Rugger, if I'd let anything significant happen afterward?

I smile, but it's not the kind that microwaves me all over.

"That's great," I say.

"I don't know." Delaney looks down again, pats the water bottles as if they're a pet. "Do you think he saw the picture?"

"Probably, yeah."

I don't tell her he claimed he didn't because, well, he's a nice kid, no doubt, but I'm still not sure I believe him. I'd be stunned if he spread it around the web like a bro-jerk, but when it was late at night and he was bored and lonely, did he look at it? Just sneak a peek? Maybe he did, maybe he didn't. That's for him and his conscience to deal with and, honestly, I wouldn't crucify him if his curiosity and/or lust won that particular battle.

"Do you think that's why he wants to go with me? Because he thinks I'm a slut and he can get something?"

"Maybe, yeah."

Her face twists and I think about what else I want to say.

"Look, Delaney, he's a high school boy. Any heterosexual guy who sees that picture is going to imagine what it'd be like to be with you. Does it mean it's the *only* reason he likes you? I don't think so. Glenn doesn't seem like that. When you were in the hospital, he was legitimately worried. The whole flowers and everything for when you came back, that was his idea. Is he attracted to you? I'm sure he is. But he doesn't strike me as the kind of boy who doesn't care about anything else, who doesn't want to get to know you beyond the physical aspect. Personally, I'd give him more credit."

"That's what I think too. I want to trust him."

"So trust him, and if you're wrong, you're wrong. If he

turns out to be a jerk, it'll say more about him than it does about you. We can't stop trusting people, right? That's what Coach says and I believe her. I'd rather trust someone and get burned than be the person who never trusts anyone."

I wonder if I'm talking to Delaney or myself.

Sydney jogs over and Delaney hands her a water bottle and I nod my head as if I'm agreeing to something.

Which I am.

I'm agreeing to go to homecoming without a date.

With Mallory and Julie B. and Aaliyah and whoever else on the team wants to go.

It's the day after the state championship final and if we get that far—win or lose—we'll show up.

A battalion of us.

We'll wear tight dresses and show off our badass legs and if the boys are intimidated, that is nobody's freakin' problem but their own.

[74]

THE NIGHT BEFORE THE CHAMPIONSHIP, I pick up Mallory and we drive to the field.

It's cold, and ten o'clock, and dark, but the sky is cloudless and the moon is out so we can see, sort of. We climb over the fence with our sticks and a bag of balls because the gate is locked, but we've known since we were twelve that there's one spot on the fence where the twisted spikes on top are blunted and you won't catch your sweatpants or scratch your legs or otherwise injure yourself when you swing over them.

We used to sneak in during summer, early in the morning before football started their two-a-days. Even after seventh grade we used to do that, passing to each other across the W, pretending we were scoring goals for the high school varsity team. We've never done it at night before though, and we're not those little girls dreaming anymore. Now we're big girls, still dreaming.

"Is your homework done?" Mallory asks.

"Yes, Mom."

She stares at me, not sure if the idea of "mother" is something we can joke about yet. Mine's home. More or less self-sufficient in a wheelchair, sleeping on a couch in the living room, trying to wean herself from painkillers. Doing a pretty good job of it, actually. We've watched a lot of movies. Her license has been suspended so even if she could physically drive, she's not allowed to. Maybe someone will give her a ride to the game, but I'm not going to organize it. If she cares enough, she'll get on the phone and do it herself.

I am in the process of forgiving her.

It will happen, we both know that, but it will happen slowly.

Mallory and I start by running two laps around the field. Mal says just to jog, it's a warm-up pace, we've got the game tomorrow, don't kill yourself.

We kill ourselves.

Mal gets a step on me after about twenty yards so I catch up and pull ahead. Then she does. Within seconds, we are at a full sprint and we stay that way until we finish, chests heaving, breath ragged, Mallory maybe half a step in front. "I hate you," she says when her mouth can form words.

"You suck," I say.

"Core," she says, and we jog over to the W and lie on our backs. Even though it's cold, we're sweating and the turf beneath us feels warm. Above, the moon splashes us with her light and the stars blink and flutter from way, way up high.

Too far away to imagine.

Mallory is sucking wind like a horse and the only thing louder than her breath is my breath. We know it's our last time by ourselves on this field, that tomorrow we will battle Beth Avery and their monster goalie for the title, and then, win or lose, we will no longer be high school field hockey players. Tonight is ours. The W is ours, sponging our sweat and no one else's.

Not Julie B.'s or Aaliyah's or Coach's.

Just ours.

"Crunches," Mal says, and we do them, two sets of fifty.

Then sit-ups, locking our ankles together as anchors, then leg lifts.

Then we flip over and do push-ups. Four sets of twenty-five.

"Grab a ball," Mallory says and, in the dark, we pass to each other. We can see, a little, but there's a zen quality to what we're doing. When she hits the ball, I have to guess where it's going by sound, by what little flash of her body I can make out in the gloom. She has to do the same. At first, we let a lot of balls by us, but as we keep going, the task becomes easier. I hear her stick make contact. I move my stick to where I think the ball will be, and it's there. I knock it back to her and she guesses and before long we don't miss any balls. There's a rhythm. There's a feeling. There's knowing your friend so well, you can make magic.

I don't think I ever want to stop. I don't want to do homework or see my mother or not be a high school field hockey player or have a boyfriend or grow up.

In a corner of my brain, I sense another car pull into the parking lot, feel it turn off its engine and headlights. I hope it's not one of the Rat Bros, now back in school after their suspension. I heard a rumor they want to come to the game tomorrow, demonstrate their support, or their regret, or some other supposedly vulnerable emotion.

Sorry, not interested.

Mom gets forgiven first, then if I have anything left in the well, I'll think about the boys.

"Corners," Mallory says, and we take turns inserting and lasering shots into the net. When we're exhausted, we shoot more. And some more after that. When our bodies are soaked and sore and we can't move anymore, we keep shooting. Two more blasts. One each. *Blam, blam* into the board.

"Let's try one more thing," Mallory says. "Then we'll be done."

I nod.

"Let's see if we can score on the run, here, in the dark. We'll pretend there's a defender coming at us, and one of us has to pass to the other at full speed for the shot."

"Are you crazy? We can't see. It's one thing if we're waiting on the circle for an insert and we kind of know where the pass has to go. No way we can do that if we're moving at full speed. We'll never see the ball."

"That's the point. Can we do it without seeing? Can we do it blind? Can we do it if all we have is listening and feeling?"

"No."

"You sure?"

I think about it for a second.

"No."

"No, you're not sure, or no, we can't do it?"

"No, you're crazy, but let's try."

The first attempt is horrible. I dribble the ball down the middle, pretend a defender's in front of me, slap the ball on the dead run to the right and it hits Mallory in the foot and she trips and falls. I tumble down next to her and, on our backs, our laughter fountains, like a geyser, toward the stars.

We get better.

On our next try, I hit Mal in the foot again, but she doesn't fall.

The third time, I hit her stick, but the pass is too bouncy and she fumbles it.

Then we get it.

Five times in a row. Six times in a row.

I pass by sense and she knows where it's going to be, how

hard it's coming. Our timing gets better and better and her shots smack the board one after another. Twenty times in a row. *Blam, blam, blam, blam.*

Then we switch and she passes to me.

It only takes us two fails to get it, and then our rhythm is like a syncopated jazz combo. She knows what I'm doing. I know what she's doing. So what if we can barely see each other? We hit. We hit. In the dark, we improvise and hit.

It's almost midnight, and we are shivering now, despite our sweat, but we don't want to leave. After tomorrow, this field will belong to Aaliyah and Sydney and Jess and the rest of the team who'll be coming back. Tonight, for a few more minutes, it's still ours.

This W, this turf, ours.

"Two more laps?" Mallory says after we're done shooting. Her eyes, wet, glisten in the moonlight

"Yeah." Mine glisten too.

"Just a cool down, OK? Let's not kill ourselves."

"OK."

We kill ourselves. We knew we would. It feels so good. The cold air flies across our faces as we sprint both laps all out. Mal's a quarter-step ahead of me, but I don't fall back. She is a fire knifing through the dark. I swear, her heat glows. It's an aura around her, outlining her rock-hard shoulders, her piston-legs, and it carries me with her. Stride for stride, grunt for grunt. I pull even and she won't give an inch and I won't either. We fly, two fires burning up the field that belongs to us.

For tonight, only to us.

When we finally drain our water bottles and wrap up in our sweatshirts, there's a man waiting for us at the fence after we climb over. He looks about fifty, with white hair and a pair of maroon ski gloves on his hands. There's a light from the parking lot not too far away and we can see him pretty well. He smiles and his face is lined and kind, a sailboat or yacht-guy's face, and he pulls in his shoulders and backs away from us, tries to look as non-threatening as possible, but it's still creepy.

Must have been his car that pulled in earlier.

"I'm sorry," he says. "Didn't mean to scare you. I've been watching. Pretty impressive."

"You could see something?" Mallory says.

"Not much," the man says, "but I could hear."

We shrink back, move closer to each other, raise our water bottles like weapons, not that they'd do any good, but Mal's stick is zipped up and mine's tucked in its straps and it would take a few seconds to pull it out.

"Your father told me you'd be out here, Mallory," the man says. "I came to watch the game tomorrow, but thought I'd try to check in tonight and see if I could chat with you for a minute. I'm Bruce Nelson, head coach at Great Lakes University."

GLU.

Perennial contenders for the Midwest regional championship.

A top-fifteen team in the country, like, every year.

Home of the coolest mahogany-colored turf anybody's ever seen.

He extends his maroon-gloved hand to shake Mallory's and I freeze for a second, then back off another couple steps, so they can have privacy to talk.

"Uh, Allison," he says, "where are you going?"

I don't say anything, wait.

My heart feels like it might explode.

"Are you insane?" he says. "The way you two work together, passing to each other in the dark? There's no coach in the world who wouldn't want you on the same team. I want you to come to Glenn Harbor. Full scholarships. Both of you. I can't wait to see how great you'll become over the next four years."

I can't say anything.

I want to, but my whole throat feels clogged.

Mallory shakes her head like she's not interested, looks at the ground. I kind of want to slap her.

"Do you know about—" she says.

"The picture? Yeah. And I know you scored something like fifty goals the next game too. Anyone can make a mistake, Mallory. You've learned from it?"

She nods.

"I know about your little blip with your grades too, Allison. Don't think I haven't been trying to find out as much as I can about both of you. You've learned from that also, I suspect?"

I nod too.

"Do you two talk or just make gestures?"

Mallory offers me her fist. I give her mine. We bump knuckles.

"Warriors," Mallory says.

"Come out to play," I say.

"I don't doubt it," Coach Nelson says, and shakes his head like he knows everything he needs to know.

[75]

BETH AVERY'S monster goalie no longer has a weakness.

Her left hip no longer opens too much and she is huge and quick and mean and snarling and it seems like there's no possible way to get anything past her. Believe me, we've tried.

Again, we're dominating play, have kept the ball in their end the entire game, or at least ninety percent of it. They've had a couple breakaways and that's it. Both times their shots went wide and, after the whistle, we brought the ball back across midfield and kept it there. We've had about a dozen corners and haven't been able to score. Mal's had two beautiful shots, one high that the goalie leapt for and got her blocker on and knocked over the goal, and the other low and screaming toward the corner and the goalie did the splits like a dang gymnast and just got the tip of her toe on it and deflected it out of bounds. Both times there was a huge whoosh of air from the crowd, like their anticipation was built up and ready to erupt with a roar, but then got sucked away with a giant deflator-vacuum as if it were our fate to disappoint their every hope.

That is not our fate though.

We were not born to disappoint them, or ourselves, and we have kept trying.

And the goalie has kept blocking.

And kicking the ball out.

And thwarting and thwarting. All she does is thwart us.

"Just keep playing your game," Coach told us at halftime. "Don't get frustrated."

We nodded, but how can we not get frustrated? Everything we do keeps getting stuffed in our faces. My mother is at the game in her wheelchair, Mallory's dad standing behind her. They look concerned, worried we might not finish off our season, our high school careers, the way we want to. As if whatever joyous celebration the team parents have planned will have to be shelved. As if they'll have to spend the night rehabbing our devastated self-esteems. I'm not worried about my self-esteem, but I am developing a sick feeling, a nausea that hisses its foul breath on my neck. We're going to keep everything down in their end, I know that, but then we're going to mess up with, like, one minute left, just mess up one time, and they'll have a breakaway and scorch down the field and this time they won't miss.

And we'll lose.

With ninety seconds remaining, it almost happens.

Mal breaks free and I see her from the middle of the field and pull past my defender and rifle a pass to her on the dead run. For a moment, I think it's over, she's going to score. She beats a defender and it's just her and the behemoth. Mal stops her sprint like a hockey skater—I can almost picture ice spraying from her blades—and draws the goalie out so she can backhand around her. Except, somehow, the goalie grows about four feet taller, her legs extend like Plasticman legs, and when Mal shoots, somehow the magnificent beast—and I do mean she is magnificent, God, I hope I get to be on a team with her someday—does the gymnast-split again, except the wingspan of her legs covers the whole field. Covers the whole region. Spreads, really, like Manifest Destiny, spanning our entire great land from coast to coast, and she gets a foot on the ball and knocks it straight to the stick of a defender.

Mal is stunned and doesn't recover quickly enough to cover the girl who whacks the ball upfield and Beth Avery's gone, a three-on-two headed toward our net. I sprint back to try to muck things up but I'm too late, a pass flies from the edge to the center and I can't reach it. Their forward receives the ball in the circle and one-times it toward the goal.

All I can do is watch.

Thankfully, the shot is right at Marty Max. She swats it, but the ball rebounds out to their other forward who, unlike me, kept running instead of watching. With Marty Max out of position, the whole left side of the net is open and the forward flicks it neatly toward the board and we're about to be losing for the first time all season.

Except Julie B. and Aaliyah are both right there.

Somehow, they got there.

Both of them.

A new wall.

Julie B. knocks down the shot and Aaliyah cracks it out of the circle and toward the sideline. It hits a Beth Avery stick and bounces out of bounds.

Our ball.

I breathe.

Shake my head at what an idiot I am for being caught spectating.

Breathe again.

Damn.

Coach calls a timeout, our only timeout, and we sprint over to her on the W. In the stands, or just in front of them, actually, my mother still looks worried. The Rat Bros did not show up, at least not as a group. Rugger is there though, by himself, up in a high corner of the bleachers. The truth is, the kid is probably an all right person. He's not going to be *my* person ever, or Delaney's, but someday, maybe, he'll be an OK boyfriend for someone else.

Martindale's also in the stands, and a couple rows behind him, Gowhatever and Ms. Waldron. He whispers something to her and I wonder if they're a couple. That's kind of gross, but then I think, *Why not?* He could do a lot worse than being called "dear" all the time by a woman who loves eighties music.

"Listen," Coach says, "you're playing great. Aaliyah, Julie B., you saved us. Now let's make that save stand up. We've got to find a way to beat that goalie. Ideas?"

I don't have any.

No one else says anything either.

Delaney gives us water bottles and we drink, maybe we think too. But I'm drawing a damn blank. I can't conjure anything, not a single thing.

After a few seconds, nobody else has an idea either.

I glance at Mallory, figure her face will show as much frustration as mine does.

It doesn't.

She catches my eye and stares at me, through me, as if she's trying to tell me something.

But I can't tell what it is.

I need to step it up?

Participate in plays instead of watching them?

What is she trying to say?

Then she smiles at me.

A moonlit smile full of warmth and magic, and it hits me.

We have a plan.

We've *always* had a plan.

"Don't worry, Coach," I say. "We got this."

I don't elaborate. Coach looks like she wants to ask me a question, but she doesn't. I nod at her. Mallory nods too.

Coach waits. We keep nodding.

"All right," Coach says, nodding herself. "Do it."

Mallory puts her fist into the middle of the circle. "Warriors," she says.

We all put our fists into the circle. "Warriors," we say.

Warriors!

Warriors!

Warriors!

Come out to play!

[76]

Aaliyah inserts to Sydney.

Sydney beats her defender and carries the ball across midfield. When another player rushes at her, she backhands the ball across to me. Two defenders swarm and cut off anywhere for me to go so I pass it back to Syd. She dribbles toward the circle, then swings it back. Ten seconds left in the game. I beat the girl who rushes at me by spinning backward, pulling the ball in a full 360-degree turn, and then exploding forward. The crowd sucks in its breath because now, it's just the goalie and me. She is huge and strong and faster than I am, but I know what she's watching.

My eyes.

Fortunately, I don't need them.

I look right at her, issue the challenge. She thunders toward me, swallows my whole field of vision. All I can see is a mammoth goalie devouring the world. She launches from her feet and there's nowhere for me to go, no angle to shoot, nothing in front of me but her pads, her immense helmet, a giant smothering mass that will end regulation in a tie, taking us to a shootout we cannot win.

CENTER-MID

At the last possible instant, I backhand the ball to my right without looking in that direction.

I don't need to look.

I know she'll be there.

I can hear her. I can feel her.

Mallory swings.

Smack!

My favorite sound in the world.

ACKNOWLEDGMENTS

Special thanks to the Pioneer High School Field Hockey team and the Fer de Lance Field Hockey club for inspiration and for letting me watch practices and games. Thanks to Karen Smyte for helping me understand what it means to be a female athlete and coach. This book also takes inspiration from all the books I read as a kid that encouraged me to love sports and love the stories of sports – writers like John R. Tunis and Ring Lardner. Thanks to Carl Deuker for letting me see what contemporary versions of these kinds of stories can look like. Of course, I wouldn't be able to write about high schoolers with any kind of imagination without the students I see every day who push me to rethink much of what I think about every forty seconds or so. Thanks too to Emma Hamstra and Jessie Hieber, teachers who share field hockey tales in the English Department office. Thanks to Steve Gillis and Patrick Flores Scott for your friendship and support of my literary adventures. Finally, thanks to Erin Helmrich and Fifth Avenue Press for believing in this project and to Nichole Christian for helping to make these words sing.

ABOUT THE AUTHOR

Jeff Kass teaches tenth-grade English and Creative Writing at Pioneer High School in Ann Arbor, MI. He is the author of *Takedown*, a thriller previously published by Fifth Avenue Press, as well as the short story collection *Knuckleheads*, Independent Publishers Best Short Fiction Collection of 2011. His poetry collections include *My Beautiful Hook-Nosed Beauty Queen Strut Wave* and *Teacher/Pizza Guy*, a 2020 Michigan Notable Book. He lives in Ann Arbor with the writer Karen Smyte and their daughter Sam and their son Julius.

Made in the USA
Monee, IL
17 January 2022